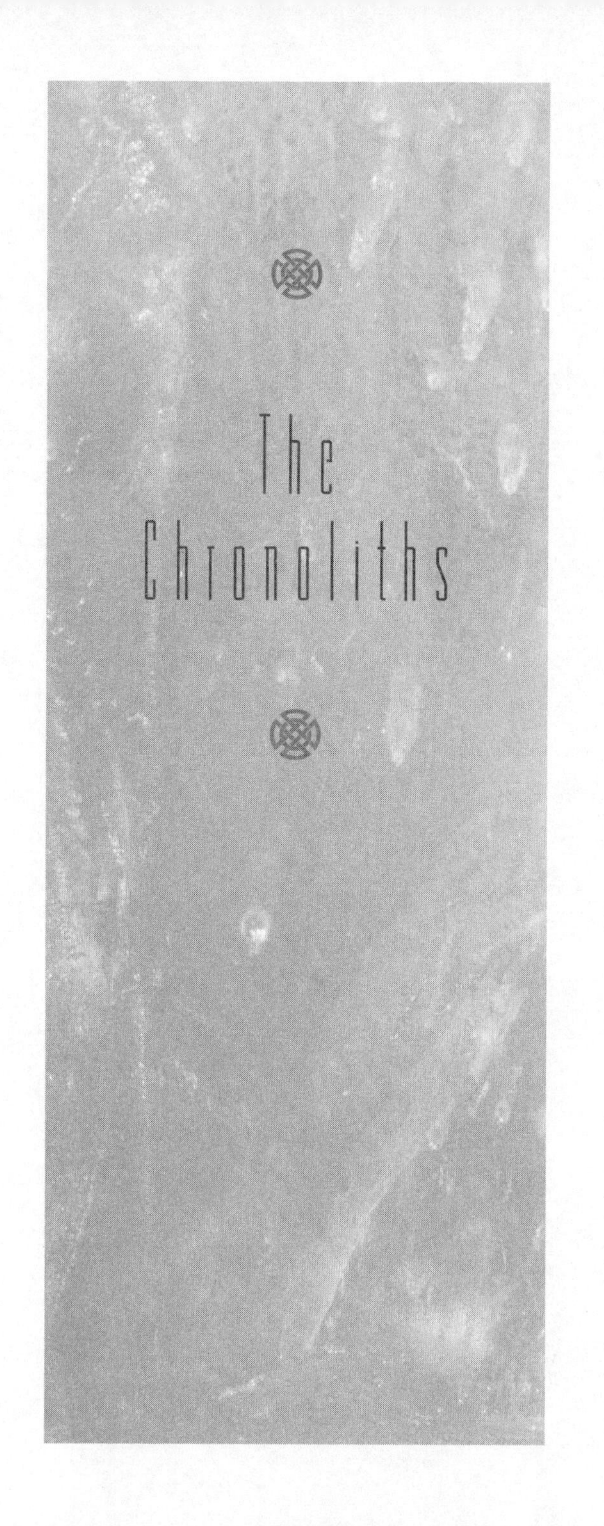
The
Chronoliths

Tor Books by Robert Charles Wilson:

Darwinia

Bios

The Perseids and Other Stories

The Chronoliths

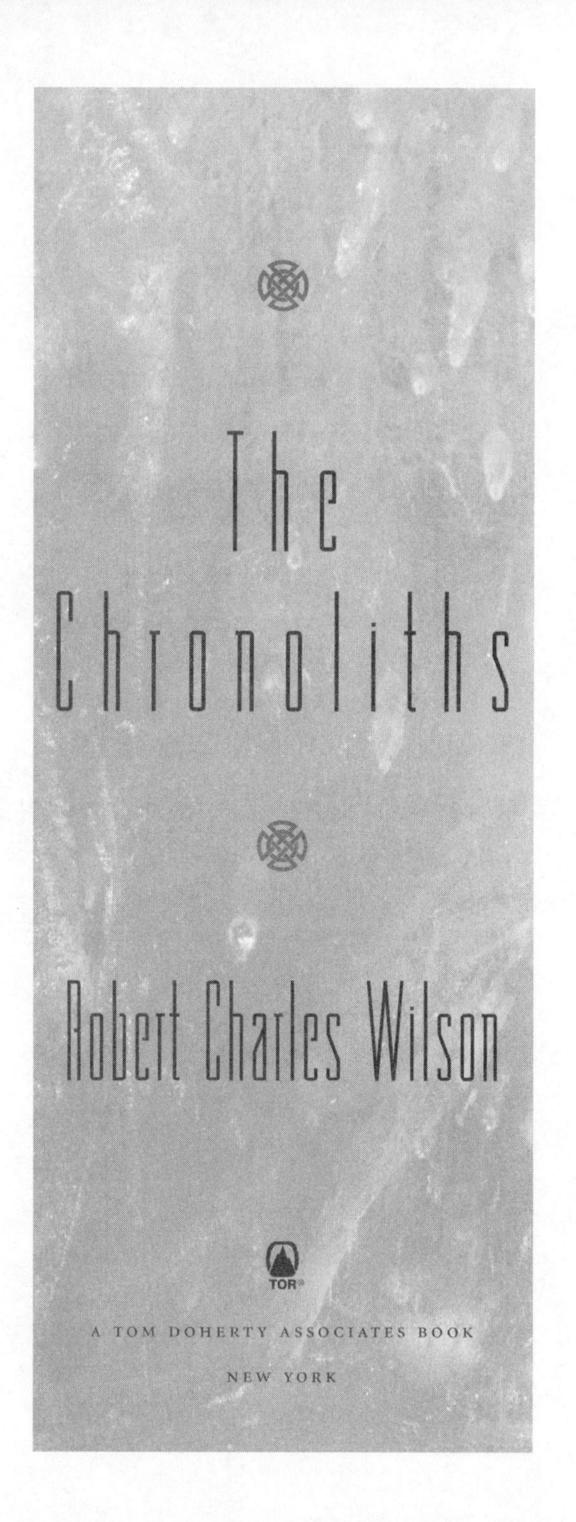

The Chronoliths

Robert Charles Wilson

TOR®

A TOM DOHERTY ASSOCIATES BOOK

NEW YORK

This is a work of fiction. All the characters and events portrayed in this novel are either fictitious or are used fictitiously.

THE CHRONOLITHS

Book design by Ellen Cipriano

Edited by Patrick and Teresa Nielsen Hayden

A Tor Book
Published by Tom Doherty Associates, LLC
175 Fifth Avenue
New York, NY 10010

Tor® is a registered trademark of Tom Doherty Associates, LLC.

"A Tom Doherty Associates book."
ISBN 0-312-87384-0

Printed in the United States of America

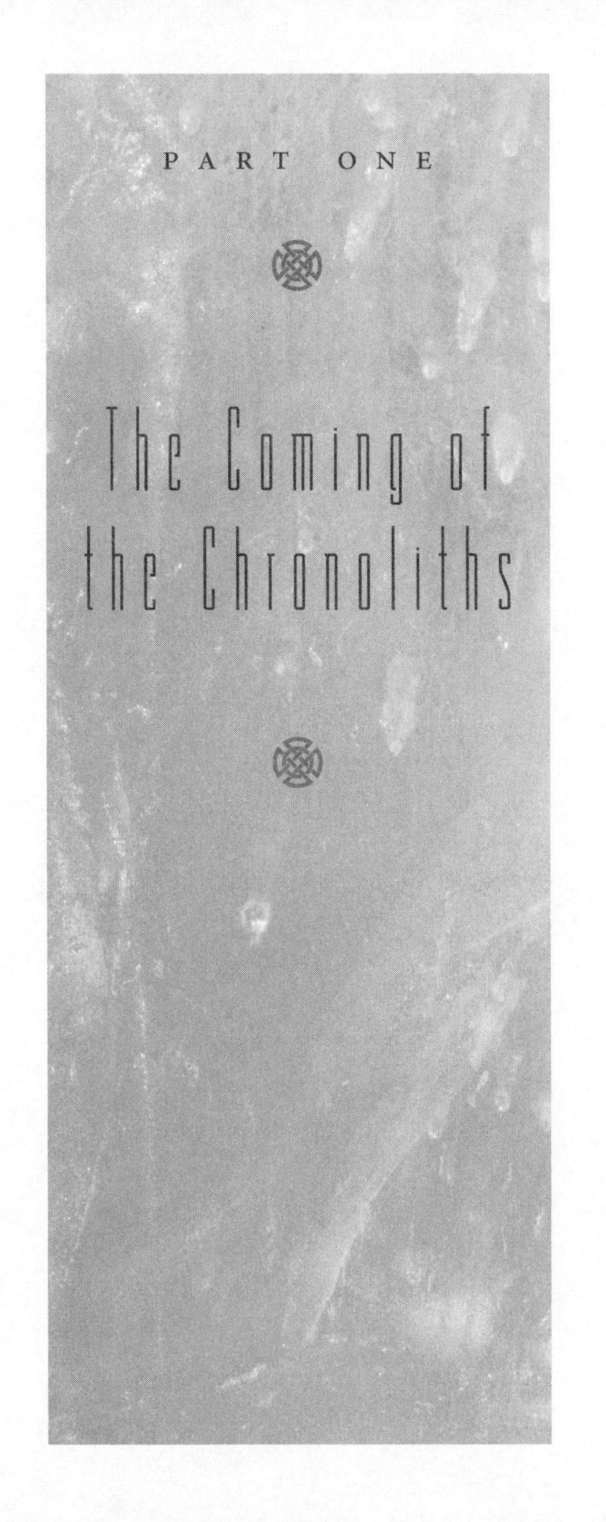

PART ONE

The Coming of the Chronoliths

One

It was Hitch Paley, rolling his beat-up Daimler motorbike across the packed sand of the beach behind the Haat Thai Dance Pavilion, who invited me to witness the end of an age. Mine, and the world's. But I don't blame Hitch.

Nothing is coincidental. I know that now.

He was grinning as he approached, generally a bad omen with Hitch. He wore the American-in-Thailand uniform of that last good summer, army shorts and John the Baptist sandals, oversized khaki T-shirt and a flowered spandex headband. He was a big man, an ex-Marine gone native, bearded and developing a paunch. He looked formidable despite his clothes, and worse, he looked mischievous.

I knew for a fact that Hitch had spent the night in the party tent, eating the hash-laced spice cookies a German diplomatic-corps functionary had given him and feeding the same to her, until she went out with him at high tide to better appreciate the moonlight on the water. He shouldn't have been awake at this hour, much less cheerful.

I shouldn't have been awake either.

After a few hours at the bonfire I had gone home to Janice, but we hadn't slept. Kaitlin had come down with a head cold, and Janice had spent the evening alternately soothing our daughter and battling an infestation of thumb-sized cockroaches that had colonized the warm and greasy passages of the gas stove. Given that, and the hot night, and the tension that already existed between us, it was probably inevitable that we had argued almost until dawn.

So neither Hitch nor I was fresh or perhaps even thinking clearly, though the morning sunlight coaxed a false alertness out of me, the conviction that a world so brightly lit must also be safe and enduring. Sunlight glossed the heavy water of the bay, picked out fishing sloops like dots on radar, promised another cloudless afternoon. The beach was as broad and flat as a highway, a road toward some nameless and perfect destination.

"So that sound last night," Hitch said, beginning this conversation the way he began most, without preamble, as if we had been apart for no significant time, "like a Navy jet, you heard that?"

I had. I'd heard it about four a.m., shortly after Janice stomped off to bed. Kaitlin was asleep at last, and I was alone at our burn-scarred linoleum kitchen table with a cup of sour coffee. The radio was linked to a U.S. jazz station, turned down to polite chatter.

The broadcast had turned brittle and strange for about thirty seconds. There was a crack of thunder and a series of rolling echoes (Hitch's "Navy jet"), and a little after that an odd cold breeze rattled Janice's potted bougainvilleas against the window. The window blinds lifted and fell in a soft salute; Kaitlin's bedroom door opened by itself, and she turned in her netted crib and made a soft unhappy sound but didn't wake.

Not quite a Navy jet, but it might have been summer thunder, a newborn or senescent storm mumbling to itself out over the Bay of Bengal. Not unusual, this time of year.

"Party of caterers stopped by the Duc this morning and bought all our ice," Hitch said. "Heading for some rich man's dacha. They said there was real action out by the hill road, like fireworks or artillery. A bunch of trees blew down. Want to go see, Scotty?"

"As well one thing as another," I said.

"What?"

"Means yes."

It was a decision that would change my life beyond repair, but I made it on a whim. I blame Frank Edwards.

Frank Edwards was a Pittsburgh radio broadcaster of the last century who compiled a volume of supposedly true miracle lore (*Stranger Than Science*, 1959), featuring such durable folktales as the Mystery of Kaspar Hauser and the "spaceship" that blew up over Tunguska, Siberia, in 1910. The book and its handful of sequels were a big item in our household when I was naive enough to take such things seriously. My father had given me *Stranger Than Science* in a battered library-discard edition and I had finished it—at the age of ten—in three late-night sessions. I suppose my father considered this the kind of material that might stimulate a boy's imagination. If so, he was right. Tunguska was a world away from the gated Baltimore compound where Charles Carter Warden had planted his troubled wife and only child.

I outgrew the habit of *believing* this sort of thing, but the word "strange" had become a personal talisman. Strange, the shape of my life. Strange, the decision to stay in Thailand after the contracts evaporated. Strange, these long days and drugged nights on the beaches at Chumphon, Ko Samui, Phuket; strange as the coiled geometry of the ancient Wats.

Maybe Hitch was right. Maybe some dark miracle had landed in the province. More likely there had been a forest fire or a narcotics shoot-out, but Hitch said the caterers had told him it was "something from outer space"—and who was I to argue? I was restless and facing the prospect of another empty day fielding Janice's complaints. And not relishing it. So I hopped on the back of Hitch's Daimler, fuck the consequences, and we motored away from the coast in a cloud of blue exhaust. I didn't stop to tell Janice I was going. I doubted she would be interested; anyway, I'd be home by nightfall.

Lots of Americans disappeared in Chumphon and Satun in those days, kidnapped for ransom or murdered for pocket change or recruited as heroin mules. I was young enough not to care.

We passed the Phat Duc, the shack where Hitch supposedly sold fishing tackle but in fact did a brisk trade in native marijuana to the party crowd, and turned onto the new coast road. Traffic wasn't heavy, just a few eighteen-wheelers out of the C-Pro fish farms, jitneys and *songthaews* decorated like carnival wagons, tourist buses. Hitch drove with the verve and fearlessness of a native, which made the journey an exercise in bladder control. But the rush of humid air was cooling, especially as we turned onto the feeder road toward the interior, and the day was young and pregnant with miracles.

Away from the coast, Chumphon is mountainous. When we turned inland we had the road very nearly to ourselves, until a phalanx of border police roared past us in a hail of gravel. So something was definitely up. We stopped long enough for Hitch to relieve himself in a gas station *hawng nam* while I tuned my portable radio to the English-language radio station out of Bangkok. Lots of U.S. and U.K. top forty, no word of Martians. But just as Hitch came ambling back from the urinal trough a brigade of Royal Thai soldiers roared past us, three troop carriers and a handful of rattletrap humvees, going the same direction the local police had been headed. Hitch looked at me, I looked at him. "Get the camera out of the saddlebag," he said, not smiling this time. He wiped his hand on his shorts.

Up ahead, a bright column of fog or smoke spiked the tumbled hills.

What I did not know was that my daughter Kaitlin, five years old, had awakened from her morning nap with a raging fever, and that Janice had wasted a good twenty minutes trying to locate me before she gave up and took Kait to the charity clinic.

The clinic doctor was a Canadian who had been in Chumphon since 2002 and had established a fairly modern surgery with funds donated by some department of the World Health Organization. Doctor Dexter, the beach people called him. The man to see for syphilis or intestinal parasites. By the time he examined Kaitlin, her fever had peaked at 105 degrees and she was only intermittently lucid.

Janice, of course, was frantic. She must have feared the worst: the Japanese encephalitis we all read about in the papers that year, or the dengue that had killed so many people in Myanmar. Doctor Dexter diagnosed a common influenza (it had been going around the Phuket and Ko Samui crowd since March) and pumped her full of antivirals.

Janice settled down in the clinic waiting room, still trying periodically to phone me. But I had left my phone in a backpack on a shelf in the rental. She would have tried Hitch, maybe, but Hitch didn't believe in unencrypted communication; he carried a GPS locator and a compass and figured that was more than enough for any truly rugged male.

When I first glimpsed the pillar through a scrim of forest I took it to be the *chedi* of a distant Wat, one of the Buddhist temples scattered throughout Southeast Asia. You can find a photograph of Angkor Wat, for instance, in any encyclopedia. You'd recognize it if you saw it: stone reliquary towers that look weirdly organic, as if some enormous troll had left its bones to fossilize in the jungle.

But this *chedi*—and I saw more of it as we followed the switchback road up a long ridge—was the wrong shape, the wrong color.

We crested the ridge into a roadblock of Royal Thai Police, border patrol cars, and assorted armed men in rust-pocked SUVs. They were turning away all traffic. Four of the soldiers had trained their weapons on an ancient Hyundai *songthaew* packed with squawking chickens. The border police looked both very young and very hostile, wearing khakis and aviator glasses and holding their rifles at a nervous angle. I didn't want to challenge them and I told Hitch so.

I don't know if he heard me. His attention was on the monument—I'll use that word for now—in the distance.

We could see it more clearly now. It sat astride a higher terrace of the hill, partially obscured by a ring of mist. Without any visible reference the size of it was difficult to judge, but I guessed it must have been at least three hundred feet tall.

In our ignorance we might have mistaken it for a spaceship or a weapon, but the truth is that I recognized it as a kind of monument as soon as I could see it clearly. Imagine a truncated Washington Monument made of sky-blue glass and gently rounded at all corners. I couldn't guess who had made it or how it had got here—apparently in a single night—but for all its strangeness it did look distinctly man-made, and men make such things for a single purpose: to announce themselves, to declare their presence and display their power. That it should be here at all was dazzlingly strange, but there was no mistaking the solidity of it—the weight, the size, the stunning incongruity.

Then the mist rose up and obscured our view.

Two uniformed men strode toward us, loose-limbed and surly. "By the look of it," Hitch said—his muted Southwestern drawl sounding a little too lazy, given the circumstances—"we'll probably have U.S. and U.N. assholes all over us before long, plus a lot more fucking BPP." Already, an unmarked but obviously military helicopter was circling the ridge, its downdraft stirring the ground haze.

"So we go back," I said.

He snapped a single photograph, then tucked the camera away. "We don't have to. There's a smuggler's trail up around that hill. It leaves the road about a half mile back. Not too many people know about it." He grinned again.

I suppose I smiled back. The second thoughts were coming thick and fast, but I knew Hitch and I knew he wouldn't be argued out of this. I also knew I didn't want to be left at this checkpoint without a ride. He wheeled the motorcycle around and we left the Thai cops glaring at our tailpipe.

This was maybe two or three in the afternoon, about the time Kaitlin began to ooze bloody pus from her left ear.

We circled up the smugglers' trail as far as the Daimler would take us, then concealed the bike in a thicket and hiked a quarter mile more.

The trail was rough, designed for maximum concealment but not maximum comfort. Steep real estate, Hitch called it. Hitch carried hiking boots in the Daimler's saddlebag but I had to make do with my high-tops, and I worried about snakes and insects.

Had we followed the trail far enough we would no doubt have arrived at some hidden drug cache, an extraction factory, maybe even the Burmese border, but twenty minutes took us as close to the monument as we cared to get—as close as we *could* get.

We came within a thousand yards of it.

We weren't the first people to see it at that proximity. It had blocked a road, after all, and it had been there for at least twelve hours, assuming the sound of last night's "Navy jet" had in fact marked the arrival of the artifact.

But we were among the first.

Hitch stopped at the fallen trees. The forest here—pines, mostly, and some wild bamboo—had collapsed in a radial pattern around the base of the monument, and the wreckage obliterated the path. The pines had obviously been toppled by some kind of pressure wave, but they hadn't been burned. Quite the opposite. The leaves of the uprooted bamboo were still green and only beginning to wither in the afternoon heat. Everything here—the trees, the trail, the ground itself—was crisply cool. *Cold*, in fact, if you put your hand down among the windfall. Hitch pointed this out. I was reluctant to take my eyes off the monument itself.

If I had known what was to come, my awe might have been tempered. This was—in light of what followed—a relatively minor miracle. But all I knew was that I had stumbled into an event immensely stranger than anything Frank Edwards had uncovered in the back numbers of the *Pittsburgh Press*, and what I felt was partly fear, partly a dizzy elation.

The monument. It was not, first of all, a *statue*; that is, it was not a representation of a human or animal figure. It was a four-sided pillar, planed to a smooth, conical apex. The material of which it was made suggested glass, but on a ridiculous, impossible scale. It was blue: the deep, inscrutable blue of a mountain lake, somehow peaceful and ominous at once. It was not transparent but carried the suggestion of translucency. From this side—the northern side—it was scabbed with patches of white: ice, I was astonished to realize, slowly sublimating in the humid daylight. The ruined forest at its base was moist with fog, and the place where the monument met the earth was invisible under mounds of melting snow.

It was the ice and the waves of unnaturally cool air wafting out from the ruined forest that made the scene especially eerie. I imagined the obelisk rising like an immense tourmaline crystal from some underground glacier . . . but such things happen only in dreams. I said so to Hitch.

"Then we must be in Dreamland, Scotty. Or maybe Oz."

Another helicopter came around the crown of the hill, too low for comfort. We knelt among the fallen pines, the cool air earthy with their scent. When the aircraft crested the hill and was gone, Hitch touched my shoulder. "Seen enough?"

I nodded. It was clearly not wise to stay, although some stubborn part of me wanted to linger until the monument made sense, to retrieve a little sanity from the ice-blue deeps of the thing. "Hitch," I said.

"What?"

"Down at the bottom of it . . . does that look like *writing* to you?"

He gave the obelisk one last hard squint. Snapped a final photograph. "Letters, maybe. Not English. Too far away to make out, and we're not getting closer."

We had stayed too long already.

What I learned later—much later—from Janice, was this.

By three p.m., the Bangkok media had obtained video footage of the monument from an American tourist. By four, half the beach-lizard population in Chumphon Province had taken off to see this prodigy for themselves and were turned away en masse at the roadblocks. Embassies were notified; the international press began to sit up and take notice.

Janice stayed with Kaitlin in the clinic. Kaitlin, by this time, was screaming with pain despite the painkillers and antivirals Doctor Dexter had given her. He examined her a second time and told Janice our daughter had acquired a rapidly necrotizing bacterial ear infection, possibly from swimming at the beach. He'd been reporting elevated levels of *e. coli* and a dozen other microbes for almost a month, but health officials had taken no action, probably because the C-Pro fish farms were worried about their export license and had flexed their muscle with the authorities.

He administered a massive dose of fluoroquinolones and phoned the embassy in Bangkok. The embassy dispatched an ambulance helicopter and cleared space for Kait at the American hospital.

Janice didn't want to leave without me. She phoned the rental shack repeatedly and, when that failed, left calls with our landlord and a few friends. Who expressed their sympathy but hadn't seen me lately.

Doctor Dexter sedated Kaitlin while Janice hurried to the shack to pack a few things. When she got back to the clinic the evac helicopter was already waiting.

She told Doctor Dexter I would almost certainly be reachable by nightfall, probably down at the party tent. If I got in touch, he would give me the hospital's number and I could make arrangements to drive up.

Then the helicopter lifted off. Janice took a sedative of her own while a trio of paramedics pumped more broad-spectrum antibiotics into Kait's bloodstream.

They would have gained considerable altitude over the bay, and Janice must have seen the cause of all this from the air—the crystalline pillar poised like an unanswerable question above the lush green foothills.

We came off the smugglers' trail into a nest of Thai military police.

Hitch made a brave attempt to reverse the Daimler and haul ass out of trouble, but there was nowhere to go except back up that dead-end trail. When a bullet kicked up dust by the front wheel, Hitch braked and killed the engine.

The soldiers bade us kneel, hands behind our necks. One of them approached us and put the barrel of his pistol against Hitch's temple, then mine. He said something I couldn't translate; his comrades laughed.

A few minutes later we were inside a military wagon, under the guard of four armed men who spoke no English or pretended not to. I wondered how much contraband Hitch was carrying and whether that made me an accomplice or an accessory to a capital offense. But no one said anything about drugs. No one said anything at all, even when the truck lurched into motion.

I asked politely where we were going. The nearest soldier—a barrel-ribbed, gap-toothed adolescent—shrugged and waved the butt of his rifle at me in a desultory threat.

They took Hitch's camera. He never got it back. Nor his motorcycle, come to that. The army was economical in such matters.

We rode in that truck for almost eighteen hours and spent the next night in a Bangkok prison, in separate cells and without communication privileges. I learned later that an American threat-assessment team wanted to "debrief" (i.e., interrogate) us before we talked to the press, so we sat in our isolation cells with buckets for toilets while, across the world, sundry well-dressed men booked flights for Don Muang Airport. These things take time.

My wife and child were less than five miles away in the embassy hospital, but I didn't know that and neither did Janice.

Kaitlin bled from her ear until dawn.

Doctor Dexter's second diagnosis had been correct. Kaitlin had been infected with some ominously poly-drug-resistant bacteria that dissolved her tympanic membrane as neatly—one doctor told me—as if someone had poured a vial of acid into her ear. The surrounding small bones and nervous tissue were also affected, in the time it took for multiple doses of fluoroquinolones to battle back the infection. By the following nightfall two things were clear.

One, Kaitlin's life was no longer in danger.

Two, she would never hear with that ear again. She would retain some hearing in her right ear, but it would be impaired.

Or maybe I should say three things became clear. Because it was plain to Janice by the time the sun went down that my absence was inexcusable and that she wasn't prepared to forgive me for this latest lapse of adult judgment. Not this time—not unless my corpse washed up on the beach, and maybe not even then.

The interrogation went like this.

Three polite men arrived at the prison and apologized contritely for the conditions in which we were being held. They were in touch with the Thai government on our behalf "even as we speak," and in the meantime, would we answer a few questions?

For instance, our names and addresses and Stateside connections, and how long had we been in Thailand, and what were we doing here?

(This must have been fun for Hitch. I simply told the truth: that I had been in Bangkok doing software development for a U.S.-based hotel chain and that I had stayed on for some eight months after my contract lapsed. I didn't mention that I had planned to write a book about the rise and fall of expatriate beach culture in what the Thai travel guides are pleased to call the Land of Smiles—which had turned from a nonfiction work into a novel before it died aborning—or that I had exhausted my personal savings six weeks ago. I told them about Janice but neglected to mention that, without the money she had borrowed from her family, we would have been destitute. I told them about Kaitlin, too, but I didn't know Kaitlin had nearly died a mere forty-eight hours earlier . . . and if the suits knew, they didn't elect to share the information.)

The rest of their questions were all about the Chumphon object: how we had heard about it, when we had first seen it, how close we had come, our "impressions" of it. A Thai prison guard looked on glumly as a U.S. medic took blood and urine samples for further analysis. Then the suits thanked us and promised to get us out of confinement ASAP.

The following day three different polite gentlemen with a fresh set of credentials asked us the same questions and made the same promises.

We were, at last, released. Some of the contents of our wallets were returned to us and we stepped out into the heat and stench of Bangkok somewhere on the wrong side of the Chao Phrya. Abandoned and penniless, we walked to the embassy and I badgered a functionary there into advancing us one-way bus fare to Chumphon and a couple of free phone calls.

I tried to reach Janice at our rental shack. There was no answer. But it was dinnertime and I imagined she was out with Kait securing a meal. I tried to contact our landlord (a graying Brit named Bedford), but I talked to his voicemail instead. At which point a nice embassy staffer reminded us pointedly not to miss our bus.

I reached the shack long after dark, still firmly convinced I'd find Janice and Kaitlin inside; that Janice would be angry until she heard what had happened; that there would follow a tearful reconciliation and maybe even some passion in the wake of it.

In her hurry to reach the hospital Janice had left the door ajar. She had taken a suitcase for herself and Kaitlin and local thieves had taken the rest, what there was of it: the food in the refrigerator, my phone, the laptop.

I ran up the road and woke my landlord, who admitted he had seen Janice lugging a suitcase past his window "the other day" and that Kaitlin had been ill, but in all the fuss about the monument the details had escaped him. He let me use his phone (I had become a phone beggar) and I reached Doctor Dexter, who filled me in on the details of Kaitlin's infection and her trip to Bangkok.

Bangkok. And I couldn't call Bangkok from Colin's phone; that was a toll call, he pointed out, and wasn't I already behind on the rent?

I hiked to the Phat Duc, Hitch's alleged bait and tackle shop.

Hitch had problems of his own—he still harbored faint hopes of tracking down the lost Daimler—but he told me I could crash in the Duc's back room (on a bale of moist sinsemilla, I imagined) and use the shop's phone all I wanted; we'd settle up later.

It took me until dawn to establish that Janice and Kaitlin had already left the country.

I don't blame her.

Not that I wasn't angry. I was angry for the next six months. But when I tried to justify the anger to myself, my own excuses seemed flimsy and inadequate.

I had, after all, brought her to Thailand when her explicit preference had been to stay in the U.S. and finish her postdoc. I had kept her there when my own contracts lapsed, and I had effectively forced her into a poverty-level existence (as Americans of those years understood poverty, anyway) while I played out a scenario of rebellion and retreat that had more to do with unresolved post-adolescent angst than with anything substantial. I had exposed Kaitlin to the dangers of an expatriate lifestyle (which I preferred to think of as "broadening her horizons"), and in the end I had been absent and unavailable when my daughter's life was threatened.

I did not doubt that Janice blamed me for Kaitlin's partial deafness. My only remaining hope was that Kait herself would not blame me. At least, not permanently. Not forever.

In the meantime what I wanted was to go home. Janice had retreated to her parents' house in Minneapolis, from which she was very firmly not returning my calls. I was given to understand that a bill of divorcement was in the works.

All of this, ten thousand miles away.

At the end of a frustrating month I told Hitch I needed a ride back to the U.S. but that my funds had bottomed out.

We sat on a drift log by the bay. Windsurfers rolled out on the long blue, undeterred by the bacteria count. Funny how inviting the ocean can look, even when it's poisoned.

The beach was busy. Chumphon had become a mecca for photojournalists and the idly curious. By day they competed for telephoto shots of the so-called Chumphon Object; by night they bid up the prices of liquor and lodging. All of them carried more money than I had seen for a year.

I didn't much care for the journalists and I already hated the monument. I couldn't blame Janice for what had happened, and I was understandably reluctant to blame myself, but I could without objection blame the mystery object that had come to fascinate much of the world.

The irony is that I hated the monument almost before anyone else did. Before very long the silhouette of that cool blue stone would become a symbol recognized and hated (or, perversely, loved) by the vast majority of the human race. But for the time being I had the field to myself.

The moral, I suppose, is that history doesn't always put its finger on the nice folks.

And of course: There is no such thing as a coincidence.

"We both need a favor," Hitch said, grinning that dangerous grin of his. "Maybe we can do one for each other. Maybe I can get you back home, Scotty. If you do something for me in return."

"That kind of proposition worries me," I said.

"A little worry is a healthy thing."

That evening, the English-language papers printed the text of the writing that had been discovered on the base of the monument—an open secret here in Chumphon.

The inscription, carved an inch deep into the substance of the pillar and written in a kind of pidgin Mandarin and basic English, was a simple declarative statement commemorating a battle. In other words, the pillar was a victory monument.

It celebrated the surrender of southern Thailand and Malaysia to the massed forces of someone (or something) called "Kuin," and beneath the text was the date of this historic battle.

December 21, 2041.

Twenty years in the future.

Two

I flew into the United States on a start-up air carrier with legal berths at Beijing, Dusseldorf, Gander, and Boston—the long way around the planet, with numbing layovers—and arrived at Logan Airport with a set of knockoff designer luggage in the best Bangkok tradition, a five-thousand-dollar grubstake, and an unwelcome obligation, all thanks to Hitch Paley. I was home, for better or for worse.

It was amazing how effortlessly wealthy Boston seemed after a season on the beaches, even before I left the terminal, as if all these gleaming cafés and newsstands had sprung up after a hard rain, bright Disney mushrooms. Nothing here was older than five years, not the terminal annex itself nor the Atlantic landfill that supported it, a facility younger than the great majority of its patrons. I submitted to a noninvasive Customs scan, then crossed the cavernous Arrivals complex to a taxi bay.

The mystery of the Chumphon Chronolith—it had been given that name by a pop-science journalist just last month—had already faded from public attention. It was still making news, but mainly in the supermarket checkout papers (totem of the Devil or trump of the Rapture) and in countless conspiracy-chronicling webjournals. Incomprehensible as it may seem to a contemporary reader, the world had passed on to more immediate concerns—Brazzaville 3, the Windsor weddings, the attempted assassination of the diva Lux Ebone at the Roma Festival just last weekend. It was as if we were all waiting for the event that would define the new century, the thing or person or abstract cause that would strike us as indelibly new, a Twenty-first Century Thing. And of course we didn't recognize it when it nudged its way into the news for the first time. The Chronolith was a singular event, intriguing but ultimately mystifying, hence ultimately boring. We set it aside unfinished, like the *New York Times* crossword puzzle.

In fact there was a lot of ongoing concern over the Thai event, but it was restricted to certain echelons of the intelligence and security communities, both national and international. The Chronolith, after all, was an avowedly hostile military incursion conducted on a large scale and with ultimate stealth, even if the only casualties had been a few thousand gnarled mountain pines. Chumphon Province was under very close scrutiny these days.

But that was not my business, and I imagined I could disentangle myself from it simply by flying a few thousand miles west.

We thought like that then.

Unusually cold weather that autumn. The sky was cast over with turbulent clouds, a high wind tormenting the last of the year's fishing fleet. Outside the street atrium of the AmMag station, a row of flags beat the air.

I paid the taxi driver, crossed the lobby, and bought a ticket for the Northern Tier Express: Detroit, Chicago, and across the prairies to Seattle, though I was only going as far as Minneapolis. Boarding at seven p.m., the vending machine informed me. I purchased a newspaper and read it on a coin monitor until the station's wall clock showed 4:30.

Then I stood up, surveyed the lobby for suspicious activity (none), and walked out onto Washington Street.

Five blocks south of the magrail station was a tiny, ancient mailbox service called Easy's Packages and Parcels.

It was a storefront business, not prosperous, with a flyblown mylar shade over the display window. While I watched, a man with a steel walker inched through the front door and emerged ten minutes later carrying a brown paper envelope. I imagined this was the typical customer at an establishment like Easy's, a golden-ager perversely loyal to what remained of the U.S. Postal Service.

Unless the gentleman with the walker was a criminal in latex makeup. Or a cop.

Did I have qualms about what I was doing? Many . . . or at least second thoughts. Hitch had bankrolled my trip home, and the favor he had asked in return had seemed simple enough when we were basking penniless on the sand. I had known Hitch for most of a year before the advent of the Chumphon Chronolith; he was one of the few Haat Thai regulars whose conversation extended to anything more advanced than personal sexual conquests and designer drugs. He was a master of unaudited deals and subterranean income, but he was essentially honest and (as I had often insisted to Janice) "not a bad person." Whatever that meant. I trusted him, at least within the boundaries of his nature.

But as I stood watching Easy's Packages for evidence of police surveillance—fully aware that I wouldn't recognize professional surveillance unless the Treasury Department happened to rent a billboard to advertise its presence—all those judgments seemed facile and naive. Hitch had asked me to show up at Easy's, give his name, and take delivery of "a package," which I was to hold until he contacted me, no questions asked.

Hitch was after all a drug dealer, though his beach trade had been confined to cannabis, exotic mushrooms, and the milder phenylethylamines. And Thailand was indeed a source country and established commercial route for the narcotics trade since the days of Marco Polo.

I wasn't modest about intoxicants and I had sampled more than a few. Virtually every psychoactive substance was legal somewhere and almost all of it decriminalized in the liberal Western nations, but the U.S. in general and Massachusetts in particular were still heavily punitive when it came to the transportation of hard narcotics. If Hitch had somehow contrived to mail himself, say, a kilo of black tar heroin—and if his sense of humor extended to giving me custody of it—I might be paying for my ticket home with penitentiary time. I might not see Kaitlin without a sheet of wire-reinforced glass between us, at least until her thirtieth birthday.

Rain came down in a sudden, sheeting torrent. I ran across the street to Easy's Packages, took a breath of damp air, and stepped inside.

Easy himself, or someone like him—a tall, intricately wrinkled, muscular black man who might have been sixty or eighty—stood behind a hardwood counter, guarding a row of aluminum mailboxes tarnished a foggy gray. He looked at me briefly. "Help you?"

"I'm here to pick up a package."

"You and everybody else. Mailbox number?"

Hitch hadn't given me a number. "Hitch Paley said there'd be a package waiting for me."

His eyes narrowed, and his head seemed to rise a quarter inch in sudden indignation. "Hitch *Paley*?"

From the tone of his voice this was already going badly, but I nodded.

"Hitch fucking Paley!" He thumped the counter with his fist. "I don't know who the fuck you are, but if you happen to be talking to Hitch Paley, you tell that asshole our scores are not settled! He can keep his fuckin' packages to himself, too!"

"You don't have anything for me?"

"Do I have anything *for* you? Do I have anything *for* you? The toe of my fucking *boot* is what I have for you!"

I managed to find the door.

Thus the failed journalist, failed husband and failed parent became a failed criminal.

Riding the AmMag coach out of Massachusetts, out of the urban corridor into shanty sprawl and dusky farmland, I tried to put these mysteries out of my mind.

Anything could have gone wrong between Hitch Paley and Easy's Packages, but I told myself it didn't really matter. I had done what Hitch had asked and I was frankly relieved not be carrying a butcher-paper-wrapped bundle of incriminating evidence. The only potential problem was that Hitch might (and in the near future) want his money back.

Midnight inched past in the rainy dark. I reclined my seat and contemplated the future. West of the Mississippi, the economy was booming. The new covalent processor platforms had enabled oceans of complex new software, and I was certain I could find at least an entry-level gig with one of the Silicon Ring NASDAQ candidates. Put my degree to use before it became obsolete. In time, I could pay Hitch back and null the debt. Thus crime engenders virtue.

In time, I imagined, I would become respectable; I would prove my worth to Janice and be forgiven, and Kait would come toddling back into my arms.

But I couldn't help thinking of my father—seeing him in my own reflection in the rain-scored window. Failure is entropy, this specter seemed to announce, and entropy is a law of nature. Love becomes pain. Eventually you learn to ignore it. You achieve the nirvana of indifference. It's not easy. But nothing worth doing is easy.

Hitch and I were among the first to witness the Chumphon Chronolith, and in the great conflation of time and mind that followed . . . well, yes, it has occurred to me to wonder how much of my own pessimism (or my father's) I fed into that loop.

Not to mention a touch of madness on the maternal side. Cold air filtered into the darkened coach, and I remembered how fervently my mother had despised the cold. She had taken it personally, especially in her last years. A personal affront. She was an enemy of ice, plagued by snow.

She told me once that snow was the fecal matter of angels: it didn't stink, being angelic in origin, but it was an insult nevertheless, so pure it burned like fire on mortal skin.

Tucking away my ticket stub in a jacket pocket, I noticed that the index number printed under the AmMag logo was 2,041—same as the due date inscribed on the Kuin stone.

At the depot in Minneapolis/St. Paul I picked up the local news and a pop-science magazine with an article about the Chronolith.

The science magazine featured a number of photos of the Thai site, much changed from the day Hitch and I had visited it. A vast blankness had been bulldozed into the brown earth surrounding the pillar, and the cleared perimeter was pockmarked with tents, polygonal equipment sheds, makeshift laboratories, and an array of ochre-painted Porta-Potties. A multinational pool of scientific investigators had been installed by the Pacific Treaty powers, mostly materials scientists who were at this point admittedly baffled. The Chronolith was spectacularly inert. It seemed not to react with its environment at all, could not be etched with acid or cut with lasers; deep digging had not yet reached the roots of it; its temperature, at least since the icy blast of its arrival, had never varied from ambient by so much as a fraction of a centigrade degree. The thing was spectacularly aloof.

Spectral analysis of the pillar had proved especially unrewarding. The Chronolith passed and scattered light in the blue-green portion of the visible spectrum and, inexplicably, at a few harmonic wavelengths both infrared and ultraviolet. At other frequencies it was either purely reflective—impossibly reflective—or purely absorptive. Net input-output appeared to sum to zero, but no one was certain of that, and even that putative symmetry defied easy explanation. The article went on to speculate about a wholly new state of matter, which was less an explanation than a confession of ignorance phrased so as not to disturb the smooth flow of investigatory funding.

Speculation about the legend inscribed on the Chronolith was even gaudier and even less enlightening. Was "time travel" really a practical possibility? Most authorities dismissed the notion. The inscription was then perhaps a form of stealthing, a clue designed to mislead. Even the name "Kuin" was spectacularly uninformative. If it was a proper name, it might have been Chinese but was more commonly Dutch; the word also turned up in Finnish and Japanese; there was even a tribe of indigenous Peruvians called the Huni Kuin, though they could hardly be held responsible.

The alternate possibility—that some Asian warlord a mere twenty years hence had created a monument to a minor victory and *projected it into the recent past*—was simply too ridiculous to be true. (If this seems shortsighted now, consider that the scientific community had already been forced to swallow a number of evident absurdities about the Kuin stone and understandably balked at this ultimate impossibility. People used the word "impossible" more freely then.)

Such was the consensus, circa autumn of 2021.

I had bought the local paper for a more practical purpose. I searched its classified pages for rental properties close to the ring of suburban digital design consortia. The search coughed up a list of possibilities, and by Wednesday I had bribed my way into a one-bedroom walkup just west of the Twin Cities Agricultural Enclave. The room was unfurnished. I bought a chair, a table, and a bed. Anything more would have been a confession of permanency. I decided I was "in transition." Then I looked for a job. I didn't call Janice, at least not right away, because I wanted something to show her, first, some token of my credibility: an income, for example. If there had been a merit badge for Good Citizenship I would have applied for that, too.

Of course, none of this helped. There is no retrieving the past, a fact the reader almost surely understands. The younger generation knows these things better than my peers ever did. The knowledge has been forced on them.

Three

By February of 2022 Janice and Kaitlin had moved into a pleasant suburban co-op, far from Janice's work but close to good schools. The divorce contract we had finalized in December included a custody agreement that gave me Kaitlin for an average of one week per month.

Janice had been reasonable about sharing Kait, and I had seen a fair amount of my daughter since the fall. I was scheduled to have Kait this Saturday. But a day together mandated by a divorce court isn't just a day together. It's something else. Strange, awkward, and uncomfortable.

I showed up at Janice's at 8:45, a sunny but viciously cold Saturday morning. Janice invited me into her home and told me Kait was at a friend's house, watching morning cartoons until the appointed hour.

The co-op apartment had a pleasant

odor of fresh broadloom and recent breakfast. Janice, in her weekend-morning blouse and denims, poured me a cup of coffee. It seemed to me that we had reached a sort of rapprochement . . . that we might even have enjoyed seeing each other, if not for the baggage of pain and recrimination each of us carried into the other's presence. Not to mention bruised affection, forlorn hope, and muted grief.

Janice sat down with the coffee table between us. She had left a couple of her antiques on the table in a faux-casual display. She collected printed-paper magazines from the last century, *Life* and *Time* and so on. They lay in their stiff plastic wrappers like advertisements for a lost age, ticket stubs from the *Titanic.* "You're still at Campion-Miller?" she asked.

"Another six-month contract." And a 3k re-up bonus. At this rate my net income might someday advance all the way from Entry Level to Junior Employee. I had spent most of that bonus on a widescreen entertainment panel so Kait and I could watch movies together. Before Christmas I'd been relying on my portable station for both work and entertainment.

"So it's looking long-term."

"As such things go." I sipped from the cup she had given me. "The coffee's lousy, by the way."

"Oh?"

"You always made very bad coffee."

Janice smiled. "And now you can bring yourself to tell me about it?"

"Mm-hm."

"All those years, you hated my coffee?"

"I didn't say I hated it. I said it was bad."

"You never turned down a cup."

"No. I never did."

Kaitlin came in from the neighbors'—crashed through the front door in dripping plastic boots and a pleated winter jacket. Her glasses immediately frosted over with condensation. The glasses were a new addition. Kaitlin was only modestly nearsighted, but they don't do corrective surgery on children as young as Kait. She swiped her lenses with her fingers and gazed at me owlishly.

Kait used to give me a big smile whenever she saw me coming. She still smiled at me. But not automatically.

Janice said, "Did you see your cartoons, love?"

"No." Kait's eyes remained fixed on me. "Mr. Levy wanted to see the news."

It didn't occur to me to ask why Janice's neighbor had insisted on seeing the news.

But then, if I had asked, I might have missed an afternoon with Kait.

"Have fun with Daddy today," Janice said. "Do you need to go to the bathroom before you leave?"

Kaitlin was scandalized by this indelicacy. *"No!"*

"All right, then." Janice straightened and looked at me. "Eight o'clock, Scott?"

"Eight," I promised.

We hummed along in my secondhand car, neatly laced into heavy Saturday traffic by proximity protocols. I had promised Kaitlin a trip to an amusement mall, and she was already cycling through waves of elation and exhaustion, jabbering for long stretches of the ride, then lapsing against the upholstery with a forlorn *are-we-there-yet?* expression on her face.

During her silences I examined my conscience . . . cautiously, the way you might handle a sedated but venomous snake. I peeked at myself through Janice's eyes and saw (yet again) the man who had taken her and her daughter to a third-world country; who had nearly stranded them there; who had exposed them to an expatriate beach culture which, though no doubt colorful and interesting, was also drug-raddled, dangerous, and hopelessly unproductive.

The kind word for that sort of behavior is "thoughtless." Synonyms include "selfish" and "reckless."

Had I changed? Well, maybe. But I still owed Hitch Paley several thousand dollars (though I hadn't heard from him in half a year and had begun to harbor hopes that I wouldn't, ever)—and a life that includes such accessories as Hitch Paley is not, by definition, stable.

Still, here was Kaitlin, unharmed, periodically bouncing against the upholstery like a harnessed capuchin monkey. I had taught her to tie her shoes. I had shown her the Southern Cross, one cloudless night in Chumphon. I was her father, and she suffered my presence gladly.

We spent three hours at the mall, enough to tire her out. Kait was fascinated, if a little intimidated, by the clowns in their morphologically adaptive character suits and makeup. She packed away an astonishing amount of mall food, sat through two half-hour Surround Adventures, and slept sitting up on the way back to my apartment.

Home, I turned up the lights and shut out the prairie-winter dusk. For dinner I heated frozen chicken and string beans, prole food but good-smelling in the narrow kitchen; we watched downloads while we ate. Kaitlin didn't say much, but the atmosphere was cozy.

And when she looked to the right, I was able to see her deaf ear cosseted in a nest of golden hair. The ear was not grossly deformed, merely puckered where the bacteria had chewed away notches of flesh, pinkly scarred.

In her other ear she wore a hearing aid like a tiny polished seashell.

After dinner I washed the dishes, then coaxed Kaitlin away from cartoons and switched to a news broadcast.

The news was from Bangkok.

"*That,*" Kaitlin said sourly as she emerged from the bathroom, "is what Mr. *Levy* wanted to see."

• • •

This was, as you will have guessed, the first of the city-busting Chronoliths—in effect, first notice that something more significant than a *Stranger Than Science* anecdote was taking place in Southeast Asia.

I sat down next to Kaitlin and let her curl up against my ribs while I watched.

Kait was immediately bored. Children Kaitlin's age possess no context; one video event is much like another. And they're ruthless with their attention. She was impressed, if confused, by the helicopter shots of the riverfront neighborhoods destroyed and ice-coated, steaming in the sunlight. But there were only a few of these segments available, and the news networks ran them repeatedly over an aural haze of casualty estimates and meaningless "interpretation." The palpable atmosphere of confusion, fear, and denial evinced by the commentators kept her frowning a few minutes more, but before long she closed her eyes and her breathing steadied into petite, phlegmatic snores.

We were there, Kait, you and I, I thought.

Ruined Bangkok from the air looked like a misprinted road map. I recognized the Chao Phrya bending through the city, and the devastated Rattanakosin district, the old Royal City, where the Khlong Lawd fed the larger river. A patch of green might have been Lumphini Park. But the gridwork of roads had been reduced to an incomprehensible wasteland of brick and rebar, tin and cardboard and frost-heaved asphalt, all glittering with ice and wound about with fog. The ice had not prevented a number of broken gas mains from catching fire, islands of flame in the glacial wreckage. A great many people had died here, as the commentators took pains to point out. Some of the baggy objects littering the streets were almost certainly human bodies.

The only intact structure closer than the suburbs was at the very center of the disaster: the Chronolith itself.

It was not much like the Chumphon Chronolith. It was taller, grander, more intricately detailed and more finely sculpted. But I immediately recognized the translucent blue surface visible where patches of frost had peeled away, that distinct, indifferent skin.

The monument had "arrived" (explosively) after dark, Bangkok time. These clips were more recent, a few from the chaotic night, most fresh this morning. As time passed, the news networks relayed more aerial video. It was possible to see the new Chronolith in a kind of montage as it shed its cloak of condensed and frozen moisture, changing from what it had seemed to be—a monstrously large, oddly bulky white pillar—into what it really was: the stylized form of a human figure.

It recalled more than anything else the public monuments of Stalinist Russia; the Winged Victory at Leningrad, say. Or maybe the Colossus of Rhodes astride its harbor. Such structures are daunting not only because they are enormous but because they are so coldly stylized. This was not an image but a *schematic* of a human being, even the face contrived to suggest some generic Eurasian perfection unattainable in the real world. Scabs of ice clung to the domes of the eyes, the crevasses of the nostrils. Beyond its apparent masculinity, the figure might have been anyone. At least, anyone in whom infinite confidence had colluded with absolute power.

Kuin, I supposed. As he would have us see him.

His torso blended into the fundamental columnar structure of the Chronolith. The base of the monument, maybe a quarter mile in diameter, straddled the Chao Phrya, and skins of ice had formed where it met the water. These were breaking up in the sunlight and floating downstream, ice floes in the tropics, bumping the half-sunken hulls of tourist barges.

Janice called at ten, demanding to know what I had done with Kait. I looked at my watch, gritted my teeth and apologized. I explained to Janice how we had spent the day and how I had become distracted by the Bangkok Chronolith.

"*That* thing," she said, as if it were already old news. And maybe for Janice it was: she had already processed the Chronoliths into a generalized symbolic threat, terrifying but distant. She seemed unhappy that I had brought it up.

"I can drive Kaitlin back tonight," I said, "or keep her until morning if that's more convenient. She's asleep on the sofa right now."

"Get her a pillow and a blanket," Janice said, as if that thought had not already crossed my mind. "I guess she might as well sleep through."

I did better than that: I carried Kaitlin to the bed and took the sofa for myself. Sat up nearly until dawn watching TV with the sound turned low. The commentary was inaudible and probably better that way. Only the images remained, growing more complex as news crews pushed deeper into the rubble. By morning Kuin's vast head was wreathed in cloud, and rain had begun to dampen the burning city.

In the summer of that year (the summer Kaitlin learned to ride the bicycle I bought her for her birthday), a third Chronolith cored the living heart out of Pyongyang, and the Asian Crisis began in earnest.

Four

Time passed.

Should I apologize for these lapses—a year here, a year there? History isn't linear, after all. It runs in shallows and narrows and bayous and bays. (And treacherous undertows and hidden whirlpools.) And even a memoir is a kind of history.

But I suppose it depends on the audience I'm writing for, and that's still unclear in my mind. Who am I addressing? My own generation, so many of whom have died or are now dying? Our heirs, who may not have experienced these events but who can at least recite them from schoolbooks? Or some more distant generation of men and women who may have been allowed, God willing and impossible as it seems, to forget a little of what passed in this century?

In other words, how much should I explain, and how thoroughly?

But it's a moot question.

Really, there are only two of us here.

Me. And you. Whoever you are.

Nearly five years passed between my visit to the mall with Kaitlin and the day Arnie Kunderson called me out of a batch-sort test to his office—which was, perhaps, the next significant turning point in my life, if you believe in linear causality and the civilized deference of the future to the past. But taste those years, first: imagine them, if you don't remember them.

Five summers—warm ones, when the news (between Kuin events) was dominated by the ongoing depletion of the Oglalla Aquifer. New Mexico and Texas had virtually lost the ability to irrigate their dry lands. The Oglalla Aquifer, a body of underground water as large as Lake Huron and a relic of the last ice age, remained essential to agriculture in Nebraska, parts of Wyoming and Colorado, Kansas and Oklahoma—and it continued to decline, sucked up from increasing depths by ruthlessly efficient centrifugal pumps. The news feeds featured the farm exodus in repetitive, blunt images: families in battered cargo trucks stalled on the interstates, their sullen children with web toys plugging their ears and masking their eyes. Men and women standing on labor lines in Los Angeles or Detroit, the dark underside of our blossoming economy. Because most of us had work, we allowed ourselves the luxury of pity.

Five winters. Our winters were dry and cold, those years. The well-to-do wore thermally adaptive clothes for the first time, which left the tonier shopping districts looking as if they had been invaded by aliens in polyester jogging suits and respirators, while the rest of us beetled down the street in bulging parkas or stuck as close as possible to the skywalks. Domestic robots (self-guided vacuum cleaners, lawnmowers bright enough not to maim local children) became commonplace; the Sony dogwalker was withdrawn from the market after a well-publicized accident involving a malfunctioning streetlight and a brace of Shi Tzus. In those years, even the elderly stopped calling their entertainment panels "TV sets." Lux Ebone announced her retirement, twice. Cletus King defeated incumbent Marylin Leahy, giving the White House to the Federal Party, though Democrats continued to control Congress.

Catchphrases of the day, now all but forgotten: "Now give me *mine.*" "Brutal but nice!" "Like daylight in a drawer."

Names and places we imagined were important: Doctor Dan Lesser, the Wheeling Courthouse, Beckett and Goldstein, Kwame Finto.

Events: the second wave of lunar landings; the Zairian pandemic; the European currency crisis and the storming of the Hague.

And Kuin, of course, like a swelling drumbeat.

Pyongyang, then Ho Chi Minh City; eventually Macao, Sapporo, the Kanto Plain, Yichang. . . .

And all the early Kuin mania and fascination, the ten thousand websources with their peculiar and contradictory theories, the endless simmering of the crackpot press, the symposia and the committee reports, the think tanks and the congressional inquiries. The young man in Los Angeles who had his name legally changed to "Kuin," and all his subsequent imitators.

Kuin, whoever or whatever he might be, had already caused the deaths of hundreds of thousands of people, perhaps more. For that reason, the name was treated with gravitas in respectable circles. For the same reason, it became popular with comedians and T-shirt designers. "Kuinist" imagery was banned from certain schools, until the ACLU intervened. Because he stood for nothing discernible except destruction and conquest, Kuin became a slate on which the disaffected scrawled their manifestos. None of this was taken terribly seriously in North America. Elsewhere, the seismic rumbling was more ominous.

I followed it all closely.

For two years I worked at the Campion-Miller research facility outside of St. Paul, writing patches into self-evolved commercial-interface code. Then I was transferred to the downtown offices, where I joined a team doing much the same work on much more secure material, Campion-Miller's own tightly-held source code, the beating heart of our major products. Mostly I drove in from my one-bedroom apartment, but on the worst winter days I rode the new elevated train, an aluminum chamber into which too many commuters shed their heat and moisture, mingled body odors and aftershave, the city a pale scrim on steaming white windows.

(It was on one of those trips that I saw a young woman sitting halfway down the car, wearing a hat with the words "TWENTY AND THREE" printed on it—twenty years and three months, the nominal interval between the appearance of a Chronolith and its predicted conquest. She was reading a tattered copy of *Stranger Than Science*, which must have been out of print for at least sixty years. I wanted to approach her, to ask her what events had equipped her with these totems, these echoes of my own past, but I was too bashful, and how could I have phrased such a question, anyway? I never saw her again.)

I dated a few times. For most of a year I went out with a woman from the quality-control division of Campion-Miller, Annali Kincaid, who loved turquoise and New Drama and took a lively interest in current events. She dragged me to lectures and readings I would otherwise have ignored. We broke up, finally, because she possessed deep and complex political convictions, and I did not; I was a Kuin-watcher, otherwise politically agnostic.

But I was able to impress her on at least one occasion. She had used someone's credentials at Campion-Miller to wangle us admission to an academic conference at the university—"The Chronoliths: Scientific and Cultural Issues." (My idea as much as hers this time. Well, mostly mine. Annali had already voiced her objection to the aerial and orbital photographs of Chronoliths with which I had decorated my bedroom, the Kuinist downloads that littered the apartment.) We sat through the presentation of three papers and most of a pleasant Saturday afternoon, at which point Annali decided the discourse was a little too abstract for her taste. But on our way through the lobby I was hailed by an older woman in loose jeans and an oversized pea-green sweater, beaming at me through monstrous eyeglasses.

Her name was Sulamith Chopra. I had known her at Cornell. Her career had taken her deep into the fundamental-physics end of the Chronolith research.

I introduced Sue to Annali.

Annali was floored. "Ms. Chopra, I know who you are. I mean, they always quote your name in the news stories."

"Well, I've done some work."

"I'm pleased to meet you."

"Likewise." But Sue hadn't taken her eyes off me. "Strange I should run into *you* here, Scotty."

"Is it?"

"Unexpected. *Significant*, maybe. Or maybe not. We need to catch up on our lives sometime."

I was flattered. I wanted very much to talk to her. Pathetically, I offered her my business card.

"No need," she said. "I can find you when I need you, Scotty. Never fear."

"You can?"

But she was gone in the crowd.

"You're well connected," Annali told me on the ride home.

But that wasn't right. (Sue didn't call me—not that year—and my attempts to reach her were rebuffed.) I was connected, not well, but not quite randomly, either. Running into Sue Chopra was an omen, like seeing the woman in the commuter car; but the meaning of it was inscrutable, a prophecy in an indecipherable language, a signal buried in noise.

• • •

Being called to Arnie Kunderson's office was never a good sign. He had been my supervisor since I joined Campion-Miller, and I had learned this about Arnie: When the news was good, he would bring it to you. If he called you into his office, prepare for the worst.

I had seen Arnie angry, most recently, when the team I was leading botched an order-sort-and-mail protocol and nearly cost us a contract with a nationwide retailer. But I knew this was something even more serious as soon as I walked into his office. When he was angry, Arnie was ebulliently, floridly angry. Today, worse, he sat behind his desk with the furtive look of a man entrusted with some repellent but necessary duty—an undertaker, say. He wouldn't meet my eyes.

I pulled up a chair and waited. We weren't formal. We had been to each other's barbecues.

He folded his hands and said. "There's never a good way to do this. What I have to tell you, Scott, is that Campion-Miller isn't renewing your contract. We're canceling it. This is official notice. I know you haven't had any warning and Christ knows I'm incredibly fucking sorry to drop this on you. You're entitled to full severance and a generous compensation package for the six months left to run."

I wasn't as surprised as Arnie seemed to expect. The Asian economic collapse had cut deeply into Campion-Miller's foreign markets. Just last year the firm had been acquired by a multinational corporation whose management team laid off a quarter of the staff and cashed in most of C-M's subsidiary holdings for their real-estate value.

I did, however, feel somewhat blindsided.

Unemployment was up that year. The Oglalla crisis and the collapse of the Asian economies had dumped a lot of people onto the job market. There was a tent city five blocks square down along the riverside. I pictured myself there.

I said, "Are you going to tell the team, or do you want me to do it?"

The team I led was working on predictive market software, one of C-M's more lucrative lines. In particular, we were factoring genuine as versus perceived randomness into such applications as consumer trending and competitive pricing.

Ask a computer to pick two random numbers between one and ten and the machine will cough up digits in a genuinely random sequence—maybe 2,3; maybe 1,9, and so on. Ask a number of human beings, plot their answers, and you'll get a distribution curve heavily weighted at 3 and 7. When people think "random" they tend to picture numbers you might call "unobtrusive"—not too near the limits nor precisely in the middle; not part of a presumed sequence (2,4,6), etc.

In other words, there is something you might call *intuitive* randomness which differs dramatically from the real thing.

Was it possible to exploit this difference to our advantage in high-volume commercial apps, such as stock portfolios or marketing or product price-placement?

We thought so. We'd made a little progress. The work had been going well enough that Arnie's news seemed (at least) oddly timed.

He cleared his throat. "You misunderstand. The team isn't leaving."

"Excuse me?"

"It's not my decision, Scott."

"You said that. Okay, it's not your fault. But if the project is going forward—"

"Don't ask me to justify this. Frankly, I can't."

He let that sink in.

"Five years," I said. "Fuck, Arnie. Five years!"

"Nothing's guaranteed. Not anymore. You know that as well as I do."

"It might help if I understood why this was happening."

He twisted in his chair. "I'm not at liberty to say. Your work has been excellent, and I'll put that in writing if you like."

"What are you telling me, I made an enemy in management?"

He halfway nodded. "The work we do here is pretty tightly held. People get nervous. I don't know if you made an enemy, exactly. Maybe you made the wrong friends."

But that wasn't likely. I hadn't made very many friends.

People I could share lunch with, catch a Twins game with, sure. But no one I confided in. Somehow, by some process of slow emotional attrition, I had become the kind of guy who works hard and smiles amiably and goes home and spends the evening with the video panel and a couple of beers.

Which is what I did the day Arnie Kunderson fired me.

The apartment hadn't changed much since I moved in. (Barring the one wall of the bedroom I used as a sort of bulletin board. News printouts and photos of Chronolith sites plus my copious notes on the subject.) To the degree that the place had improved, it was mostly Kaitlin's doing. Kait was ten now, eager to criticize my fashion sense. Probably it made her feel grown up. I had replaced the sofa because I had gotten tired of hearing how "uncontemporary" it was—Kait's favorite word of derision.

At any rate, the old sofa had gone; in its place was an austere blue padded bench that looked great until you tried to get comfortable on it.

I thought about calling Janice but decided not to. Janice didn't appreciate spontaneous phone calls. She preferred to hear from me on a regular and predictable schedule. And as for Kaitlin . . . better not to bother her, either. If I did, she might launch into a discourse on what she had done today with Whit, as she was encouraged to call her stepfather. Whit was a great guy, in Kait's opinion. Whit made her laugh. Maybe I should talk to Whit, I thought. Maybe Whit would make *me* laugh.

So I did nothing that evening except nurse a few beers and surf the satellites.

Even the cheap servers carried a number of science-and-nature feeds. One of them was showing fresh video from Thailand, of a genuinely dangerous expedition up the Chao Phrya to the ruins of Bangkok, sponsored by the National Geographic Society and a half-dozen corporate donors whose logos were prominently featured in the start-up credits.

I turned off the sound, let the pictures speak for themselves.

Not much of Bangkok's urban core had been rebuilt in the years since 2021. No one wanted to live or work too close to the Chronolith—rumors of "proximity sickness" frightened people away, though there was no such diagnosis in the legitimate clinical literature. The bandits and the revolutionary militias, however, were quite real and omnipresent. But despite all this there was still a brisk river trade along the Chao Phrya, even in the shadow of Kuin.

The program began with overflight footage of the city. Crude, canted docks allowed access to rough warehouses, a marketplace, stocks of fresh fruits and vegetables, order emerging from the wreckage, streets reclaimed from the rubble and open to commerce. From a great enough altitude it looked like a story of human perseverance in the face of disaster. The view from the ground was less encouraging.

As the expedition approached the heart of the city the Chronolith was present in every shot: from a distance, dominating the brown river; or closer, towering into a tropical noon.

The monument was conspicuously clean. Even birds and insects avoided it. Airborne dust had collected in the few protected crevices of the sculpted face, faintly softening Kuin's abstracted gaze. But nothing grew even in that protected soil; the sterility of it was absolute. Where the base of the monument touched ground on one bank of the river a few lianas had attempted to scale the immense octagonal base; but the mirror-smooth surface was ungraspable, unwelcoming.

The expedition anchored mid-river and went ashore for more footage. In one sequence, a storm swirled over the ancient city. Rainwater cascaded from the Chronolith in miniature torrents, small waterfalls churning plumes of silt from the river bottom. The dockside vendors covered their stalls with tarpaulins and sheet plastic and retreated beneath them.

Cut to a shot of a wild monkey on a collapsed Exxon billboard, barking at the sky.

Clouds parting around the promontory of Kuin's vast head.

The sun emerging near the green horizon, the Chronolith shadowing the city like the gnomon of a great bleak sundial.

There was more, but nothing revelatory. I turned off the monitor and went to bed.

We—the English-speaking world—had by this time agreed on certain terms to describe the Chronoliths. What a Chronolith did, for instance, was to *appear* or to *arrive* . . . though some favored *touched down*, as if it were a kind of stalled tornado.

The newest of the Chronoliths had appeared (arrived, touched down) more than eighteen months ago, leveling the waterfront of Macao. Only half a year earlier a similar monument had destroyed Taipei.

Both stones marked, as usual, military victories roughly twenty years in the future. Twenty and three: hardly a lifetime, but arguably long enough for Kuin (if he existed, if he was more than a contrived symbol or an abstraction) to mass forces for his putative Asian conquests. Long enough for a young man to become a middle-aged man. Long enough for a young girl to become a young woman.

But no Chronolith had arrived anywhere in the world for more than a year now, and some of us had chosen to believe that the crisis was, if not exactly finished, at least purely Asian—confined by geography, bound by oceans.

Our public discourse was aloof, detached. Much of southern China was in a condition of political and military chaos, a no-man's-land in which Kuin was perhaps already gathering his nucleus of followers. But an editorial in yesterday's paper had wondered whether Kuin might not, in the long term, turn out to be a *positive* force: a Kuinist empire was hardly likely to be a benevolent dictatorship, but it might restore stability to a dangerously destabilized region. What was left of the tattered Beijing bureaucracy had already detonated a tactical nuclear device in an unsuccessful attempt to destroy last year's so-called Kuin of Yichang. The result had been a breached dam and a flood that carried radioactive mud all the way to the East China Sea. And if crippled Beijing was capable of that, could a Kuin regime be worse?

I had no opinion of my own. We were all whistling through the graveyard in those years, even those of us who paid attention, analyzing the Chronoliths (by date, time, size, implied conquest and such) so that we could pretend to understand them. But I preferred not to play that game. The Chronoliths had shadowed my life since things went bad with Janice. They were emblematic of every malign and unpredictable force in the world. There were times when I was profoundly afraid of them, and as often as not I admitted that fact to myself.

Is this obsession? Annali had thought so.

I tried to sleep. Sleep that knits the raveled sleeve, etc. Sleep that kills the awkward downtime between midnight and dawn.

But I didn't get even that. An hour before sunrise, my phone buzzed. I should have let the server pick it up. But I groped for the handset and flipped it open, afraid—as always when the phone rings late at night—that something had happened to Kait. "Hello?"

"Scott," a coarse male voice said. "Scotty"

I thought for one panicky moment of Hitch Paley. Hitch, with whom I had not spoken since 2021. Hitch Paley, riding out of the past like a pissed-off ghost.

But it wasn't Hitch.

It was some other ghost.

I listened to the phlegmy breathing, the compression and expansion of night air in a withered bellows. "Dad?"

"Scotty . . ." he said, as if he couldn't get past the name.

"Dad, have you been drinking?" I was courteous enough to refrain from adding, *again*.

"No," he said angrily. "No, I—ah, well, fuck it, then. This is the kind of—the kind of treatment—well, you know, *fuck* it."

And he was gone.

I rolled out of bed.

I watched the sun come up over the agricultural co-ops to the east, the great corporate collective farms, our bulwark against famine. A dusting of snow had collected in the fields, sparkling white between empty cornrows.

Later I drove to Annali's apartment, knocked on her door.

We hadn't dated for more than a year, but we were still friendly when we met in the coffee room or the cafeteria. She took a slightly maternal interest in me these days—inquiring after my health, as if she expected something to go terribly wrong sooner or later. (Maybe that day had come, though I was still healthy as a horse.)

But she was startled when she opened the door and saw me. Startled and obviously dismayed.

She knew I'd been fired. Maybe she knew more than that.

Which was why I had come here: on the off chance that she could help make sense of what had happened.

"Scotty," she said, "hey, you should have called first."

"You're busy?" She didn't look busy. She was wearing loose culottes and a faded yellow shirt. Cleaning the kitchen, maybe.

"I'm going out in a few minutes. I'd ask you in, but I have to get dressed and all that. What are you doing here?"

She was, I realized, actually *afraid* of me—or of being seen with me.

"Scott?" She looked up and down the corridor. "Are you in trouble?"

"Why would I be in trouble, Annali?"

"Well—I heard about you being fired."

"How long ago?"

"What do you mean?"

"How long have you known I was going to be fired?"

"You mean, was it general knowledge? No, Scott. God, that would be humiliating. No. Of course, you hear rumors—"

"What kind of rumors?"

She frowned and chewed her lip. That was a new habit. "The kind of work Campion-Miller does, they don't need trouble with the government."

"The fuck does that have to do with me?"

"You know, you don't have to shout."

"Annali—trouble with the *government?*"

"The thing I heard is that some people were asking about you. Like government people."

"Police?"

"No—are you in trouble with the police? No, just people in suits. Maybe IRS, I don't know."

"That doesn't make sense."

"It's just people talking, Scott. It could all be bullshit. Really, I don't know why they fired you. It's just that CM, they depend on keeping all their permits in order. All that tech stuff they ship overseas. If somebody comes in asking questions about you, it could endanger everybody."

"Annali, I'm not a security risk."

"I know, Scott." She knew nothing of the sort. She wouldn't meet my eyes. "Honestly, I'm sure it's all bullshit. But I really do have to get dressed." She began to ease the door shut. "Next time, phone me, for God's sake!"

She lived on the second floor of a little three-story brick building in the old part of Edina. Apartment 203. I stared at the number on the door for a while. Twenty and three.

I never saw Annali Kincaid again. Occasionally I wonder what sort of life she led. How she fared during the long hard years.

• • •

I didn't tell Janice that I had lost my job. Not that I was still trying to prove anything to Janice. To myself, maybe. To Kaitlin, almost certainly.

Not that Kait cared what I did for a living. At ten, Kait still perceived adult business as opaque and uninteresting. She knew only that I "went to work" and that I earned enough money to make me a respectable if not wealthy member of the grownup world. And that was fine. I liked that occasional reflection of myself in Kait's eyes: Stable. Predictable. Even boring.

But not disappointing.

Certainly not dangerous.

I didn't want Kait (or Janice or even Whit) to know I'd been fired . . . at least not immediately, not until I had something to add to the story. If not a happy ending, then at least a second chapter, a what-comes-next . . .

It came in the form of another unexpected phone call.

Not a happy ending, no. Not an ending at all. Definitely not happy.

Janice and Whit invited me to dinner. They did this on a quarterly basis, the way you might contribute to a pension plan or a worthy charity.

Janice was no longer a single mom in a rent-controlled townhouse. She had shed that stigma when she married her supervisor at the biochem lab where she worked, Whitman Delahunt. Whit was an ambitious guy with serious managerial talent. Clarion Pharmaceuticals had prospered despite the Asian crisis, feeding Western markets suddenly deprived of cut-rate Chinese and Taiwanese biochemical imports. (Whit sometimes referred to the Chronoliths as "God's little tariff," which made Janice smile uneasily.) I don't think Whit liked me much, but he accepted me as a sort of country cousin, attached to Kaitlin by an unpleasant and unmentionable accident of paternity.

To be fair, he tried to make me feel welcome, at least this night. He opened the door of his two-story house, framing himself in warm yellow light. He grinned. Whit was one of those big soft men, teddy-bear-shaped and about as hairy. Not handsome, but the sort women call "cute." He was ten years older than Janice. Balding, but wearing it well. His grin was expansive if inauthentic, and his teeth were blazing white. Whit almost certainly had the best dentistry, the best radial kariotomy, and the best car on the block. I wondered if it was hard on Janice and Kaitlin, being the best wife and the best daughter.

"Come on in, Scott!" he exclaimed. "Take off those boots, warm yourself by the fire."

We ate in the spacious dining room, where leaded windows of distinguished provenance rattled in their frames. Kait talked a little about school. (She was having trouble this year, particularly in math.) Whit talked with vastly greater enthusiasm about his work. Janice was still running fairly routine protein syntheses at Clarion and talked about it not at all. She seemed content to let Whit do the bragging.

Kait excused herself first, dashing off to an adjacent room where the television had been mumbling counterpoint to the sound of the wind. Whit brought out a brandy decanter. He served drinks awkwardly, like a Westerner attempting a Japanese tea ceremony. Whit wasn't much of a drinker.

He said, "I'm afraid I've been doing all the talking. How about you, Scott? How's life treating you?"

" 'Fortune presents gifts not according to the book.' "

"Scotty's quoting poetry again," Janice explained.

"What I mean is, I've been offered a job."

"You're thinking of leaving Campion-Miller?"

"I parted ways with Campion-Miller about two weeks ago."

"Oh! Gutsy decision, Scott."

"Thank you, Whit, but it didn't seem that way at the time."

Janice said, out of what appeared to be a profounder understanding, "So who are you with now?"

"Well, it's not for certain, but—you remember Sue Chopra?"

Janice frowned. Then her eyes widened. "Yes! Cornell, right? The junior professor who taught that flaky first-year course?"

Janice and I had met at university. The first time I had seen her she had been walking through the chemistry lab with a bottle of lithium aluminum hydroxide in her hand. If she had dropped it, she might have killed us both. First rule of a stable relationship: Don't drop the fucking bottle.

It was Janice who had introduced me to Sulamith Chopra when Sue was a ridiculously tall and chunky post-doc building a reputation in the physics department. Sue had been handed (probably as punishment for some academic indiscretion) a second-year interdisciplinary course of the kind offered to English students as a science credit and to science students as an English credit. For which she turned around and wrote a curriculum so intimidating that it scared off everybody but a few naive artsies and confused computer science types. And me. The pleasant surprise was that Sue had no interest in failing anyone. She had put together the course description to scare away parvenus. All she wanted with the rest of us was an interesting conversation.

So "Metaphor and Reality-Modeling in Literature and the Physical Sciences" became a kind of weekly salon, and the only requirement for a passing grade was that we demonstrate that we'd read her syllabus and that she must not be bored with what we said about it. For an easy mark all you had to do was ask Sue about her pet research topics (Calabi-Yau geometry, say, or the difference between prior and contextual forces); she would talk for twenty minutes and grade you on the plausibility of the rapt attention you displayed.

But Sue was fun to bullshit with, too, so mostly her classes were extended bull sessions. And by the end of the semester I had stopped seeing her as this six-foot-four-inch bug-eyed badly-dressed oddity and had begun to perceive the funny, fiercely intelligent woman she was.

I said, "Sue Chopra offered me a job."

Janice turned to Whit and said, "One of the Cornell profs. Didn't I see her name in the paper recently?"

Probably so, but that was awkward territory. "She's part of a federally-funded research group. She has enough clout to hire help."

"So she got in touch with *you*?"

Whit said, "That's maybe not the kindest way to put it."

"It's okay, Whit. What Janice means is, what would a high-powered academic like Sulamith Chopra want with a keyboard hack like myself? It's a fair question."

Janice said, "And the answer is—?"

"I guess they wanted one more keyboard hack."

"You told her you needed work?"

"Well, you know. We stay in touch."

(*I can find you when I need you, Scotty. Never fear.*)

"Uh-huh," Janice said, which was her way of telling me she knew I was lying. But she didn't press.

"Well, that's great, Scott," Whit said. "These are tough times to be out of a job. So, that's great."

We said no more about it until the meal was finished and Whit had excused himself. Janice waited until he was out of earshot. "Something you're not mentioning?"

Several things. I gave her one of them. "The job is in Baltimore."

"Baltimore?"

"Baltimore. Maryland."

"You mean you're moving across the country?"

"If I get the job. It's not for sure yet."

"But you haven't told Kaitlin."

"No. I haven't told Kaitlin. I wanted to talk to you about it first."

"Uh-huh. Well, I don't know what to say. I mean, this is really sudden. The question is how upset Kait will be. But I can't answer that. No offense, but she doesn't talk about you as much as she used to."

"It's not like I'll be out of her life. We can visit."

"Visiting isn't parenting, Scott. Visiting is . . . an *uncle* thing. But I don't know. Maybe that's best. She and Whit are bonding pretty well."

"Even if I'm out of town, I'm still her father."

"Insofar as you ever were, yes, that's true."

"You sound angry."

"I'm not. Just wondering whether I *should* be."

Whit came back downstairs then, and we chatted some more, but the wind grew louder and hard snow ticked on the windows and Janice fretted out loud over the condition of the streets. So I said goodbye to Whit and Janice and waited at the door for Kait to give me her customary farewell hug.

She came into the foyer but stopped a few feet away. Her eyes were stormy and her lower lip was trembling.

"Kaity-bird?" I said.

"Please don't call me that. I'm not a baby."

Then I figured it out. "You were listening."

Her hearing impairment didn't prevent her from eavesdropping. If anything, it had made her stealthier and more curious.

"Hey," she said, "it doesn't matter. You're moving away. That's all right."

Of all the things I could have said, what I chose was: "You shouldn't listen in on other people's conversations, Kaitlin."

"Don't tell me what to do," she said, and turned and ran to her room.

Five

Janice called me a day before I was due to leave for Baltimore and an interview with Sue Chopra. I was surprised to hear her voice on the phone—she seldom called except at our agreed-on times.

"Nothing wrong," Janice said at once. "I just wanted to, you know, wish you luck."

The kind of luck that would keep me out of town? But that was petty. I said, "Thanks."

"I mean it. I've been thinking this over. And I wanted you to know—yes, Kaitlin's taking it pretty hard. But she'll come around. If she didn't care about you, she wouldn't be so upset."

"Well—thank you for saying so."

"That's not all." She hesitated. "Ah, Scott, we fucked up pretty badly, didn't we? Those days in Thailand. It was just too weird. Too strange."

"I've apologized for that."

"I didn't call you up for an apology. Do you hear what I'm saying? Maybe it was partly my fault, too."

"Let's not play whose fault it was, Janice. But I appreciate you saying so."

I couldn't help surveying my apartment as we spoke. It seemed empty already. Under the stale blinds, the windows were white with ice.

"What I want to tell you is that I know you've been trying to make it up. Not to me. I'm a lost cause, right? But to Kaitlin."

I said nothing.

"All the time you spent at Campion-Miller. . . . You know, I was worried when you came back from Thailand, way back when. I didn't know whether you were going to hang on my doorstep and harass me, whether it would be good for Kaitlin even to see you. But I have to admit, whatever it takes to be a divorced father, you had the right stuff. You brought Kait through all that trauma as if you were walking her through a minefield, taking all the chances yourself."

This was as intimate a conversation as we had had in years, and I wasn't sure how to respond.

She went on: "It seemed like you were trying to prove something to yourself, prove that you were capable of acting decently, taking responsibility."

"Not proving it," I said. "Doing it."

"Doing it, but punishing yourself, too. Blaming yourself. Which is part of taking responsibility. But past a certain point, Scott, that becomes a problem in itself. Only monks get to lacerate themselves full-time."

"I'm not a monk, Janice."

"So don't act like one. If this job looks like a good choice, take it. *Take* it, Scott. Kait won't stop loving you just because you can't see her on a weekly basis. She's upset now, but she's capable of understanding."

It was a long speech. It was also Janice's best effort to date to grant me absolution, give me full marks for owning up to the disaster I had made of our lives.

And that was good. It was generous. But it was also the sound of a closing door. She was giving me permission to look for a better life, because any lingering suspicion that we could recreate what was once between us was desperately misplaced.

Well, we both knew that. But what the head admits isn't always what the heart allows.

"I have to say goodbye, Scotty."

There was a little catch in her voice, almost a hiccup.

"Okay, Janice. Give Whit my best wishes."

"Call when you find work."

"Right."

"Kait still needs to hear from you, whatever she may think. Times like this, you know, the world being what it is . . ."

"I understand."

"And be careful on the way to the airport. The roads are slippery since that last big snow."

I came into the Baltimore airport expecting a hired driver with a name card, but it was Sulamith Chopra herself who met me.

There was no mistaking her, even after all these years. She towered above the crowd. Even her head was tall, a gawky brown peanut topped with black frazzle. She wore balloon-sized khaki pants and a blouse that might once have been white but appeared to have shared laundry rounds with a few non-colorfast items. Her look was so completely Salvation Army Thrift Shop that I wondered whether she was really in a position to offer anyone a job . . . but then I thought *academia* and *the sciences.*

She grinned. I grinned, less energetically.

I put out my hand, but Sue was having none of it; she grabbed me and bear-hugged me, breaking away about a tenth of a second before the grip became painful. "Same old Scotty," she said.

"Same old Sue," I managed.

"I've got my car here. Have you had lunch yet?"

"I haven't had breakfast."

"Then it's my treat."

She had called me two weeks ago, waking me out of a dreamless afternoon sleep. Her first words were, "Hi, Scotty? I hear you lost your job."

Note, this was a woman I hadn't spoken with since our chance meeting in Minneapolis. A woman who hadn't returned any of my calls since. It took me a few groggy seconds just to place the voice.

"Sorry I haven't got back to you till now," she went on. "There were reasons for that. But I kept track of you."

"You kept *track* of me?"

"It's a long story." I waited for her to tell it. Instead, she reminisced for a while about Cornell and gave me the highlights of her career since then—her academic work with the Chronoliths, which interested me enormously. And distracted me, as I'm sure Sue knew it would.

She talked about the physics in greater detail than I was able to follow: Calabi-Yau spaces, something she called "tau turbulence."

Until at last I asked her, "So, yeah, I lost my job—how did you know?"

"Well, that's part of why I'm calling. I feel a certain amount of responsibility for that."

I recalled what Arnie Kunderson had said about "enemies in management." What Annali had told me about "men in suits." I said, "Whatever you need to tell me, tell me."

"Okay, but you have to be patient. I assume you don't have anywhere to go? No urgent bathroom calls?"

"I'll keep you posted."

"Okay. Well. Where to begin? Did you ever notice, Scotty, how hard it is to sort out cause and effect? Things get tangled up."

Sue had published a number of papers on the subject of exotic forms of matter and C-Y transformations ("nonbaryonic matter and how to untie knots in string") by the time the Chumphon Chronolith appeared. Many of these dealt with problems in temporal symmetry—a concept she seemed determined to explain to me, until I cut her short. After Chumphon, when Congress began to take seriously the potential threat of the Chronoliths, she had been invited to join an investigatory effort sponsored by a handful of security agencies and funded under an ongoing federal appropriation. The work, they told her, would be basic research, would be part-time, would involve the collaboration of the Cornell faculty and various elder colleagues, and would look impressive on her *curriculum vitae.* She said it was "Like Los Alamos, you understand, but a little more relaxed."

"Relaxed?"

"At least at first. So I accepted. It was in those first few months I came across your name. It was all pretty wide-open back then. I saw all kinds of security shit. There was a master list of eyewitnesses, people they had debriefed in Thailand. . . ."

"Ah."

"And of course your name was on it. We were thinking of bringing all those people in, anybody we could find, for blood testing and whatever, but we decided against it—too much work, too invasive, not likely to produce any substantive results. Plus there were civil-liberties problems. But I remembered your name on that list. I knew it was you because they had practically your entire life history down there, including Cornell, including a hypertext link to *me.*"

And again I thought of Hitch Paley. His name would have been on that list, too. Maybe they had looked a little more deeply into his business activities since then. Maybe Hitch was in jail. Maybe that was why there had been no pickup that day at Easy's Packages and no word from him since.

But of course I didn't say any of this to Sue.

She went on, "Well, I made a kind of mental note of it, but that was that, at least until recently. What you have to understand, Scotty, is that the evolution of this crisis has made everyone a lot more paranoid. Maybe *justifiably* paranoid. Especially since Yichang; Yichang just drove everybody completely bugfuck. You know how many people were killed by floodwater *alone*? Not to mention that it was the first nuclear device detonated in a kind-of-sort-of war since before the turn of the century."

She didn't have to tell me. I'd been paying attention. It was not even slightly surprising to learn that the NSA or CIA or FBI was profoundly involved with Sue's research. The Chronoliths had become, at bottom, a defense issue. The image lurking at the back of everyone's mind—seldom spoken, seldom explicit—was of a Chronolith on American soil: Kuin towering over Houston or New York or Washington.

"So when I saw your name again . . . well, it was on a different kind of list. The FBI is looking into witnesses again. I mean, they've been sort of keeping an eye on you since the word go. Not exactly *surveillance*, but if you moved out of state or something like that, it would be noted, it would go in your file. . . ."

"Christ, Sue!"

"But all that was harmless busywork. Until lately. Your work at Campion-Miller came up on the radar."

"I write business software. I don't see—"

"That's way too coy, Scotty. You've done some really sensitive work with marketing heuristics and collective anticipation. I've looked at your code—"

"You've seen Campion-Miller source code?"

"Campion-Miller elected to share it with the authorities."

I began to put this together. An interrogatory FBI visit at

Campion-Miller could easily have alarmed management, especially if it was core code that had come under scrutiny. And it would explain Arnie Kunderson's strange intransigence, the don't-ask-don't-tell atmosphere that had surrounded the firing.

"You're telling me you got me fired?"

"It was nobody's intention for you to lose your job. As it happens, though, that's kind of handy."

Handy was about the last word I would have used.

"See, Scotty, how this hooks together? You're on the spot when the Chumphon Chronolith arrives, which marks you for life all by itself. Now, five years later, it turns out you're evolving algorithms that are deeply pertinent to the research we're doing here."

"Are they?"

"Trust me. It flagged your file. I put in a good word for you, and that kept them off your tail a little bit, but I have to be frank with you, some very powerful people are getting way too excited. It's not just Yichang, it's the economy, the riots, all that trouble during the last election . . . the level of nervousness is indescribable. So when I heard you got fired I had the brilliant idea of getting you placed *here*."

"As what, a prisoner?"

"Hardly. I'm serious about your work, Scotty. In terms of code husbandry, it's absolutely fine. And very, very pertinent. Maybe it doesn't seem so, but a great deal of what I've been looking at lately is modeling the effect of anticipation on mass behavior. Applying feedback and recursion theory to both physical events and human behavior."

"I'm a keyboard hack, Sue. I've grown algorithms I don't pretend to understand."

"You're too modest. This is key work. And it would be much nicer, frankly, if you were doing it for *us*."

"I don't understand. Is it my work you're interested in, or the fact that I was at Chumphon?"

"Both. I suspect it's not coincidental."

"But it is."

"Yes, in the *conventional* sense, but—oh, Scotty, this is too much to talk about over the phone. You need to come see me."

"Sue—"

"You're going to tell me you feel like I put your head in a blender. You're going to tell me you can't make a decision like this while you're standing in your PJs drinking bottled beer and feeling sorry for yourself."

I was wearing jeans and a sweatshirt. Otherwise, she was on the mark.

"So *don't* decide," she said. "But do come see me. Come to Baltimore. My expense. We can talk about it then. I'll make arrangements."

One of the salient facts about Sulamith Chopra is that when she says she means to do a thing, she does it.

The recession had hit Baltimore harder than it hit Minneapolis/St. Paul. The city had done all right in the young years of the century, but the downtown core had lost that brief sheen of prosperity, had faded into empty storefronts, cracked plasma displays, gaudy billboards turned pastel by sun and weather.

Sue parked at the back of a small Mexican restaurant and escorted me inside. The restaurant staff recognized her and greeted her by name. Our waitress was dressed as if she had stepped out of a 17th-century mission but recited the daily specials in a clipped New England accent. She smiled at Sue the way a tenant farmer might smile at a benevolent landlord—I gathered Sue was a generous tipper.

We talked for a while about nothing in particular—current events, the Oglalla crisis, the Pemberton trial. This was Sue's attempt to re-establish the tone of the relationship between us, the familial intimacy she had established with all her students at Cornell. She had never liked being treated as a figure of authority. She deferred to no one and hated being deferred to. Sue was old-fashioned enough to envision working scientists as equal plaintiffs before the absolute bar of truth.

Since Cornell, she said, the Chronolith project had taken up more and more of her time; had become, in effect, her career. She had published important theoretical papers during this time, but only after they had been vetted by national security. "And the most important work we've done can't be published at all, for fear that we'd be putting the weapon into Kuin's hands."

"So you know more than you can say."

"Yes, lots . . . but not *enough*." The waitress brought rice and beans. Sue tucked into her lunch, frowning. "I know about you, too, Scotty. You divorced Janice, or vice versa. Your daughter lives with her mom now. Janice remarried. You did five years of good but extremely circumscribed work at Campion-Miller, which is a shame, because you're one of the brightest people I know. Not genius-in-a-wheelchair smart, but *bright*. You could do better."

"That's what they always used to write on my report cards—'could do better.' "

"Did you ever get over Janice?"

Sue asked intimate questions with the brusqueness of a census taker. I don't think it even occurred to her that she might be giving offense.

Hence no offense taken.

"Mostly," I said.

"And the girl? Kaitlin, is it? God, I remember when Janice was pregnant. That big belly of hers. Like she was trying to shoplift a Volkswagen."

"Kait and I get on all right."

"You still love your daughter?"

"Yes, Sue, I still love my daughter."

"Of course you do. How Scotty of you." She seemed genuinely pleased.

"Well, how about you? You have anything going?"

"Well," she said. "I live alone. There's somebody I see once in a while, but it's not a *relationship*." Sue lowered her eyes and added, "She's a poet. The kind of poet who works retail by daylight. I can't bring myself to tell her the FBI already looked into her background. She'd go ballistic. Anyway, she sees other people too. We're non-monogamous. Polyamorous. Mostly we're barely even *together*."

I raised a glass. "Strange days."

"Strange days. *Skol.* By the way, I hear you're not speaking to your father."

I almost choked.

"Saw your phone records," she explained. "He makes the calls. They don't last more than thirty seconds."

"It's kind of a race," I said. "See who hangs up first. Goddammit, Sue, those are *private* calls."

"He's sick, Scotty."

"Tell me about it."

"No, really. You know about the emphysema, I guess. But he's been seeing an oncologist. Liver cancer, nonresponsive, metastatic."

I put down my fork.

"Oh, Scotty," she said. "I'm sorry."

"You realize, I don't know you."

"Of course you know me."

"I knew you a long time ago. Not intimately. I knew a junior academic, not a woman who gets me fired—and bugs my fucking phone."

"There's no such thing as privacy anymore, not really."

"He's, what, dying?"

"Probably." Her face fell when she realized what she'd said. "Oh, God—forgive me, Scott. I speak before I think. It's like I'm some kind of borderline autistic or something."

That, at least, I did know about her. I'm sure Sue's defect has been named and genetically mapped, some mild inability to read or predict the feelings of others. And she loved to talk—at least in those days.

"None of my business," she said. "You're right."

"I don't need a surrogate parent. I'm not even sure I need this job."

"Scotty, I'm not the one who started logging your calls. You can take this job or not, but walking away won't give you a normal life. You surrendered that in Chumphon, whether you knew it or not."

I thought, *My father is dying.*

I wondered whether I cared.

Back in the car, Sue remained apologetic. "Is it wrong of me to point out that we're both in a bind? That both our lives have been shaped by the Chronoliths in ways we can't control? But I'm trying to do the best thing, Scotty. I need you here, and I think the work would be more satisfying than what you were doing at Campion-Miller." She drove through a yellow light, blinking at the reprimand that flashed on her heads-up. "Am I wrong to suspect that you *want* to get involved with what we're doing?"

No, but I didn't give her the satisfaction of saying so.

"Also—" Was she blushing? "Frankly, I'd enjoy your company."

"You must have lots of company."

"I have *colleagues*, not company. Nobody real. Besides, you *know* it's not a bad offer. Not in the kind of world we're living in." She added, almost coyly, "And you get to travel. See foreign lands. Witness miracles."

Stranger than science.

Six

In the grand tradition of federal employment, I waited three weeks while nothing happened. Sulamith Chopra's employers put me up in a motel room and left me there. My calls to Sue were routed through a functionary named Morris Torrance, who advised me to be patient. Room service was free, but man was not meant to live by room service alone. I didn't want to give up my Minneapolis apartment until I had signed something permanent, and every day I spent in Maryland represented a net fiscal loss.

The motel terminal was almost certainly tapped, and I presumed the FBI had found a way to read my portable panel even before its signal reached a satellite. Nevertheless I did what they probably expected me to do: I continued to collect Kuin data, and looked a little more closely at some of Sue's publications.

She had published two important papers in the *Nature* nexus and one on the *Science* site. All three were concerned with matters I wasn't competent to judge and which seemed only distantly related to the question of the Chronoliths: "A Hypothetical Tauon Unification Energy," "Non-Hadronic Material Structures," "Gravitation and Temporal Binding Forces." All I could discern from the text was that Sue had been breeding some interesting solutions to fundamental physical problems. The papers were focused and, to me, opaque, not unlike Sue herself.

I spent some of that time thinking about Sue. She had been, of course, more than a teacher to those of us who came to know her. But she had never been very forthcoming about her own life. Born in Madras, she had immigrated with her parents at the age of three. Her childhood had been hermetic, her attention divided between schoolwork and her burgeoning intellectual interests. She was gay, of course, but seldom spoke about her partners, who never seemed to stick around for long, and she hadn't discussed what her coming out might have meant to her parents, whom she described as "fairly conservative, somewhat religious." She gave the impression that these were trivial issues, unworthy of attention. If she harbored old pain, it was well concealed.

There was joy in her life, but she expressed it in her work—she worked with an enthusiasm that was unmistakably authentic. Her work, or her capacity to do her work, was the prize life had handed her, and she considered it adequate compensation for whatever else she might lack. Her pleasures were deep but monkish.

Surely there was more to Sue than this. But this was what she had been willing to share.

"A Hypothetical Tauon Unification Energy." What did that mean?

It meant she had looked closely at the clockwork of the universe. It meant she felt at home with fundamental things.

• • •

I was lonely but too unsettled to do anything about it and bored enough that I had begun to scan the cars in the motel parking lot to see if I could spot the one with my FBI surveillance crew inside, should there be such a vehicle.

But when I finally did interact with the FBI there was nothing subtle about the encounter. Morris Torrance called to tell me I had an appointment at the Federal Building downtown and that I should expect to provide a blood sample and submit to a polygraph examination. That it should be necessary to hurdle these obstacles in order to obtain gainful employment as Sue Chopra's code herder was an indication of how seriously the government took her research, or at least the congressional investment in it.

Even so, Morris had underestimated what would be required of me at the Federal Building. I submitted not only to the drawing of blood but to a chest X-ray and a cranial laser scan. I was relieved of urine, stool, and hair samples. I was fingerprinted, I signed a release for chromosomal sequencing, and I was escorted to the polygraph chamber.

In the hours since Morris Torrance mentioned the word "polygraph" on the telephone I had entertained but a single thought: Hitch Paley.

The problem was that I knew things about Hitch that could put him in prison, assuming he wasn't there already. Hitch had never been my closest friend and I wasn't sure what degree of loyalty I owed him, these many years later. But I had decided over the course of a sleepless night that I would turn down Sue's job offer sooner than I would endanger his freedom. Yes, Hitch was a criminal, and putting him in jail may have been what the letter of the law required; but I didn't see the justice in caging a man for selling marijuana to affluent dilettantes who would otherwise have invested their cash in vodka coolers, coke, or methamphetamines.

Not that Hitch was particularly scrupulous about what he sold. But I was scrupulous about who *I* sold.

The polygraph examiner looked more like a bouncer than a doctor, despite his white coat, and the unavoidable Morris Torrance joined us in the bare clinic room to oversee the test. Morris was plainly a federal employee, maybe thirty pounds above his ideal weight and ten years past his prime. His hair had receded in the way that makes some middle-aged men look tonsured. But his handshake was firm, his manner relaxed, and he didn't seem actively hostile.

I let the examiner fix the electrodes to my body and I answered the baseline questions without stammering. Morris then took over the dialogue and began to walk me detail-by-detail through my initial experience with the Chumphon Chronolith, pausing occasionally while the polygraph guru added written notations to a scrolling printout. (The machinery seemed antiquated, and it was, designed to specifications laid down in 20th-century case law.) I told the story truthfully if carefully, and I did not hesitate to mention Hitch Paley's name if not his occupation, even adding a little fillip about the bait shop, which was after all a legitimate business, at least some of the time.

When I came to the part about the Bangkok prison, Morris asked, "Were you searched for drugs?"

"I was searched more than once. Maybe for drugs, I don't know."

"Were any drugs or banned substances found on your person?"

"No."

"Have you carried banned substances across national or state borders?"

"No."

"Were you warned of the appearance of the Chronolith before it arrived? Did you have any prior knowledge of the event?"

"No."

"It came as a surprise to you?"

"Yes."

"Do you know the name Kuin?"

"Only from the news."

"Have you seen the image carved into the contemporary monuments?"

"Yes."

"Is the face familiar? Do you recognize the face?"

"No."

Morris nodded and then conferred privately with the polygraph examiner. After a few minutes of this I was cut loose from the machine.

Morris walked me out of the building. I said, "Did I pass?"

He just smiled. "Not my department. But I wouldn't worry if I was you."

Sue called in the morning and told me to report for work.

The federal government, for reasons probably best known to the senior senator from Maryland, operated this branch of its Chronolith investigation out of a nondescript building in a suburban Baltimore industrial park. It was a low-slung suite of offices and a makeshift library, nothing more. The hard end of the research was performed by universities and federal laboratories, Sue explained. What she ran here was more like a think tank, collating results and acting as a consultancy and clearing house for congressional grant money. Essentially, it was Sue's job to assess current knowledge and identify promising new lines of research. Her immediate superiors were agency people and congressional aides. She represented the highest echelon, in the Chronolith research effort, of what could plausibly be called science.

I wondered how someone as research-driven as Sue Chopra could have ended up with a glorified management job. I stopped wondering when she opened the door of her office and beckoned me in. The large room contained a lacquered secondhand desk and too many filing cabinets to count. The space around her work terminal was crowded with newspaper clippings, journals, hard copies of e-mail missives. And the walls were papered with photographs.

"Welcome to the *sanctum sanctorum*," Sue said brightly.

Photographs of Chronoliths.

They were all here, crisp professional portraits side by side with tourist snapshots and cryptic false-color satellite photos. Here was Chumphon in more detail than I had ever seen it, the letters of its inscription picked out in a raking light. Here was Bangkok, and the first graven image of Kuin himself. (Probably not a true representation, most experts felt. The features were too generic, almost as if a graphics processor had been asked to come up with an image of a "world leader.")

Here were Pyongyang and Ho Chi Minh City. Here were Taipei and Macao and Sapporo; here was the Kanto Plain Chronolith, towering over a brace of blasted granaries. Here was Yichang, both before and after the futile nuclear strike, the monument itself aloofly unchanged but the Yellow River transformed into a gushing severed artery where the dam had been fractured by the blast.

Here, photographed from orbit, was the brown outflow draining into the China Sea.

Throughout was Kuin's immaculately calm face, observing all this as if from a throne of clouds.

Sue, watching me inspect the photographs, said, "It's almost a complete inversion of the idea of a monument, when you think about it. Monuments are supposed to be messages to the future—the dead talking to their heirs."

" 'Look upon my works, ye mighty, and despair.' "

"Exactly. But the Chronoliths have it exactly backward. Not, 'I was here.' More like, 'I'm coming. I'm the future, whether you like it or not.' "

"Look upon my works and be *afraid*."

"You have to admire the sheer perversity of it."

"Do you?"

"I have to tell you, Scotty, sometimes it takes my breath away."

"Me, too." Not to mention my wife and daughter: It had taken those away, too.

I was disturbed to see my own obsession with the Chronoliths recreated on Sue Chopra's wall. It was as if I had discovered we shared a common lung. But this was, of course the reason she had been seduced into the work she did here: It gave her the chance to know virtually everything it was possible to know about the Chronoliths. Hands-on research would have confined her to some far narrower angle, counting refraction rings or hunting elusive bosons.

And she was still able to do the deep math—better able, with virtually every piece of highly classified research work crossing her desk on a daily basis.

"This is it, Scotty," she said.

I said, "Show me where I work."

She took me to an outer office furnished with a desk, a terminal. The terminal, in turn, was connected to serried ranks of Quantum Organics workstations—more and more sophisticated crunching power than Campion-Miller had ever been able to afford.

Morris Torrance was perched in one corner on a wooden chair tilted against the wall, reading the print edition of *Golf.*

"Is he part of the package?" I asked.

"You can share space for a while. Morris needs to be close to me, physically."

"Morris is a good friend?"

"Morris is my bodyguard, among other things."

Morris smiled and dropped his magazine. He scratched his head, an awkward gesture probably meant to reveal the pistol he wore under his jacket. "I'm mostly harmless," he said.

I shook hands with him again . . . more cordially this time, since he wasn't nagging me for a urine sample.

"For now," Sue said, "you just want to acquaint yourself with the work I'm doing. I'm not a code herder of your class, so take notes. End of the week, we'll discuss how to proceed."

I spent the day doing that. I was looking, not at Sue's input or results, but at the procedural layers, the protocols by which problems were translated into limiting systems and solutions allowed to reproduce and die. She had installed the best commercial genetic apps, but these were frankly inappropriate (or at least absurdly cumbersome) for some of what she was attempting—"sliderule apps," we used to call them, good to a first approximation, but primitive.

Morris finished looking at *Golf* and brought in lunch from the deli down the road, along with a copy of *Fly Fisherman* to while away the shank of the afternoon. Sue emerged periodically to give us a happy glance: We were her buffer zone, a layer of insulation between the world and the mysteries of Kuin.

It dawned on me, driving home to another nearly-empty apartment after my first week with the project, exactly how suddenly and irrevocably my life had changed.

Maybe it was the tedium of the drive; maybe it was the sight of the roadside tent colonies and abandoned, rust-ribbed automobiles; maybe it was just the prospect of a lonely weekend. "Denial" has a bad reputation, but stoicism is supposed to be a virtue, and the key act of stoicism is denial, the firm refusal to capitulate to an awful truth. Lately I had been very stoic indeed. But I changed lanes to pass a tanker truck, and a yellow Leica utility van crowded me from behind, and then the truck began edging out of his lane and into mine. The driver must have had his proximity overrides pulled, a highly illegal act not uncommon among gypsy truckers. And I was in his blind spot, and the Leica refused to brake, and for a good five seconds all I could see was a premonitory vision of myself pancaked behind the steering column.

Then the trucker caught sight of me in his side mirror, careened right and let me pass.

The Leica zoomed on by as if nothing had happened.

And I was left in a cold sweat at the wheel—untethered, essentially lost, hurrying down a gray road between oblivion and oblivion.

There was good news a week later: Janice called to tell me Kait was getting a new ear.

"It's a complete fix, Scott, or at least it ought to be, given that she was born with normal hearing and probably retains all the neural pathways. It's called a mastoid-cochlear prosthesis."

"They can do that?"

"It's a relatively new procedure, but the success rate has been almost one hundred percent on patients with Kait's kind of history."

"Is it dangerous?"

"Not especially. But it is a major surgery. She'll be hospitalized for at least a week."

"When?"

"Scheduled for six months from now."

"How are you paying for it?"

"Whit has good coverage. His insurance cooperative is willing to take on at least a percentage of the cost. I can get some help through my plan, too, and Whit's prepared to cover the remainder out of his own pocket. It might mean a second mortgage on the house. But it also means Kaitlin can have a normal childhood."

"Let me help."

"I know you're not exactly wealthy right now, Scott."

"I have money in the bank."

"And I thank you for that offer. But . . . frankly, Whit would be more comfortable taking care of it himself."

Kait had adjusted well to her hearing loss. Unless you noticed the way she cocked her head, the way she frowned when conversations grew quiet, you might not know she was impaired. But she was inevitably marked as different: condemned to sit at the front of the classroom, where too many teachers had addressed her by exaggerating their vowels and acting as if her hearing problem was an intellectual deficiency. She was awkward in schoolyard games, too easily surprised from behind. All this, plus her own natural shyness, had left her a little net-focused, self-absorbed, occasionally surly.

But that would change. The damage would be undone, apparently, thanks to some recent advances in biomechanical engineering. And thanks also to Whitman Delahunt. And if his intervention on behalf of my daughter was a little ego-bruising . . . well, I thought, fuck ego.

Kaitlin would be whole again. That was what mattered.

"But I want to contribute to this, Janice. This is something I've owed Kaitlin for a long time."

"Not really, Scott. The ear thing was never your fault."

"I want to help make it better."

"Well . . . Whit would probably let you chip in, if you insist."

It had been a frugal five years for me. I "chipped in" half the cost of the operation.

"So, Scotty," Sue Chopra said, "are you rigged for travel?"

I had already told her about Kaitlin's operation. I said I wanted to be with Kait when she was in recovery—that was nonnegotiable.

"That's half a year off," Sue said. "We won't be gone nearly that long."

Cryptic. But she seemed prepared, finally, to explain what she had lately been hinting about.

We sat in the spacious but largely empty cafeteria, four of us at a table by the only window, which overlooked the thruway. Me, Sue, Morris Torrance, and a young man by the name of Raymond Mosely.

Ray Mosely was a physics post-grad from MIT who worked with Sue on the hard-science inventories. He was twenty-five, pot-bellied, badly-groomed, and bright as a fresh dime. He was also absurdly timid. He had avoided me for weeks, apparently because I was an unfamiliar face, but gradually accepted me once he decided I wasn't a rival for Sue Chopra's affections.

Sue, of course, was at least a dozen years his senior, and her sexual tastes didn't incline to men of any sort, much less bashful young physicists who thought a lengthy chat on the subject of mu-meson interactions was an invitation to physical intimacy. Sue had explained all this to him a couple of times. Ray, supposedly, had accepted the explanation. But he still gave her mooncalf glances across the sticky cafeteria table and deferred to her opinion with a lover's loyalty.

"What's amazing," Sue began, "is how much we *haven't* learned about the Chronoliths in the years since Chumphon. All we can do is characterize them a little bit. We know, for instance, that you can't topple a Kuin stone even if you dig out its foundations, because it maintains a fixed distance from the Earth's center of gravity and a fixed orientation—even if that means hovering in midair. We know it's spectacularly inert, we know it has a certain index of refraction, we know from inspection that the objects are more likely molded than sculpted, and so on and so forth. But none of this is genuine understanding. We understand the Chronoliths the way a medieval theologian might understand an automobile. It's heavy, the upholstery gets hot in direct sunlight, parts of it are sharp, parts of it are smooth. Some of these details might be important, most are probably not; but you can't sort them out without an encompassing theory. Which is precisely what we lack."

The rest of us nodded sagely, as we usually did when Sue began to expound a thesis.

"But some details are more interesting than others," she continued. "For instance. We have some evidence that there's a gradual, stepwise increase in local background radiation in the weeks before a Chronolith manifests itself. Not dangerous but definitely measurable. The Chinese did some work on this before they stopped sharing their research with us. And the Japanese had a lucky hit, too. They have a grid of radiation monitors routinely in use around their

Sapporo/Technics fusion reactor. Tokyo was trying to pin down the source of all this stray radiation days before the Chronolith appeared. Readings peaked with the arrival of the monument, then fell very rapidly to normal ambient levels."

"Which means," Ray Mosely said as if interpreting for the stupid, "although we can't stop the appearance of a Chronolith, we have a limited ability to predict it."

"Give people some warning," Sue said.

"Sounds promising," I said. "If you know where to look."

"Aye," Sue admitted, "there's the rub. But lots of places monitor for airborne radiation. And Washington has arranged with a number of friendly foreign governments to set up detectors around major urban sites. From the civil-defense point of view, it means we can get people out of the way."

"Whereas we," Ray added, "have an interest in *being* there."

Sue gave him a sharp look, as if he had stepped on her punch line. I said, "A little dangerous, wouldn't that be?"

"But to be able to record the event, get accurate measurements of the arrival burst, see the process as it happens . . . that could be priceless."

"A view from a distance," Morris Torrance put in. "I hope."

"We can minimize any physical danger."

I said, "This is happening soon?"

"We leave in a couple of days, Scotty, and that may be pushing it a little. I know it's short notice. Our outposts are already set up and we have specialists in place. Evidence suggests a big manifestation in just about fifteen days. News of the evacuation should hit the papers this evening."

"So where are we going?"

"Jerusalem," Sue said.

She gave me a day to pack and get my business in order.

Instead, I went for a drive.

Seven

When I was ten years old, I came home one day from school and found my mother scrubbing the kitchen—which seemed normal enough, until I watched her for a while. (I had already learned to watch her carefully.)

My mother was not a beautiful woman, and I think I knew that, even then, in the distant way children are aware of such things. She had a hard, narrow face and she seldom smiled, which made her smiles a memorable event. If she laughed, I would lie in bed at night reliving the moment. She was, at the time, just thirty-five years old. She never wore makeup and some days didn't even bother to brush her hair; she could get away with it because her hair was dark and naturally lustrous.

She hated buying clothes. She wore every item in her wardrobe until it was explicitly unwearable. Sometimes, when she took me shopping, I was embarrassed by her blue sweater, which had a cigarette burn on the side, through which I could see the strap of her brassiere; or her yellow blouse, with a bleach stain like a map of California running down the right shoulder.

If I mentioned these things to her she would gaze at me wordlessly, go back into the house, change into something vaguely more presentable. But I hated saying anything because it made me feel priggish and effeminate, the kind of little boy who Cares About Clothing, and that wasn't it at all. I just didn't want people looking sideways at her in the aisle of the Food Mart.

She was wearing bluejeans and one of my father's oversized shirts when I came home that day. Yellow rubber gloves covered her arms up to the elbows—disguising, I failed to notice, a number of deep and freely bleeding scratches. This was her cleaning outfit, and she had cleaned with a vengeance. The kitchen reeked of Lysol and ammonia and the half-dozen other cleansers and disinfectants she kept in the cupboard under the sink. She had tied her hair back under a red bandana, and her attention was focused on the tiled floor. She didn't see me until I rattled my lunch box down on the counter.

"Keep out of the kitchen," she said tonelessly. "This is your fault."

"My fault?"

"He's your dog, isn't he?"

She was talking about Chuffy, our Springer Spaniel, and I began to be afraid . . . not because of what she said, exactly, but because of the way she said it.

It was like the way she said goodnight. Every night she would come into my room and lean over my bed, straighten the cotton sheet and quilted blanket, kiss her fingertips and brush them against my forehead. And 90 percent of the time that was exactly as comforting as it sounds. But some nights . . . some nights she might have been drinking a little, and then she would loom over me with the feral stink of sweat and alcohol radiating from her like heat from a coal stove, and although she said the same words, the same "Goodnight, Scotty, sleep well," it sounded like an impersonation, and her fingers against my skin were cold and abrasive. Those nights, I pulled the covers over my head and counted the seconds (*one-one-thousand, two-one-thousand*) until her footsteps faded down the hall.

She sounded that way now. Her eyes were too round and her mouth was clamped into a narrow line, and I suspected that if I got close to her I would smell the same repulsive salty stench, like a beach at low tide.

She went on cleaning, and I crept into the living room and turned on the TV and stared at a syndicated rerun of *Seinfeld* until I got to thinking about the remark she'd made about Chuffy.

My mother had never liked Chuffy. She tolerated him, but he was my father's dog and mine, not hers. If Chuffy had peed on the kitchen floor, say, might that not explain her reaction? And where *was* Chuffy, anyway? Usually, this time of day, he was up on the sofa wanting his ears scratched. I called his name.

"That animal is filthy," my mother said from the kitchen. "Leave that animal alone."

I found Chuffy upstairs, locked in the half-bath that adjoined my parents' bedroom. His hindquarters and his legs had been scrubbed raw, probably with one of the steel Brillo pads we kept for greasy cookware. His skin where the fur had come away was bleeding in a dozen different places, and when I tried to comfort him he sank his teeth into my forearm.

The years hadn't been kind to the Maryland suburb where my father lived. The once semi-rural neighborhood had become a nest of strip malls, erotica retailers, and high-rise worker housing. The gated community still existed, but its gatehouse was untended and covered with Arabic graffiti. The house on Provender Lane, the house where I had grown up, was almost unrecognizable behind lumpy hedges of snow. One of the eavestroughs had worked loose from the roof, and the shingles behind it sagged alarmingly. It was not the house as I remembered it, but it seemed very much the kind of house my father would (or maybe ought to) inhabit—unkempt, inhospitable.

I parked, turned off the engine, sat in the car.

Of course it was stupid to have come here. It was one of those reckless impulses, all drama and no content. I had decided I ought to see my father before I left the country (implicitly, *before he died*)—but what did that mean exactly? What did I have to say to him, and what could he possibly say to me?

I was reaching for the ignition key when he came out onto the creaking wooden porch to pick up his evening paper. The porch light, in a blue dusk, turned his skin jaundiced yellow. He looked at the car, bent to pick up the paper, then looked again. Finally he walked out to the curb wearing his house slippers and a white strap undershirt. The unaccustomed exercise left him panting.

I rolled down the window.

He said, "I thought it was you."

The sound of his voice set loose a regiment of unpleasant memories. I said nothing at all.

"So come on in," he said. "Cold out here."

I locked the car behind me and set the security protocols. Down the street, three blank-faced Asiatic youths watched me follow my dying father to the door.

Chuffy recovered from his injuries, though he never went near my mother again. It was my mother whose injuries were permanent and disabling. I was told, at some point during her decline, that she was the victim of a neurological disease called adult-onset schizophrenia; that it was a medical condition, a failure somewhere in the mysterious but natural processes of the brain. I didn't believe it, because I knew by direct experience that the problem was both simpler and more frightening: A good mother and a bad mother had begun to cohabit the same body. And because I loved the good mother it became possible, even necessary, to hate the bad one.

Alas, they bled into each other. The good mother might kiss me goodbye in the morning, but when I came home (late, reluctantly) from school, the crazed usurper would have taken control. I had no close friends beyond the age of ten, because when you have friends you have to let them into your house; and the last time I had tried that, when I brought home a timid red-haired boy named Richard who had befriended me in geography class, she lectured him for twenty minutes on the danger posed by video monitors to his future fertility. The language she actually used was considerably more graphic. The next day Richard was aloof and unresponsive, as if I done something unspeakable. It wasn't my fault, I wanted to tell him, and it wasn't even my mother's. We were the victims of a haunting.

Because she disbelieved in her own illness she saw this as my weakness, not hers, and I cannot count the number of times during my teenage years when she demanded that I stop looking at her "like that"—that is, with obvious, wincing dread. One of the ironies of paranoid schizophrenia is that it fulfills its own darkest expectations with almost mathematical rigor. She thought we were conspiring to drive her mad.

None of this brought my father and me closer together. The opposite. He resisted the diagnosis almost as fiercely as my mother did, but his form of denial was more direct. I think he always felt that he had married beneath him, that he had done a favor to my mother's family in Nashua, New Hampshire, by taking this moody and reclusive daughter off their hands. Maybe he had imagined that marriage would improve her. It hadn't. She had disappointed him, and perhaps vice-versa. But he continued to hold her to a high standard. He blamed her for every one of her irrational acts just as if she were capable of moral and ethical judgment—which she *was*, but only sporadically. Thus the good mother suffered for the sins of the bad mother. The bad mother might be bitter and obscene, but the good mother could be cowed and bullied. The good mother could be reduced to a state of craven apology, and he performed this alchemy on her on a regular basis. He shouted at her, occasionally struck her, regularly humiliated her, while I hid in my room trying to imagine a world in which the good mother and I could abandon both him and the invading pseudo-mom. We would live contentedly, I told myself, in the kind of loving home she had once at least attempted to create, while my father continued battling his irrational *faux* wife in some distant, isolated place—a jail cell, say; a madhouse.

Later, after I had turned sixteen and learned to drive, but before she was committed to the residential home in Connecticut where she spent her final years, my father took us all on a trip to New York City. I think he believed—and he must have been desperate to have grasped at such a fragile straw—that a vacation would be good for her, would "clear her head," as he was fond of saying. So we packed up the car, had the oil changed and the gas tank filled, and set out like dour pilgrims. My mother insisted on having the back seat to herself. I sat up front, the navigator, occasionally turning back to beg her to stop picking at the skin of her lip, which had begun to bleed.

I have only two vivid memories of the weekend in New York City.

We visited the Statue of Liberty on Saturday, and in my mind's eye I can practically count the burnished stairs we climbed on the way to the top. I remember the simultaneous sense of smallness and largeness when we arrived there, the smell of perspiration and hot copper on the windless July air. My mother shrank away from the view of Manhattan, keening quietly to herself, while I watched with rapt attention the seagulls diving toward the sea. I brought home from that journey a hollow brass model of Liberty as tall as my hand.

And I remember Sunday morning the same weekend, when my mother wandered out of the hotel room while my father was showering and I was down the hallway pumping quarters into a soft-drink machine. When I came back and found the room empty I panicked, but I couldn't bring myself to interrupt my father's bath, probably because he would have blamed me (or I imagined he would have) for misplacing her. Instead I walked the red-carpeted hallway up and down, past room-service trays and carts of snowy linen, and then rode the elevator to the lobby. I saw my mother's dark hair disappearing through the rotunda, out the revolving doors. I did not call her name, because that would alarm strangers and provoke a public embarrassment, but I ran after her, almost tripping over the newspaper rack outside the gift shop. But by the time I pushed through the glass door onto the sidewalk she was invisible. The red-suited doorman was blowing his whistle, I didn't know why, and then I saw my mother lying sprawled across the curb and moaning to herself, while the driver of the floral delivery van that had just broken her legs jumped out of his truck and stood trembling above her, his eyes wide as two full moons. And all I felt was brutally, icily cold.

My mother was committed to the long-term care facility after the New York trip—after her legs had mended, and after the doctors at Central Mercy had been forced to pump her full of Haldol until the casts came off. The living room where I sat with my father had changed remarkably little since that time. It was not that he had made an effort to keep the house as a shrine to her. He simply hadn't changed anything. It hadn't occurred to him.

"I was getting all kinds of phone calls about you," he said. "Thought for a while you'd robbed a bank."

The curtains were closed. It was the kind of house where not much light gets inside no matter what. Nor did the ancient floor lamp do much to dispel the gloom.

He sat in his tired green easy chair, breathing shallowly, waiting for me to speak.

"It was about a job," I said. "They were doing a background check."

"Some job, if you got the FBI making house calls."

The undershirt exposed his skinny frame. He had been a big man once. Big and easily angered, not the kind of man you trifled with. Now his arms were skeletal, the flesh sagging. His barrel chest had shrunk back to the ribs, and his belt was at least five notches in, the loose end flapping against his high hip joints.

I told him, "I'm going out of the country for a while."

"How long?"

"Tell you the truth, I don't know."

"Did the FBI tell you I was sick?"

"I heard."

"Maybe I'm not as sick as they think. I don't feel good, but—" He shrugged. "These doctors know fuck-all, but they charge like Moses. You want a cup of coffee?"

"I can get it. I guess the coffee maker's still where it was."

"You think I'm too fragile to make coffee?"

"I didn't say that."

"I can still make coffee, for Christ's sake."

"Don't let me stop you."

He went to the kitchen. I got up to follow but stopped at the doorway when I saw him sneaking a big dollop of Jack Daniel's into his own cup. His hands shook.

I waited in the living room, looking at the bookshelves. Most of the books had been my mother's. Her tastes had run to Nora Roberts, *The Bridges of Madison County*, and endless volumes of Tim LaHaye. My father contributed the ancient Tom Clancy novels and *Stranger Than Science*. I had owned a lot of books when I lived here—I was a straight-A student, probably because I dreaded leaving school and going home—but I had kept my mystery novels segregated on a shelf in my room, primly unwilling to let Conan Doyle or James Lee Burke mingle with the likes of V. C. Andrews and Catherine Coulter.

My father came back with two mugs of coffee. He handed me the one with CORIOLIS SHIPPING, the name of his last employer, still faintly legible on the side. He had managed the Coriolis distribution network for twenty-three years and still collected a pension check every month. The coffee was both bitter and weak. "I don't have any regular milk or cream," he said. "I know you like it white. I used powdered milk."

"It's fine," I said.

He settled back into his chair. There was a remote control on the coffee table in front of him, presumably for his video panel. He looked at it wistfully but didn't reach for it. He said, "That must be some job you applied for, because those FBI people asked some peculiar questions."

"Like what?"

"Well, there was I guess the usual, where you went to school and what kind of grades you got and where did you work and all that. But they wanted lots of details. Did you go out for sports, what did you do in your spare time, did you talk about politics or history much. Did you have lots of friends or did you keep to yourself. Who was your family doctor, did you have any unusual childhood diseases, did you ever see a shrink. A lot about Elaine, too. They knew she'd been sick. In that area, I mainly told them to fuck off. But they knew a lot already, obviously."

"They asked about Mom?"

"Didn't I just say that?"

"What kind of questions?"

"Her, you know, symptoms. When did they come on and how did she behave. How you took it. Things that aren't anybody's business but family, frankly. Christ, Scotty, they wanted into *everything*. They wanted to look at your old stuff that was in the garage. They took samples of the tap water, if you can believe that."

"You're telling me they came to the house?"

"Uh-huh."

"Did they take anything besides tap water?"

"Not as I noticed, but there was a bunch of 'em and I couldn't keep an eye on everybody. If you want to check your old stuff, the box is still there, back of the Buick."

Curious and unsettled, I excused myself long enough to step into the unheated garage.

The box he was talking about contained unsorted detritus from my high-school years. Yearbooks, a couple of academic awards, old novels and DVDs, a few toys and keepsakes. Including, I noticed, the brass Statue of Liberty I had brought home from New York. The green felt base was frayed, the hollow brass body tarnished. I picked it up and tucked it into my jacket pocket. If there was anything missing from this assortment, I couldn't place it. But the idea of anonymous FBI agents rummaging through boxes in the garage was chilling.

Beneath this, at the bottom of the box, was a layer of my schoolboy drawings. Art was never my best subject, but my mother had liked these well enough to preserve them. Flaking water-based paints on stiff brown paper the consistency of fallen leaves. Snow scenes, mostly. Bent pines, crude snowbound cabins—lonely things in a large landscape.

Back in the house my father was nodding in his chair. The coffee cup teetered on the padded arm. I moved it onto the table. He stirred when the telephone rang. An old handset-style telephone with a digital adapter where the cord joined the wall.

He picked it up, blinked, said, "Yeah," a couple of times, then offered the receiver. "It's for you."

"For me?"

"You see anybody else here?"

The call was Sue Chopra, her voice thin over the old low-bandwidth line.

"You had us worried, Scotty," she said.

"It's mutual."

"You're wondering how we found you. You should be glad we did. You caused us a lot of anxiety, running away like that."

"Sue, I didn't run away. I'm spending the afternoon with my father."

"I understand. It's just that we could have used some warning up front, before you left town. Morris had you followed."

"Morris can fuck himself. Are you telling me I have to ask permission to leave town?"

"It's not a written rule, but it would have been nice. Scotty, I know how angry you must feel. I went through the same thing myself. I can't justify it to you. But times change. Life is more dangerous than it used to be. When are you coming back?"

"Tonight."

"Good. I think we need to talk."

I told her I thought so, too.

I sat with my father a few more minutes, then told him I had to leave. The faint daylight beyond the window had faded altogether. The house was drafty and smelled of dust and dry heat.

He stirred in his chair and said, "You came a long way just to drink coffee and mumble. Look, I know why you're here. I'll tell you, I'm not especially afraid of dying. Or even of talking about it. You wake up, you read the mail, you say to yourself, well, it won't be today. But that's not the same as not knowing."

"I understand."

"No you don't. But I'm glad you came."

It was an astonishing thing for him to say. I couldn't muster a response.

He stood up. His pants rode low on his bony hips. "I didn't always treat your mother the way I should have. But I was there, Scotty. Remember that. Even when she was at the hospital. Even when she was raving. I didn't take you there unless I knew she was having a good day. Some of the things she said would peel your skin. And then you were off at college."

She had died of complications of pneumonia the year before I graduated. "You could have called me when she got sick."

"Why? So you could carry away the memory of your own mother cursing you from her deathbed? What's the point?"

"I loved her, too."

"It was easy for you. Maybe I loved her and maybe I didn't. I don't remember anymore. But I was with her, Scotty. All the time. I wasn't necessarily nice to her. But I was *with* her."

I went to the door. He followed a few paces, then stopped, breathless.

"Remember that about me," he said.

Eight

When we came into Ben Gurion the airport was chaotic, crowded with fleeing tourists. The inbound El Al flight—delayed for four hours by weather, after a three-day "diplomatic" delay Sue refused to talk about—had been nearly empty. It would be filled to capacity on the way out, however. The evacuation of Jerusalem continued.

I left the aircraft in a core group with Sue Chopra, Ray Mosley, and Morris Torrance, surrounded by a cordon of FBI agents with enhanced-vision eyetacts and concealed weapons, escorted in turn by five Israeli Defense Force conscripts in jeans and white T-shirts, Uzis slung over their shoulders, who met us at the foot of the ramp. We were conducted quickly through Israeli Customs and out of Ben Gurion to what looked like a *sheruti*, a private taxi van, commandeered for the emergency. Sue scooted into the seat beside me, still dazed by travel. Morris and Ray climbed in behind us, and the power plant hummed softly as the van pulled away.

A monotonous rain slicked Highway One. The long line of cars crawling toward Tel Aviv glistened dully under a rack of clouds, but the Jerusalem-bound lanes were utterly empty. Ahead of us, vast public-service roadside screens announced the evacuation. Behind us, they marked the evacuation routes.

"Makes you a little nervous," Sue said, "going someplace everybody else is leaving."

The IDF man—he looked like a teenager—in the seat behind us snickered.

Morris said, "There's a lot of skepticism about this. A lot of resentment, too. The Likkud could lose the next election."

"But only if nothing happens," Sue said.

"Is there a chance of that?"

"Slim to none."

The IDF man snorted again.

A gust of rain rattled down on the *sheruti*. January and February are the rainy season in Israel. I turned my head to the window and watched a grove of olive trees bend to the wind. I was still thinking about what Sue had told me on the plane.

She had been inaccessible for days after I drove back from my father's house, smoothing over whatever diplomatic difficulty it was that had kept us in Baltimore until very nearly the last minute.

I spent the week revising code and wasted a couple of evenings at a local bar with Morris and Ray.

They were more pleasant company than I would have guessed. I was angry with Morris for tracking me down to my father's house . . . but Morris Torrance was one of those men who make an art of affability. An art, or maybe a tool. He rebuffed anger like Superman bouncing bullets off his chest. He wasn't dogmatic about the Chronoliths, nursed no particular convictions about the significance of Kuin, but his interest obviously ran deep. What this meant was that we could bullshit with him: float ideas, some wild, without fear of tripping over a religious or political fixation. Was this genuine? He did, after all, represent the FBI. Likely as not, everything we said to him found its way into a file folder. But Morris's genius was that he made it seem not to matter.

Even Ray Mosely opened up in Morris's company. I had pegged Ray as one of those bright but socially-challenged types, his sexual radar locked hopelessly and inappropriately on Sue. There was some truth in this. But when he relaxed he revealed a passion for American League baseball that gave us some common ground. Ray liked the expansion team from his native Tucson and managed to piss off a guy at the neighboring table with some remarks about the Orioles. From which he did not back down when challenged. Ray was not a coward. He was lonely, but much of this was sheer intellectual loneliness. His conversation tended to trail off when he realized he had progressed to a level we couldn't follow. He wasn't condescending about it—at least, not very often—only visibly sad that he couldn't share his thoughts.

It was this loneliness, I think, that Sue satisfied for him. No matter that she reserved her physical affection for brief contacts carefully segregated from her work. I think, in some sense, when Ray talked physics with her, he *was* making love.

Of Sue we saw very little. "This is what it was like at Cornell," I told Morris and Ray. "For her students, I mean. She brought us together, but we did some of our best talking after class, without her."

"Must have been kind of like a dress rehearsal," Morris mused.

"For what? For this? The Chronoliths?"

"Oh, she couldn't have known anything about that, of course. But don't you once in a while get that feeling, that your life has been one big rehearsal for some critical event?"

"Maybe. Sometimes."

"Like she had the wrong cast back there at Cornell," Morris said, "and the script still needed work. But you must have been good, Scott." He smiled. "You made the final cut."

"So what's the event?" I asked. "This thing in Jerusalem?"

"This thing in Jerusalem . . . or whatever comes after."

Sue and I didn't have a chance to talk privately until we were well over the Atlantic, when she beckoned me to the back of the deserted economy section and said, "I'm sorry about keeping you in the dark, Scotty. And I'm sorry about the thing with your dad. I thought we could make this a day job for you, not . . ."

"House arrest," I offered.

"Right, house arrest. Because I guess that's what it is, in a sense. But not just for you. I'm in the same situation. They want to keep us together and under observation."

Sue had a head cold and was bulling through it with her usual determination. She sat with her hands in her lap, twisting a handkerchief in a beam of sunlight, as apparently contrite and as fundamentally immovable as Mahatma Gandhi. Up front, an El Al steward was delivering scrambled eggs and toast in plastic trays. I said, "Why *me*, Sue? That's the question no one wants to answer. You could have hired a better code herder. I was at Chumphon, but that doesn't explain anything."

"Don't underestimate your talent," she said. "But I know what you're asking. The FBI surveillance, the agents at your father's house. Scotty, I made the mistake a few years ago of attempting to publish a paper about a phenomenon I called 'tau turbulence.' Some influential people read it."

An answer that veered into abstract theory promised to be no answer at all. I waited, frowning, while she blew her nose, loudly.

"Excuse me," she said. "The paper was about causality, I suppose you could say, with regard to questions of temporal symmetry and the Chronoliths. Mostly math, and most of that dealing with some contentious aspects of quantum behavior. But I also speculated about how the Chronoliths might reconfigure our conventional understanding of macroscopic cause and effect. Basically, I said that in a localized tau event—the creation of a Chronolith, hypothetically—effect naturally precedes cause, but it also creates a kind of fractal space in which the most significant connectors between events become not deterministic but correlative."

"I don't know what that means."

"Think of a Chronolith as a local event in spacetime. There's an interface, a border, between the conventional flow of time and the negative-tau anomaly. It's not just the future talking to the present. There are ripples, eddies, currents. The future transforms the past, which in turn transforms the future. You follow?"

"More or less."

"So what you get is a kind of turbulence, marked not so much by cause and effect or even paradox as by a froth of correlation and coincidence. You can't look for the *cause* of the Bangkok manifestation, because it doesn't exist yet, but you can look for clues in the turbulence, in the unexpected correlatives."

"Like what?"

"When I wrote the paper I didn't offer examples. But somebody took me seriously enough to work out the implications. The FBI went back and looked at all the people who had been interviewed after Chumphon, which was the smallest and most complete statistical sample at hand. Then they compiled a database with the names and histories of anyone who had ever expressed a public opinion about the Chronoliths, at least in the early days; everyone who did science at the Chumphon site, including the guys who ran the tractors and installed the johns; everybody they interrogated after the touchdown. Then they looked for connections."

"And found some, I presume?"

"Some strange ones. But one of the strangest was you and I."

"What, because of Cornell?"

"Partly; but put it all together, Scotty. Here's a woman who's been talking about tau anomalies and exotic matter since well before Chumphon. Who has since become a highly-regarded expert on the Chronoliths. And here's an ex-student of hers, an old friend who just happened to be on the beach at Chumphon and who was arrested a mile or so from the first recorded Chronolith, a few hours after it appeared."

"Sue," I said, "it doesn't *mean* anything. You know that."

"It has no *causal* significance, you're right, but that's not the point. The point is, it marks us. Trying to figure out the genesis of a Chronolith is like trying to unravel a sweater before it's been knitted. You can't. At best, you can find certain threads that are the appropriate length or similarly colored and make certain guesses about how they might be looped together."

"That's why the FBI investigated my father?"

"They're looking at absolutely everything. Because we don't know what might be significant."

"That's the logic of paranoia."

"Well, yeah, that's exactly what we're dealing with, the logic of paranoia. That's why we're both under surveillance. We're not suspected of anything criminal, certainly not in the conventional sense. But they're worried about what we might *become*."

"Maybe we're the bad guys, is that what you mean?"

She peered out the airliner's window at the intermittent cumulus cloud, at the ocean down below us like a burnished blue mirror.

"Remember, Scotty. Whatever Kuin is, he probably didn't originate this technology. Conquerors and kings tend not to be physics majors. They use what they can take. Kuin could be anyone, anywhere, but in all likelihood he'll *steal* this technology, and who's to say he won't steal it from us? Or maybe we're the good guys. Maybe we're the ones who solve the puzzle. That's possible too—a different kind of connection. We're not just prisoners, or we'd be in jail now. They're watching us, but they're also protecting us."

I checked the aisle to see if anyone was listening, but Morris was up front chatting with a flight attendant and Ray had lost himself in a book. "I can go along with this up to a point," I said. "I'm reasonably well paid when a lot of people aren't getting paid at all and I'm seeing things I never thought I'd see." Feeding my own obsession with the Chronoliths, I did not add. "But only up to a point. I can't promise—"

To stick with it indefinitely, I meant to say. To become an acolyte, like Ray Mosely. Not when the world was going to hell and I had a daughter to protect.

Sue interrupted with a pensive smile. "Don't worry, Scotty. Nobody's promising anything, not anymore. Because nobody's sure of anything. Certainty is one of the luxuries we'll have to learn to live without."

I had learned to do without certainty a long time ago. One of the rules of living with a schizophrenic parent is that weirdness is tolerable. You can endure it. At least—as I had told Sue—up to a point.

Past that point, madness spills all over everything. It gets inside you and makes itself at home, until there's no one you can trust, not even yourself.

The first Highway One checkpoint was the hardest to get through. This was where the IDF turned away would-be pilgrims attracted, perversely, by the evacuation.

"Jerusalem Syndrome" had been named as a psychiatric condition decades ago. Visitors are occasionally overwhelmed by the city's cultural and mythological significance. They identify too deeply, dress in bedsheets and sandals, proclaim sermons from the Mount of Olives, attempt to sacrifice animals on the Temple Mount. The phenomenon has kept the Kfar Shaul psychiatric hospital in business since well before the turn of the century.

The wave of global uncertainty generated by the Chronoliths had already triggered a new wave of pilgrimages, and the evacuation had turned it up to a fever pitch. Jerusalem was being evacuated for the safety of its inhabitants, but when had that ever mattered to a fanatic? We wormed our way through a line of vehicles, some abandoned at the checkpoint when the drivers refused to turn away. There was a steady transit of police cars, ambulances, tow trucks.

We cleared this obstacle at dusk and arrived at a major hotel on Mt. Scopus just as the last light was fading from the sky.

Observation posts had been established all over the city: not just ours, but military stations, a U.N. post, delegations from a couple of Israeli universities, and a site for the international press on the Haas Promenade. Mt. Scopus (*Har HaTsofim*, in Hebrew, which also happens to mean "looking over") was something of a choice spot, however. This was where the Romans had camped in 70 A.D., shortly before they moved to crush the Jewish rebellion. The Crusaders had been here, too, for similar reasons. The view of the Old City was spectacular but dismaying. The evacuation, especially of the Palestinian zones, hadn't gone easily. The fires were still burning.

I followed Sue through the vacant hotel lobby to a suite of adjoining rooms on the top floor. This was the heart of the operation. The curtains had been taken down and a crew of technicians had set up photographic and monitoring devices and, more ominously, a bank of powerful heaters. Most of these people were part of Sue's research project, but only a few of them had met her personally. A number of them hurried to shake her hand. Sue was gracious about it but obviously tired.

Morris showed us our private rooms, then suggested we meet in the lobby restaurant once we'd had a chance to shower and change.

Sue wondered aloud how the restaurant had managed to stay open for business during the evacuation. "The hotel's outside the primary exclusion zone," Morris said. "There's a skeleton staff to look after us, all volunteers, and a heated bunker for them back of the kitchen."

I took a few minutes in my room just to look at the city folded like a stony blanket across the Judean hills. The nearby streets were empty except for security patrols and occasional ambulances out of Hadassah Mt. Sinai a few streets away. Stoplights twitched in the wind like palsied angels.

The IDF man in the car had said something interesting as we passed the checkpoint. In the old days, he said, the fanatics who came to Jerusalem usually imagined they were Jesus, come again, or John the Baptist, or the first and only true, original Messiah.

Lately, he said, they tended to claim to be Kuin.

A city that had seen far too much history was about to see some more.

I found Sue, Morris and Ray waiting for me in the hotel's immense atrium. Morris gestured at the five stories of hanging plants and said, "Check it out, Scotty, it's the Garden of Babylon."

"Babylon's considerably east of here," Sue said. "But yeah."

In the lobby restaurant we seated ourselves at a table across the room from the only other patrons, a group of IDF men and women crowded into a red vinyl booth. Our waitress (the only waitress) was an older woman with an American accent. She claimed not to be troubled by the evacuation even though it meant she had to sleep at the hotel: "I don't like the idea of driving around these empty streets anyway, much as I used to complain about the traffic." The entree for tonight was chicken almondine, she said. "And that's about it, unless you're allergic or anything, in which case we can ask the chef to make an adjustment."

Chicken all around, and Morris ordered us a bottle of white wine.

I asked about the agenda for tomorrow. Morris said, "Apart from the scientific work, we have the Israeli Defense Minister visiting in the afternoon. Plus photographers and video people." He added, "There's no substance to it. We wouldn't be here if the Israeli government didn't already have all the information we can give them. It's a dog-and-pony show for the news pools. But Ray and Sue get to do some interpretation for the laypeople."

Ray asked, "Are we giving him Minkowski ice or feedback?"

Morris and I looked blank. Sue said, "Don't leave people out of the conversation, Ray. It's bad manners. Morris, Scotty, you must have picked up some of this from the congressional briefs."

"Slow reading," Morris said.

"We spend a lot of time translating math into English."

"Hunting metaphors," Ray said.

"It's important to make people understand. At least as much as *we* understand. Which is not very much."

"Minkowski ice," Ray persisted, "or positive feedback?"

"Feedback, I think."

Morris said, "I still feel left out."

Sue frowned and collected her thoughts. "Morris, Scotty, do you savvy feedback?"

Half of what I did with Sue's code involved recursion and self-amplification. But she was talking far more generally. I said, "It's what happens when you stand up in the high school auditorium to give the valedictory address and the PA starts to squeal like a pig in a slaughterhouse."

She grinned. "That's a good example. Describe the process, Scotty."

"You have an amplifier between the mike and the speakers. Worst case, they talk to each other. Whatever goes into the microphone comes out of the speakers, louder. If there's any noise in the system, it makes a loop."

"Exactly. Any little sound the microphone picks up, the speaker plays it louder. And the microphone hears that and multiplies it again, and so on, until the system starts ringing like a bell . . . or squealing like a pig."

"And this is relevant to the Chronoliths," Morris said, "because—?"

"Because time itself is a kind of amplifier. You know the old saw about how a butterfly flapping in China can eventually brew up a storm over Ohio? It's a phenomenon called 'sensitive dependence.' A large event is often a small event amplified through time."

"Like all those movies where a guy travels into the past and ends up changing his own present."

"Either way," Sue said, "what you have is an example of amplification. But when Kuin sends us a monument commemorating a victory twenty years from now, that's like pointing the microphone at the speaker, it's a feedback loop, a *deliberate* feedback loop. It amplifies itself. We think that may be why the Chronoliths are expanding their territory so quickly. By marking his victories Kuin creates the expectation that he'll be victorious. Which makes the victory that much more likely, even inevitable. And the next. And so on."

This was not new territory for me. I had inferred this much from Sue's work and from speculation in the popular press. I said, "Couple of questions."

"Okay."

"I guess the first is, how does this look to Kuin? How does it play out, that first time he sends us the Chumphon stone? Wouldn't he be changing his own past? Are there two Kuins now, or what?"

"Your guess is as good as mine. You're asking me whether we understand this better on the theoretical level. Well, yes and no. We'd like to avoid a many-worlds model, if possible—"

"Why? If that's the easiest answer?"

"Because we have reason to believe it's not true. And if it *is* true, it limits what we can do about the problem. However, the alternative—"

"The alternative," Ray supplied, "is that Kuin is committing a kind of suicide every time he does this."

The waitress brought us our meals on a cart covered with linen, then rolled the emptied cart back toward the kitchen. Across the room the IDF people had finished dinner and were working on dessert. I wondered if this was their first time in a four-star hotel restaurant. They were eating that way—with great attention and a few remarks about what this would have cost them if they'd had to pay for it.

"Changing what he's been," Sue said between mouthfuls. "Erasing it, replacing it, but that's not exactly *suicide,* is it? Imagine a hypothetical Kuin, some backcountry warlord who somehow gets hold of this technology. He pulls the switch and suddenly he's not just Kuin, he's *the* Kuin, the one everyone was waiting for, he's the fucking Messiah for all practical purposes, and for him it was never any different. At least some part of his personal history is gone, but it's a painless loss. He's glorified, he has lots of troops now, lots of credibility, a bright future. Either that, or the original Kuin's place has been taken by some more ambitious individual who grew up *wanting* to be Kuin. At worst it's a kind of death, but it's also a potential ticket to glory. And you can't mourn what you never had, can you?"

I wondered about that. "It still seems like a big risk. Once you've done it, why push the button a second time?"

"Who knows? Ideology, delusions of grandeur, blind ambition, a self-destructive impulse. Or just because he *has* to, as a last resort in the face of military reversals. Maybe it's a different reason every time. Anyway you look at it, he's right in the middle of the feedback loop. He's the signal that generates the noise."

"So a small noise becomes a loud noise," Morris said. "A fart becomes a thunderclap."

Sue nodded eagerly. "But the amplification factor isn't just time. It's human expectation and human interaction. The rocks don't care about Kuin, the trees don't give a shit, it's *us.* We act on what we anticipate, and it gets easier and easier to anticipate the all-conquering Kuin, Kuin the god-king. The temptation is to give in, to collaborate, to idealize the conqueror, to be part of the process so you don't get ground under."

"You're saying *we're* creating Kuin."

"Not us specifically, but people, yeah, people in general."

Morris said, "That's how it was with my wife before we broke up. She hated the idea of disappointment so much, it was always on her mind. It didn't matter what I did, how much I reassured her, what I earned, whether I went to church every week. I was on permanent probation. 'You'll leave me one day,' she used to say. But if you say something like that often enough, it has a way of coming true."

Morris thought about what he'd said, pushed away his glass of wine, reddened.

"Expectation," Sue said, "yes, feedback. Exactly. Suddenly Kuin embodies everything we fear or secretly want—"

"Slouching toward Jerusalem," I said, "to be born."

It was an idea that seemed to cast a chill across the room. Even the rowdy IDF teenagers were quieter now.

"Well," I said, "that's not especially reassuring, but I can follow the logic. What's Minkowski ice?"

"A metaphor of a different color. But that's enough of this talk for tonight. Wait till tomorrow, Scotty. Ray's explaining it to the Defense Minister."

She smiled forlornly as Ray puffed up.

We broke up after coffee, and I went to my room alone.

I thought about calling Janice and Kaitlin, but the desk manager interrupted my dial-out to tell me the bandwidth was at capacity and I would have to wait at least an hour. So I took a beer from the courtesy cooler and put my feet up on the windowsill and watched a car race down the dark streets of the exclusion zone. The floodlights on the Dome of the Rock made that structure look as venerable and solid as history itself, but in less than forty-eight hours there would be a taller and more dramatic monument a scant few miles away.

• • •

I woke at seven in the morning, restless but not hungry. I showered and dressed and wondered how far the security people would let me go if I tried to do a little sightseeing—a walk around the hotel, say. I decided to find out.

I was stopped at the elevator by one of two natty FBI men, who looked at me blankly. "Whereabouts you headed, chief?"

"Breakfast," I said.

"We'll need to see your badge first."

"Badge?"

"Nobody gets on or off this floor without a badge."

I don't need no stinkin' badge—but I did, apparently. "Who's handing out badges?"

"You need to talk to the people who brought you, chief."

Which didn't take long, because Morris Torrance came hurtling up behind me, bade me a cheerful good morning and pinned a plastic I.D. tag to the lapel of my shirt. "I'll come down with you," he said.

The two men parted like the elevator doors they were guarding. They nodded to Morris, and the less aggressive of the two told me to have a nice day.

"Will do," I said. "Chief."

"It's just a precaution," Morris said as we rode down.

"Like harassing my father? Like reading my medical records?"

He shrugged. "Didn't Sue explain any of this to you?"

"A little. You're not just her bodyguard, are you?"

"But that, too."

"You're the warden."

"She's not in prison. She can go anywhere she wants."

"As long as you know about it. As long as she's watched."

"It's a kind of deal we made," Morris said. "So where do you want to go, Scotty? Breakfast?"

"I need some air."

"You want to do the tourist thing? You realize what a bad idea that is."

"Call me curious."

"Well—I can get us an IDF car with the right tags, I suppose. Even get us into the exclusion zone, if that's really what you want."

I didn't answer.

"Otherwise," he said, "you're pretty much stuck in the hotel, the situation being what it is."

"Do you enjoy this kind of work?"

"Let me tell you about that," Morris said.

He borrowed a blue unmarked automobile with all-pass stickers pasted to the windshield and an elaborate GPS system sprawling onto the passenger side of the dash. He drove down Lehi Street while I stared (yet again) out the window.

It was another rainy day, date palms drooping along the boulevards. By daylight the streets were far from empty: there were civil-defense wardens at the major intersections, cops and IDF patrols everywhere, and only the exclusion zone around the anticipated touchdown site had been wholly evacuated.

Morris drove into the New City and turned onto King David Street, the heart of the exclusion zone.

The evacuation of a major urban area is more than just people-moving, though it's that, certainly, on an almost unmanageably large scale. Some of it is engineering. Most of the damage a Chronolith causes is a result of the initial cold shock, the so-called thermal pulse. Close enough to the arrival, any container with liquid water in it will burst. Property owners in Jerusalem had been encouraged to drain their pipes before leaving, and the municipal authorities were trying to preserve the waterworks by depressurizing the core zone, though that would make firefighting difficult—and inevitably there would be fires, when volatile liquids and gases escaped containers ruptured or weakened by the cold. The gas mains had already been shut off. Theoretically, every toilet tank should have been emptied, every gas tank drained, every propane bottle removed. In reality, without an exhaustive door-to-door search, no such outcome could be guaranteed. And close to the arrival point, the thermal pulse would turn even a bottle of milk into a potentially lethal explosive device.

I didn't speak as we drove past the shuttered businesses, windows striped with duct tape; the darkened skyscrapers, the King David Hotel as lifeless as a corpse.

"An empty city is an unnatural thing," Morris said. "Unholy, if you know what I mean." He slowed for a checkpoint, waved at the soldiers as they spotted his stickers. "You know, Scotty, I really don't take any pleasure in dogging you and Sue."

"Am I supposed to be reassured by that?"

"I'm just making conversation. The thing is, though, you have to admit it makes sense. There's a logic to it."

"Is there?"

"You've had the lecture."

"The thing about coincidence? What Sue calls 'tau turbulence'? I'm not sure how much of that to believe."

"That," Morris said, "but also how it looks to Congress and the Administration. Two true facts about the Chronoliths, Scotty. First, nobody knows how to make one. Second, that knowledge is being brewed up somewhere even as we speak. So we give Sue and people like Sue the means to figure out how to build such a thing, and maybe that's precisely the *wrong* thing to do, the knowledge is set loose, maybe it gets into the wrong hands, and maybe none of this would have happened if we hadn't opened the whole Pandora's box in the first place."

"That's circular logic."

"Does that make it wrong? In the situation we're in, are you going to rule out a possibility because it doesn't make a nice tight syllogism?"

I shrugged.

He said, "I'm not going to apologize for the way we looked into your past. It's one of those things you do in a national emergency, like drafting people or holding food drives."

"I didn't know I'd been drafted."

"Try thinking of it that way."

"Because I went to school with Sue Chopra? Because I happened to be on the beach at Chumphon?"

"More like, because we're all tied together by some rope we can't quite see."

"That's . . . poetic."

Morris drove silently for a time. The sun came through gaps in the cloud, pillars of light roaming the Judean hills.

"Scotty, I'm a reasonable person. I like to think so, anyhow. I still go to church every Sunday. Working for the FBI doesn't make a person a monster. You know what the modern FBI is? It isn't cops and robbers and trench coats and all that shit. I did twenty years of desk work at Quantico. I'm qualified on the firing range and all, but I've never discharged a weapon in a police situation. We're not so different, you and I."

"You don't know what I am, Morris."

"Okay, you're right, I'm assuming, but for the sake of the argument let's say we're both normal people. Personally, I don't believe in anything more supernatural than what you read about in the Bible, and I only believe that one day out of seven. People call me levelheaded. Boring, even. Do I strike you as boring?"

I let that one go.

He said, "But I have dreams, Scotty. The first time I saw the Chumphon thing was on a TV set in D.C. But the amazing thing is, I recognized it. Because I'd seen it before. Seen it in dreams. Nothing specific, nothing like prophecy, nothing I could prove to anybody. But I knew as soon as I saw it, that this was something that would be part of my life."

He stared straight ahead. "It'll be good if these clouds pass by tomorrow night," he said. "Good for observation."

"Morris," I said, "is any of this the truth?"

"I wouldn't shit you."

"Why not?"

"Why not? Well, maybe because I recognized you, too, Scotty. From my dreams, I mean. First time I saw you. You and Sue both."

Nine

Looking back at these pages, it seems to me I've said too much about myself and not enough about Sue Chopra. But I can only tell my own story as I experienced it. Sue, I thought, was preoccupied with her work and blind to the forces that had infantilized her, made her a ward of the state. Her acceptance of her condition bothered me, probably because I was chafing under the same restraints and reaping the same rewards. I had access to the best and newest processor platforms, the sleekest code incubators. But I was at the same time an object of scrutiny, paid to donate DNA and urine samples to the infant science of tau turbulence.

I had promised myself that I would endure this until I had financed at least the lion's share of Kaitlin's surgery. Then all bets were off. If the march of the

Chronoliths continued, I wanted to be home and near Kaitlin as the crisis worsened.

As for Kait . . . the most I could be for Kait right now was emotional backup, a refuge if things went bad with Whit, a second-string parent. But I had a feeling, maybe as powerful and specific as Morris's dream, that sooner or later she would need me.

We were in Jerusalem because the Chronolith had announced itself with murmurs of ambient radioactivity, like the premonitory rumbling of a volcano. Was there also, I wondered, a premonitory tau turbulence, whatever that might mean? A trace of strangeness in the air, a fractal cascade of coincidence? And if so, was it perceptible? Meaningful?

We were less than fifteen hours from the estimated time of touchdown when I woke Thursday morning. Today the entire floor was in lockdown, nobody allowed in or out except for technicians transiting between the indoor monitors and the antenna array on the roof. There had been threats, apparently, from unnamed radical cadres. Meals were delivered from the hotel kitchen on a strict schedule.

The city itself was still and calm under a dusty turquoise sky.

The Israeli Minister of Defense arrived for his photo-op that afternoon. Two press-pool photographers, three junior military advisors, and a couple of cabinet ministers followed him into the tech suite. The press guys wore cameras clamped to their shoulders on gymbal mounts. The Minister of Defense, a bald man in khaki, listened to Sue's description of the reconnaissance equipment and paid dutiful attention to Ray Mosley's stumbling account of "Minkowski ice"—a clumsy metaphor, in my opinion.

Minkowski was a twentieth-century physicist who asserted that the universe could be understood as a four-dimensional cube. Any event can be described as a point in four-space; the sum of these points is the universe, past present and future.

Try to imagine that Minkowski cube, Ray said, as a block of liquid water freezing (as contrary as this seems) from the bottom up. The progression of the freeze represents at least our human experience of the march of time. What is frozen is past, immutable, changeless. What is liquid is future, indeterminate, uncertain. We live on the crystallizing boundary. To travel into the past, you would have to uncreate (or, I suppose, *thaw*) an entire universe. Clearly absurd: what power could rewind the planets, wake dead stars, dissolve babies into the womb? But that wasn't what Kuin had done, though what he had done was marvelous enough. A Chronolith, Ray said, was like a hot needle driven into Minkowski ice. The effects were striking but strictly local. In Chumphon, in Thailand, in Asia, perhaps ultimately in all the world, the consequences were strange and paradoxical; but the moon didn't care; the comets were unmoved in their orbits; the stars looked blindly on. The Minkowski ice crystallizes once more around the cooling needle and time flows as before, subtly wounded, perhaps, but substantially unchanged.

The Defense Minister accepted this with the obvious private skepticism of a Moslem cleric touring the Vatican. He asked a few questions. He admired the blast-proof glass that had replaced the hotel windows and commented approvingly on the dedication of the men and women operating the machinery. He hoped we would all learn something useful in the next several hours if, God forbid, the predicted tragedy actually took place. Then he was escorted upstairs for a look at the antenna arrays, the photographers trailing after, gulping coffee from paper cups.

All this, of course, would be edited for public consumption, a display of governmental calm in the face of crisis.

Invisibly, inevitably, the Minkowski ice was melting. The hotel's links were overwhelmed by our extremely broad-band data-sharing, but I took one call that day: Janice, letting my know my father had died in his sleep.

It had snowed over most of Maryland that day—about six inches of fine powder. My father wore a medical tag which had issued an alert when he entered cardiac distress, but by the time the ambulance arrived he was beyond resuscitation.

Janice offered to make the necessary arrangements while I was overseas (there was no other surviving family). I agreed and thanked her.

"I'm sorry, Scott," she said. "I know he was a difficult man. But I'm sorry."

I tried to feel the loss in a meaningful way.

Nevertheless I caught myself wondering how much trauma he had avoided by ducking out of history at this juncture, what tithes he would not be obliged to pay.

Morris knocked at my door as dusk was falling and escorted me back to the tech suite, monitors radiating blue light into the room. As observers, Morris and I were relegated to the line of chairs along the rear wall where we wouldn't be underfoot. The room was hot and dry, ranks of portable heaters already glowing ferociously. The techs seemed overdressed and were sweating at their consoles.

Outside, the cloudless sky faded to ink. The city was preternaturally still. "Not long now," Morris whispered. This was the first time the arrival of a Chronolith had been predicted with any accuracy, but the calculations were still approximate, the countdown tentative. Sue, passing, said, "Keep your eyes open."

Morris said, "What if nothing happens?"

"Then the Likkud loses the election. And we lose our credibility."

The minutes drained away. Quilted jackets were handed out to those of us who hadn't donned protective clothing. Morris leaned out of the shadows again, sweating and obviously restless. "Best guess for touchdown point is in the business district. It's an interesting choice. Avoids the Old City, the Temple Mount."

"Kuin as Caesar," I said. "Worship whatever gods you like, as long as you bow to the conqueror."

"Not the first time for Jerusalem."

But maybe the last. The Chronoliths had re-ignited all the apocalyptic fears the 20th Century had focused on nuclear weapons: the sense that a new technology had raised the stakes of conflict, that the long parade of empires rising and empires falling might have reached its final cycle. Which was, just now, all too easy to believe. The valley of Megiddo, after all, was only a few miles from here.

We were reminded to keep our jackets zipped despite the heat. Sue wanted the room as hot as we could tolerate, a buffer against thermal shock.

Intense analysis of previous arrivals had given us an idea of what to expect. A Chronolith doesn't displace the air and bedrock where it appears; it transforms these materials and incorporates them into its own structure. The shockwave is a result of what Sue had dubbed "radiant cooling." Within a few yards of the Kuin stone the air itself would condense, solidify, and fall to the ground; for some part of a second, air rushing to replace it would be acted upon similarly. Within a slightly broader area the atmosphere would freeze in fractions of its constituent gases—oxygen, nitrogen, and carbon dioxide. Water vapor is precipitated over a much wider perimeter.

The presence of groundwater causes a similar phenomenon in soil and bedrock, cracking stone and radiating a ground-borne shockwave.

All this cooled and moving air creates convection cells, thus severe wind at ground zero and unpredictable and pervasive fogs for miles around.

Which was why no one objected to the dry heat, the sealed room.

The white-garbed technicians, most of them graduate students out on loan, manned the row of terminals facing the windows. Their telemetry came from the roof arrays or from remote sensors placed closer to the touchdown zone. Periodically they sang out numbers, none of which meant anything to me. But the level of tension was clearly rising. Sue paced among these eager young people like a fretful parent.

She paused before us, crisp in fresh bluejeans and a white blouse. "Background counts are way up," she said, "on extremely steep curves. That's like a two-minute warning, guys."

Morris said, "Should we have goggles or something?"

"It's not an H-bomb, Morris. It won't blind you."

And then she turned away.

One of the monitoring technicians, a young blond woman who looked not much older than Kaitlin, had risen from her chair and approached Sue with a supplicating smile. The IDF security contingent looked sharply at her. So did Morris.

The girl seemed dazed, maybe a little out of control. She hesitated. Then, in a gesture almost touchingly childlike, she reached for Sue's hand and took it in her own.

Sue said, "Cassie? What is it?"

"I wanted to say . . . thank you." Cassie's voice was timid but fervent.

Sue frowned. "You're welcome, but—for what?"

But Cassie just ducked her head and backed away as if the thought had gone out of her head as quickly as it had entered. She covered her mouth with her hand. "Oh! I'm sorry. I just—I guess I just felt like I should say it. I don't know what I was thinking. . . ." She blushed.

"Best stay in your chair," Sue said gently.

We were deep in the tau turbulence now. The room smelled hot and electric. Beyond the window, the city core quivered under a sudden auroral glow.

• • •

It all happened in a matter of seconds, but time was elastic; we inhabited seconds as if they were minutes. I will admit that I was afraid.

The incidental light created by the arrival was a curtain of quickly shifting color, blue-green deepening to red and violet, hovering over the city and filling the room in which we sat with eerie shadow.

"Nineteen hundred and seven minutes," Sue said, checking her watch. "Mark."

"It's already cold," Morris said to me. "You notice?"

It felt as if the temperature in the room had dropped by several degrees. I nodded.

One of the IDF men stood up nervously, fingering his weapon. As quickly as it had come, the light began to fade; and then—

Then the Chronolith was simply and suddenly present.

It flashed into existence beyond the Dome of the Rock, taller than the hills, grotesquely large, white with ice under a brittle moon.

"Touchdown!" someone at the consoles announced. "Ambient radiation dropping. External temps way, way down—"

"Hold on," Sue said.

The shockwave flexed the window glass and roared like thunder. Almost immediately the Chronolith vanished in a white whirlwind, moisture gigged out of the atmosphere by thermal shock. A few miles away, temperature differentials cracked concrete, split timbers, and surely destroyed the living tissue of any creature unfortunate enough to have strayed into the exclusion zone. (There were a few: cats, dogs, pilgrims, skeptics.)

A wave of whiteness rayed out from the central storm, frost climbing the Judean hills like fire, and a host of urban lights dimmed as power-grid transformers shorted in fountains of sparks. Cloud engulfed the hotel; a hard, fast wind rattled the windows. Suddenly the room was dark, console lights quivering like stars reflected in a pond.

"Cold as a son of a bitch," Morris muttered.

I wrapped my arms around myself and saw Sue Chopra do likewise as she turned away from the window.

The IDF man who had stood up moments ago raised his automatic rifle. He shouted something that was incomprehensible in the noise of the storm. Then he began to fire into the darkened room.

The name of the shooter was Aaron Weiszack.

What I know about him is what I read in the next day's newspapers, and wouldn't it save a world of grief if we could read tomorrow's headlines before they happened?

Or maybe not.

Aaron Weiszack had been born in Cleveland, Ohio, and immigrated to Israel with his family in 2011. He spent his teenage years in suburban Tel Aviv and had already flirted with a number of radical political organizations before he was drafted in 2020; Weiszack had been briefly detained, but not charged, during the Temple Mount riots of 2025. His IDF record, however, was impeccable, and he had been careful to conceal from his superiors his ongoing association with a fringe "Kuinist" cell called Embrace the Future.

He was, if not deranged, at least unbalanced. His motives remain unclear. He had not fired more than a couple of rounds before another of the IDF soldiers, a woman named Leah Agnon, cut him down with a brief burst from her own weapon.

Weiszack died almost instantly of his wounds. But he wasn't the only casualty in the room.

I have often thought Aaron Weiszack's act was at least as portentous as the arrival of the Kuin of Jerusalem—in its way, a far more precise imaging of the shape of things to come.

• • •

Weiszack's last rifle burst cracked one of the allegedly blast-proof (but apparently not bulletproof) windows, which collapsed in a shower of silvery nuggets. Cold wind and dense fog swept into the room. I stood up, deafened by the gunshots, blinking stupidly. Morris leaped out of his chair toward Sue Chopra, who had fallen to the floor, and covered her with his body. None of us knew whether the attack had finished or had just begun. I couldn't see Sue under Morris's bulk, didn't know whether she was seriously injured, but there was blood everywhere—Weiszack's blood all over the wallpaper, and the blood of the young technicians speckled across their consoles. I took a breath and began to hear sounds again, the scream of human voices, the scream of the wind. Fine grains of ice flew through the room like shrapnel, propelled by the impossibly steep thermoclines sweeping the city.

The IDF force surrounded the fallen Weiszack, rifles aimed at his inert body. The FBI contingent spread out to secure the scene, and some of Sue's post-docs hovered over their fallen companions attempting first aid. Voices, and I thought I heard Morris's among them, shouted for help. We had a paramedic in the room, but he was surely overwhelmed if he hadn't been injured.

I ducked and crawled across the floor to Morris. He had rolled off Sue and was cradling her head in his arms. She was hurt. There was blood on the carpet here, a smattering of red droplets steaming in the brutal cold. Morris glanced at me. "It's not serious," he said, mouthing the words broadly over the roar of the wind. "Help me drag her into the hallway."

"*No!*" Sue surged up against him, and I saw the bloody gash where her jeans had been torn by a bullet or shrapnel, a freely-bleeding divot along the fleshy part of her right thigh. But if this was her only wound then Morris was right, she was in no immediate danger.

"Let us take care of it," Morris told her firmly.

"People are hurt!" Her eyes darted toward the row of terminals where her students and technicians were variously paralyzed with terror or slumped in their chairs. "Oh, God—*Cassie!*"

Cassie, the winsome postgraduate student, had lost part of her skull to the gunfire.

Sue closed her eyes and we dragged her out of the cold and Morris spoke intently into his pocket phone as I pressed my palm against her bloody leg.

By this time the ambulances from Hadassah Mt. Sinai were already on their way, skidding over the crusts of ice still clinging to Lehi Street.

The paramedics set up triage in the lobby of the hotel, where they covered broken windows with thermal blankets and ran heaters from the hotel's generator. One of them put a pressure bandage on Sue's injury and directed arriving aid to the more critically injured, some whom had been carried to the lobby, some of whom remained immobilized upstairs. IDF and civilian police cordoned the building while sirens wailed from all points of the compass.

"She died," Sue said bleakly.

Cassie, of course.

"She died. . . . Scotty, you saw her. Twenty years old. MIT diploma program. A sweet, nice child. She thanked me, and then she was killed. What does that mean? Does that *mean* something?"

Outside, ice fell from the cornices and rooftops of the hotel and shattered on the sidewalks. Moonlight penetrated the glassy white ruins and limned the emerging contours of the Kuin of Jerusalem.

The Kuin of Jerusalem: a four-sided pillar rising to form a throne on which the figure of Kuin is seated.

Kuin gazes placidly past the fractured Dome of the Rock, scrutinizing the Judean desert. He is clothed in peasant trousers and shirt. On his head is a band which might be a modest crown, worked with images of half-moons and laurel leaves. His face is formal and regal, the features unspecific.

The immense base of the monument meets the earth deep in the ruins of Zion Square. The peak achieves an altitude of fourteen hundred feet.

PART TWO

Lost Children

Ten

What strikes me now—if you can forgive an old man second-guessing the text of his own memoirs—is how strange the advent of the Chronoliths must have seemed to the generation that came of age after the fall of the Soviet Union . . . my father's generation, though he didn't live to see the worst of it.

They were a generation that had looked on third-world dictatorships less with outrage than with impatience, a generation to whom grandiose palaces and monuments were the embarrassments of an earlier age, haunted houses ready to topple in the stiff winds blowing from the Nikkei and the NASDAQ.

The rise of Kuin caught them utterly off guard. They were serious about the threat but deaf to its appeal. They could imagine a million underfed Asians paying fealty to the name of Kuin. That was at least distantly plausible. But when they were scorned by their own children and grandchildren, their confidence evaporated.

They escaped, by and large, into the shelter of arms. Kuin's monuments might seem magical but they predicted and were ultimately derived from military conquests, and a well-defended nation could not be conquered. Or so the reasoning went. The Jerusalem arrival provoked a second surge of federal investment: in research, detector satellite arrays, a new generation of missile-hunting drones, smart mines, battlefield and supply robots. The draft was reintroduced in 2029 and the standing army increased by half a million inductees. (Which helped to disguise the decline in the civilian economy that followed the aquifer crisis, the battered condition of Asian trade, and the beginning of the years-long Atchafalaya Basin disaster.)

We would have bombed Kuin in his infancy if anyone had been able to find him. But southern China and most of Southeast Asia were in a state of ungoverned barbarism, a place where warlords in armored ATVs terrorized starving peasants. Any or all of these petty tyrants might have been Kuin. Most of them claimed to be. Probably none of them was. It was far from certain that Kuin was even Chinese. He could have been anywhere.

What seems obvious now (but wasn't then) is that Kuin was dangerous precisely because he hadn't declared himself. He possessed no platform but conquest, no ideology but ultimate victory. Promising nothing, he promised everything. The dispossessed, the disenfranchised, and the merely unhappy all were drawn toward an identification with Kuin. Kuin, who would level the mountains and make the valleys high. Kuin, who must speak with their voice, since no one else did.

For the generation that followed mine Kuin represented the radically new, the overthrow of antiquated structures of authority and the ascension of powers as cold and ruthlessly modern as the Chronoliths themselves.

In brief, he took our children from us.

• • •

When I got the call about Kait (from Janice, her video window blanked to hide her tears) I understood that I would have to leave Baltimore and that I would have to do so without Morris Torrance tailing me across seven states.

Which wouldn't be easy, but might be easier than it would have been before Jerusalem. Before Jerusalem, Sue Chopra had been overseeing Chronolith research under a generous federal dispensation. That preeminence had been compromised by her devotion to the purely theoretical aspects of Chronolith theory—her obsession with the mathematics of tau turbulence, as opposed to practical questions of detection and defense—and by her disastrous congressional appearance in June of '28. In public questioning she had refused to accommodate Senator Lazar's theory that the Jerusalem Chronolith might be a signal of the End Times. (She called the senator "poorly educated" and the notion of impending apocalypse "an absurd mythology that abets the very process we're struggling to contain." Lazar, a former Republican turned Federal Party hatchetman, called Sue "an ivory-tower atheist" who needed to be "weaned from the public teat.")

She was, of course, too valuable to cut loose entirely. But she ceased to be the central figure in the effort to coordinate Chronolith research. She was, instead, kept away from public scrutiny. She remained the nation's foremost expert on the esoterica of tau turbulence but had ceased to be its poster child.

The upside of this was that the FBI took a less direct interest in such small fish as myself, even if my files still languished in the digital catacombs of the Hoover Building.

Morris Torrance had resigned from the Bureau rather than accept reassignment. Morris was a believer. He believed in the divinity of Jesus Christ, the goodness of Sulamith Chopra, and the veracity of his own dreams. The age of the Chronoliths had made such conversions possible. I think, too, he was a little in love with Sue, though (unlike Ray Mosely) he had never harbored any illusions about her sexuality. He remained as her bodyguard and chief of security, drawing a salary that could only have been a fraction of his government income.

Both Sue and Morris wanted to keep me close to the project—Sue because I figured into her evolving pattern of meaningful coincidence; Morris because he believed I was important to Sue. Whether they could use legal leverage to keep me there had become debatable. Morris was a civilian now. But I didn't doubt he would pursue me if I announced I was leaving. Maybe even pull a few strings to keep me in my place. Morris liked me, in his cautious style, but his first loyalty was to Sue.

Sue was meanwhile trying to reconstruct her fragmented Chronolith project as an Internet circle, sharing any data the Defense Department left unclassified, deepening and expanding the mathematics of tau turbulence. In February of 2031 she lost her Department of Energy bursary and was reduced to another round of fundraising, while money flowed copiously into the glamor projects: the gamma-ray laser collider at Stanford; the Exotic Matter Group working out of Chicago.

I spent the morning cleaning up some code I had grown for her, a little routine that would go out into the world and search media nodes for relevant synchronicities, according to a noun-sorting algorithm Sue herself had cooked up. Morris passed in and out of the office a couple of times, looking leaner than he used to. Older, too. But still obstinately cheerful.

Sue was in her own office, and I stopped and knocked to tell her I was leaving. For lunch, I meant, but she must have heard something in my voice. "Long lunch? How far are you planning to go, Scotty?"

"Not far."

"We're not done, you know."

She might have been talking about the code we'd been evolving, but I doubted it.

Sue's leg wound had healed years ago, but the Jerusalem experience had left other scars. Jerusalem, she told me once, had made clear to her how dangerous her work was—that by placing herself near the center of the tau turbulence she had put at risk not only herself but the people around her.

"But I suppose it's inevitable," she had said sadly, "that's the worst of it. You stand on the train tracks long enough, sooner or later you meet a train."

I told her I'd finish the debugging that afternoon. She gave me a long, skeptical glare. "Anything else you want to tell me?"

"Not at the moment."

"We'll talk again," she said.

Like most of her prophecies, this one would come true, too.

Morris offered to join me for lunch but I told him no, I had some errands to do and I'd probably just grab a sandwich on the run. If he found this suspicious, he didn't show it.

I closed out my account at Zurich American, transferred most of the funds to a transit card and took the rest in old-fashioned folding green. I drove around a while longer to make sure Morris wasn't tailing me, unlikely as that was. More probably he had tapped the locator in my car. So I traded in the Chrysler at a downtown dealership, told the salesperson there was nothing I liked on the lot and would she mind if I shopped the other franchises? No, she said, and she'd be happy to walk me through the virtual inventory in the back room. I tentatively selected a snub-nosed Volks Edison in dusty blue, possibly the most anonymous-looking automobile ever manufactured; left my Chrysler at the lot and accepted a courtesy ride halfway across the city. Up close, the Volks looked a little more battered than it had in the virts, but its power plant was sturdy and clean, as near as I could judge.

All of this amateur espionage bullshit left an e-trail as wide as the Missouri, of course. But while Morris Torrance could surely make a few connections and hunt me down, he couldn't do it fast enough to keep me in Baltimore. I was two hundred miles west by nightfall, driving into a warm June evening with the windows open, popping antacids to calm the churning in my stomach.

There was a big ration camp where the highway crossed the Ohio, maybe a thousand threadbare canvas tents flapping in the spring breeze, dozens of barrel fires burning fitfully. Most of these people would have been refugees from the Louisiana bottomlands, unemployed refinery and petrochemical workers, farmers flooded out of their property. The consolidating clay of the Atchafalaya Basin had at last begun to draw the Mississippi River out of its own silted birdfoot deltas, despite the best efforts of the U.S. Army Corps of Engineers. More than a million families had been displaced by this spring's floods, not to mention the chaos that resulted from collapsed bridges and navigational locks and mud-choked roads.

Men lined the breakdown lane begging rides in both directions. Hitchhiking had been illegal here for fifty years and rides were scarce. But these men (almost all men) had ceased caring. They stood stiff as scarecrows, blinking into the glare of the headlights.

I hoped Kait had found a safe place to sleep tonight.

When I reached the outskirts of Minneapolis I registered at a motel. The desk clerk, an ancient turtle of a man, opened his eyes wide when I took cash out of my wallet. "I'll have to go to the bank with that," he said. So I added fifty dollars for his trouble and he was kind enough not to process my ID. The room he gave me was a cubicle containing a bed and a courtesy terminal and a window that overlooked the parking lot.

I desperately needed sleep, but before that I needed to talk to Janice.

It was Whit who answered the phone. "Scott," he said, cordially but not happily. He looked like he needed some sleep himself. "I assume you're calling about Kaitlin. I'm sorry to say there's been no further information. The police seem to think she's still in the city, so we're cautiously optimistic. Obviously, we're doing all we can."

"Thank you, Whit, but I need to talk to Janice right now."

"It's late. I hate to disturb her."

"I'll be quick."

"Well," Whit said, and wandered away from the terminal. Janice showed up a few moments later, wearing her nightgown but obviously wide awake.

"Scotty," she said. "I tried to call you but there was nobody home."

"That's all right. I'm in town. Can we get together tomorrow and talk this over?"

"You're in town? You didn't have to come all this way."

"I think I did. Janice? Can you make an hour for me? I can drop by the house, or—"

"No," she said, "I'll meet you. Where are you staying?"

"I'd as soon not meet here. What about that little steak house on Dukane, you know the one?"

"I think it's still in business."

"Meet you at noon?"

"Make it one."

"Try to get some sleep," I said.

"You, too." She hesitated. "It's been four days now, Scotty. Four nights. I think about her all the time."

"We'll talk tomorrow," I said.

Eleven

There's a difference between seeing someone in a phone window and seeing the same person in the flesh. I had phoned Janice half a dozen times in the last couple of months. But I almost failed to recognize her when she walked through the door of the steak house.

What had changed her, I think, was the combination of prosperity and dread.

Whit had done well despite the economic downturn. Janice wore a visibly expensive blue tweed suit and day jacket, but she wore it as if she had reached into her closet and yanked it off the hanger—collar bent, pockets unbuttoned. Her eyes were red, the skin under them swollen and gray.

We hugged cordially but neutrally and she took the chair opposite mine.

"No news," she said. She fingered her

handbag, where her phone undoubtedly was. "The police said they would call if anything turned up."

She ordered a salad she didn't touch and a Margarita she drank too eagerly. It might have been nice to talk about something else, but we both knew why we were there. I said, "I'm going to have to walk you through this whole thing one more time. Can you deal with that?"

"Yes," she said, "I think I can, but Scott, you have to tell me what you intend to do."

"What I intend to do?"

"About—all this. Because it's in the hands of the police now, and you could create a problem if you get too involved."

"I'm her father. I think I have a right to know."

"To know, yes, certainly. But not to interfere."

"I'm not planning to interfere."

She offered a wan smile. "Why do I find that less than convincing?"

I began a question, but Janice said, "No, wait a minute. I want you to have this."

She took a manila envelope from her handbag and passed it to me. I opened it and found a recent photograph of Kaitlin. Janice had printed it on slick stock; the image was crisp and defined.

Kait, at sixteen, was tall for her age and undeniably pretty. Fate had spared her the curse of adolescent acne and, judging by the poise in her expression, adolescent awkwardness as well. She looked somber but healthy.

For a moment I didn't recognize what was unusual about the picture. Then I thought: Her hair. Kait had tied back her long dirty-blond hair in a braid, showing off her ears.

Both of them.

"That's what you gave her, Scott. I wanted to thank you for that."

The inner-ear prosthesis was of course invisible, but the cosmetic work was flawless. As it should be. The ear wasn't false; genetically, it was hers, grown from Kaitlin's own stem cells. There were no scars except for a faded suture line. But she had been self-conscious for years after the operation.

"When the bandages came off it was all still pink, you know, but perfect. Just like a new rose."

I had been there for the surgery but not for the unveiling. That had happened during the crisis provoked by the Damascus arrival, and I'd been with Sue.

Janice went on, "I told her she was beautiful, right there in the hospital in front of the doctor and the nurses. She cocked her head, as if she wasn't sure where my voice was coming from. It takes time to, you know, adjust. You know what she said to me?"

"What?"

A single tear tracked down Janice's cheek. "She said, 'You don't have to shout.' "

The trouble started, Janice said, when Kaitlin failed to come home from a youth group meeting.

"What kind of youth group?"

"It's just a—well—" Janice faltered.

"There's no point doing this if we're not honest," I said.

"It's a youth division of this organization Whit belongs to. You have to understand, Scott. It's not a pro-Kuin thing. It's just people who want to talk about alternatives to armed conflict."

"Jesus Christ," I said. "Janice—Whit is a *Copperhead*?"

Lately the newspapers had revived the Civil War term "Copperhead" as a blanket insult for the various Kuinist movements. Janice lowered her eyes and said, "We don't use that term," by which I gathered she meant Whit didn't like it. "I'm not into politics. You know that. Even Whit, he only got involved because some of the people in upper management were joining. Preparing for a war we probably won't even have to fight, that's just not good economic sense, Whit says."

This was a standard Copperhead argument, and it was disturbing to hear it from Janice's lips. Not that it didn't contain a mote of truth. But beating under it was the Kuinist disdain for democratic process, the notion that Kuin might bring order to a planet divided along too many economic, religious, and ecological fracture lines.

I had followed the rise of the Copperhead movement on the web—inevitably, since Sue considered it significant and Morris considered it a potential threat. What I had seen, I disliked.

"And he dragged Kaitlin into this?"

"Kait wanted to go. At first he took her to the grownup meetings, but then she got interested in the youth arm."

"So you let her join—just like that?"

She looked at me pleadingly. "Honestly, Scotty, I didn't see anything wrong with it. They weren't making pipe bombs, for God's sake. It was just a social thing. I mean, they played baseball. They put on plays. *Teenagers*, Scott. She was making all these new friends—she had real friends for the first time in her life. What was I supposed to do, lock her in the house?"

"I'm not here to judge."

"Right."

"Just tell me what happened."

She sighed. "Well, I guess there were some radicals in the membership. It's hard to get away from it, you know. The young people are especially vulnerable. It's in the news, the net. She used to talk about it sometimes, about—" She lowered her voice. "About Kuin, and how you shouldn't condemn what you don't understand, that kind of thing. She was more serious about it than I imagined."

"She went to a meeting and didn't come back."

"No, nor did ten others, most of them older than Kait. Apparently they had been talking for weeks about the idea of a pilgrimage, what they call a haj."

I closed my eyes.

"But the police say they're probably still in town," Janice hurried on, "probably squatting in an empty building with a bunch of other would-be radicals, talking big and shoplifting food. I hope that's true, but it's . . . bad enough."

"Have you looked for her yourself?"

"The police said not to."

"How about Whit?"

"Whit says we should cooperate with the police. And that goes for you, too, Scott."

"Can you give me the name of somebody on the police force I can talk to?"

She took out her address book, copied a name and phone address onto a paper napkin, but she did it grudgingly, giving me long sour looks.

I said, "Also the name of this Copperhead club Whit belongs to."

At that she balked. "I don't want you making trouble."

"That's not why I'm here."

"Bullshit. You come to town with all this, this *moral outrage*—"

"My daughter's missing. That's why I'm here. What part of that are you afraid of?"

She paused.

Then she said, "Kait's been away less than a week. She could come home tomorrow. I have to believe that. I have to believe the police are doing all they can. But I can see that look in your eyes. And I hate it."

"What look?"

"Like you're getting ready to grieve."

"Janice—"

She slapped the table with her open hand. "*No*. Scott. I'm sorry. I'm grateful for all you've done for Kait. I know how hard you tried. But I can't tell you what organizations Whit belongs to. That's his private life. We discussed all this with the police and that's it, for now, anyway. So don't look at me with those, those fucking *funeral eyes.*"

I was hurt, but I didn't blame Janice, even when she stood up and stalked out into the sun-bleached street. I knew how she felt. Kaitlin was in danger, and Janice was asking herself what she could have done better, how she had dropped the ball, how things had gone so bad so fast.

I had been asking myself those same questions for ten years now. But it was a new experience for Janice.

After lunch I drove to Clarion Pharmaceuticals, a big industrial compound out where the suburbs met the wheat fields, and told the gate guard I wanted to see Mr. Delahunt. The guard stuck a card under the left front wiper and reminded me to pick up a visitor's pass at the main entrance. But Clarion's security was lax. I parked and walked through an open door near the loading bays and took an elevator up to what the directory said was Whit's office.

And walked past his secretary as if I belonged there, into a warren of doorless rooms where men and women in crisp suits held phone conferences, until I found Whitman Delahunt himself draining filtered spring water from a cooler in the narrow hall. His eyes went wide when he saw me.

Whit was as impeccable as ever. A little grayer at the temples and wider at the waist, but he carried it well. He had even been smiling faintly to himself, though the smile vanished when he spotted me. He threw his paper cup into the trash. "Scott," he said. "Jesus. You could have called."

"I thought we should talk in person."

"We should, and I don't want to seem callous, I know what you're going through, but this isn't a good time for me."

"I'd rather not wait."

"Scott, be reasonable. Maybe tonight—"

"I don't think I'm being unreasonable. My daughter has been God-knows-where for five days. Sleeping in the streets for all I know. So I'm sorry, Whit, if it interferes with your work and all, but we really do need to have a talk."

He hesitated, then puffed himself up. "I would hate to have to call Security."

"While you're thinking it over, tell me about that Copperhead club you joined."

His eyes widened. "Watch what you say."

"Or we could discuss this in private."

"Fuck, Scotty! All *right*. Jesus! Follow me."

He took me to the executive cafeteria. The steam tables were empty, the food service finished for the day. The room was deserted. We sat at a lacquered wooden table like civilized people.

Whit loosened his tie. "Janice told me this might happen. That you'd come into town and complicate everything. You really should talk to the police, Scott, because I sure as hell intend to let them know what you're up to."

"You mentioned the Copperhead club."

"No, *you* mentioned it, and will you please stop using that obscene word? It's no such thing. It's a *citizen's committee*, for Christ's sake. Yes, we talk about disarmament from time to time, but we talk about civil defense, too. We're just average, churchgoing people. Don't judge us by the fringe element you read about in the papers."

"What should I call it, then?"

"We're—" He had the grace to look embarrassed. "We're the Twin Cities Peace with Honor Committee. You have to understand, there's a lot at stake here. The kids have a point, Scott—the military buildup is distorting the economy, and there's no evidence at all that guns and bombs are useful against Kuin, assuming he constitutes a threat to the United States, which is far from proven. We're challenging the widespread belief that—"

"I don't need the manifesto, Whit. What kind of people belong to this committee?"

"Prominent people."

"How many?"

He blushed again. "Roughly thirty."

"And you initiated Kait into the children's auxiliary?"

"Far from it. The young people take these issues more seriously than we do. Than our generation, I mean. They're not cynical about it. Kaitlin is a perfect example. She'd come home from youth group talking about all the things a leader like Kuin could do, if we weren't fighting him at every turn. As if you could fight a man who controls time itself! Instead of finding a way to make the future a *functional* place."

"You ever discuss this with her?"

"I didn't indoctrinate her, if that's what you're insinuating. I respect Kaitlin's ideas."

"But she fell in with radicals, is that right?"

Whit shifted in his seat. "I wouldn't necessarily categorize them as radicals. I know some of those kids. They can be a little over the top, but it's enthusiasm, not fanaticism."

"None of them has been seen since Saturday."

"My feeling is that they're all right. Things like this happen sometimes. Kids dump their GPS tags, take an automobile and go off somewhere for a few days. It's not good, but it's hardly unique. I'm sorry if Kaitlin was misled by a few bad apples, Scott, but adolescence is never an easy time."

"Did they ever talk about a haj?"

"Pardon me?"

"A haj. Janice used the word."

"She shouldn't have. We discourage that word, too. A haj is a pilgrimage to Mecca. But that's not how the kids use it. They mean a trip to see a Kuin stone, or a place where one is supposed to arrive."

"You think that's what they had in mind?"

"I don't know what they might have had in mind, but I doubt it was a haj. You can't drive a Daimler to Madras or Tokyo."

"So you're not worried."

He drew back and looked like he wanted to spit. "That's a vicious thing to say. Of course I'm worried. The world is a dangerous place—more dangerous than it's ever been, in my opinion. I dread what might happen to Kaitlin. That's why I intend to let the police do their work without interference. I would suggest you do the same."

"Thank you, Whit," I said.

"Don't make it worse for Janice than it already is."

"I don't see how I could do that."

"Talk to the police. I mean it. Or I'll talk to them on your behalf."

He had recovered his poise. I stood up: I didn't want to hear any more homilies about Kait, not from this man. He sat in his chair like a wounded princeling and watched me leave.

I called Janice again from the car—I wanted to speak to her once more before Whitman did.

Hard times had changed the city. I drove past barred or boarded windows, discount retailers where decent shops used to be, storefront churches of obscure denomination. The trash collectors' strike had filled the sidewalks with garbage.

I told Janice over the phone that I'd talked to Whit.

"You had to do that, didn't you? Just when I thought things couldn't get worse."

There was a note in her voice I didn't like. "Janice—are you afraid of him?"

"Of course not, not physically, but what if he loses his job? What then? You don't *understand*, Scotty. A lot of what Whit does is just . . . he has to go along to get along, you know what I mean?"

"My concern is with Kaitlin right now."

"I'm not sure you're doing Kait any good, either." She sighed. "There's a parents' group the police told me about, you might want to look into it."

"Parents' group?"

"Parents whose kids ran off, usually kids with Kuinist ideas. Haj parents, if you know what I mean."

"The last thing I'm looking for is a support group."

"You could compare notes, see what other people are doing."

I doubted it. But she zipped me the address and I copied it into my directory.

"Meanwhile," she said, "I'll apologize to Whit for you."

"Has he apologized for letting Kait get mixed up in this?"

"That's none of your business, Scott."

Twelve

A month or so after the Jerusalem arrival I had taken myself to a doctor and had a long talk about genetics and madness.

It had occurred to me that Sue's logic of correlation might have a personal side to it. She was saying, in effect, that our expectations shape the future, and that those of us exposed to extreme tau turbulence might influence it more than most.

And if what was happening to the world was madness, could I have factored in some of it from my own deepest psychic vaults? Had I inherited from my mother a faulty genetic sequence, and was it my own latent insanity that had filled a hotel suite on Mt. Scopus with bullets and glass?

The physician I talked to drew a blood sample and agreed to look at my genes for any markers that might suggest late-onset schizophrenia. But it wasn't as simple as that, he said. Schizophrenia isn't a purely heritable disorder, although susceptibility has a genetic aspect. That's why they don't gene-patch for it. There are complex environmental triggers. The most he could tell me was whether I *might* have inherited a *tendency* toward adult-onset schizophrenia—an almost meaningless factoid and utterly without predictive value.

I thought of it again when I used the motel terminal to call up a map of the world marked with Chronolith sites. If this was madness, here were its tangible symptoms. Asia was a red zone, dissolving into feverish anarchy, though fragile national governments continued to exist in Japan, where the ruling coalition had survived a plebiscite (barely), and in Beijing, though not in the Chinese countryside or far from the coast. The Indian subcontinent was pockmarked with arrivals and so was the Middle East, not only Jerusalem and Damascus but Baghdad, Tehran, Istanbul. Europe was free of the physical manifestation of Kuinism, which had so far stalled at the Bosporus, but not its political counterpart; there had been massive street riots in both Paris and Brussels staged by rival "Kuinist" factions. Northern Africa had endured five disastrous arrivals. A small Chronolith had cored the equatorial city of Kinshasa just last month. The planet was sick, sick unto death.

I dumped the map window and called one of the numbers Janice had given me, a police lieutenant by the name of Ramone Dudley. His interface told me he was unavailable but that my call had been logged for return.

While I waited I entered the other number Janice had pressed on me, the "support group," which turned out to be the home terminal of a middle-aged woman named Regina Lee Sadler. She wore a bathrobe when she answered, and her hair was dripping. I apologized for calling her out of the shower.

"Makes no mind," she said, her voice a Southern contralto as dark as her complexion. "Unless you're calling from that goddamned collection agency, pardon my French."

I explained about Kaitlin.

"Yes," she said, "in fact I know about that. We have a couple other parents from that incident just joined us—mostly moms, of course. The dads tend to resist the kind of help we offer, God knows why. You seem not be a member of that stiff-necked clan, however."

"I wasn't here when Kait disappeared." I told her about Janice and Whit.

"So you're an absentee father," she said.

"Not by choice. Mrs. Sadler, can I ask you a frank question?"

"I would prefer that to the other kind. And most people call me Regina Lee."

"Do I have anything to gain by meeting these folks? Will it help me get my daughter home?"

"No. No, I can't promise you that. Our group exists for our own purposes. We save *ourselves.* A lot of parents in this situation, they are very vulnerable to despair. It helps some people to be able to share their feelings with others in similar straits. And I suspect you are tuning me out right now, saying to yourself, 'Well, I don't need that touchy-feely crap.' And maybe you don't. But some of us do, and we are not ashamed of it."

"I see."

"Not to say there isn't a certain amount of networking. A lot of our people have hired private investigators, freelance skip-tracers, deprogrammers, and so on, and they do compare notes and share information, but I will tell you frankly that I have very little faith in such activity and the results I've seen bear that out."

I told her those were the people I'd like to talk to, if only to learn from their failures.

"Well, if you come to our gathering tonight—" She gave me the address of a church hall. "If you show up, you'll certainly be able to have a conversation of that nature. But may I ask something of you in return? Don't come as a skeptic. Bring an open mind. About yourself, I mean. You seem all calm and collected, but I know from personal experience what you're going through, how easy it is to grasp at straws when a loved one is in danger. And make no mistake, your Kaitlin *is* in danger."

"I do know that, Mrs. Sadler."

"There's knowing it and there's knowing it." She looked over her shoulder, perhaps at a clock. "I ought to be getting fixed up, but may I say I hope to see you this evening?"

"Thank you."

"I pray you find a positive outcome, Mr. Warden, whatever you do."

I thanked her again.

The meeting took place in the assembly hall of a Presbyterian church in what had been a working-class neighborhood before it slipped into outright poverty some few years ago. Regina Lee Sadler, strutting across the stage in a flowered dress and with an old-fashioned handless mike bobbing in front of her head, looked both more robust and about twenty pounds heavier than she had looked in the video window. I wondered if Regina Lee was vain enough to have installed a slimming ap in her interface.

I didn't introduce myself, just lurked in the back of the hall. It wasn't exactly a Twelve-Step meeting, but it wasn't far off. Five new members introduced themselves and their problems. Four had lost children to Kuinist or haj cells within the last month. One had been missing her daughter for more than a year and wanted a place where she could share her grief . . . not that she had given up hope, she insisted, not at all, but she was just very, very tired and thought she might be able to sleep through the night for a change, if only she had someone to talk to.

There was muted, sympathetic applause.

Then Regina Lee stood up again and read from a printed sheet of news and updates—children recovered, rumors of new Kuinist movements in the West and South, a truckload of underage pilgrims intercepted at the Mexican border. I took notes.

At that point the meeting became more personal as attendees divided up into "workshops" to discuss "coping strategies," and I slipped quietly out the door.

I would have gone directly back to the motel if not for the woman sitting on the church steps smoking a cigarette.

She was about my age, her expression careworn but thoughtful and focused. Her hair was short and lustrous in the street light. Her eyes were shadowed as she glanced up at me. "Sorry," she said automatically, stubbing out the cigarette.

I told her it was all right. Under a recent statute tobacco preparations were illegal for trade without an addict's certificate and a prescription, but I considered myself broadminded—I had grown up in the days of legal tobacco. "Had enough?" she asked, waving a hand at the church door.

"For now," I said.

She nodded. "Regina Lee is good for a lot of people, and God knows she's unstoppable. But I don't need what she's handing out. I don't think so, anyhow."

We introduced ourselves. She was Ashlee Mills, and her son was Adam. Adam was eighteen years old, deeply involved in the local Kuinist network; he had been missing for six days now. Just like Kaitlin. So we compared notes. Adam had been involved with Whit Delahunt's junior auxiliary, as well as a handful of other radical organizations. So they probably would have known each other.

"That's a coincidence," Ashlee said.

I told her no, there was no such thing.

We were still talking when Regina Lee's meeting began to break up, crowding us off the church steps. I offered to buy her coffee somewhere nearby—she lived in the neighborhood.

Ashlee gave me a thoughtful look, frank and a little intimidating. She struck me as a woman who harbored no illusions about men.

Then she said, "Okay. There's an all-night coffee shop next to the drugstore, just around the corner." We walked there.

Ashlee was conspicuously not wealthy. Her skirt and blouse looked like Goodwill purchases, cared-for but a long way from new. But she wore them with a dignity that was innate, not practiced. At the restaurant she counted out dollar coins to pay for her coffee; I told her not to bother and pushed my card across the counter. She gave me another long look, then nodded. We found a quiet corner table away from the jabbering video panels.

She said, "You'll want to know about my son."

I nodded. "But this isn't one of Regina Lee's workshops. What I really want to know is how I can help my daughter."

"I can't promise you anything to that effect, Mr. Warden."

"That's what everybody tells me."

"Everybody is right, I'm sorry to say. At least in my experience."

Ashlee had been born and educated in Southern California, had come to Minneapolis to work as a medical receptionist for her uncle, a podiatrist who had since died of an aneurysm. At the reception desk she had met Tucker Kellog, a tool and dye programmer, and married him at the age of twenty. Tucker left home when their son Adam was five years old. He had been unavailable since. Ashlee filed for divorce and could have sued for child support but chose not to. She was better off without Tucker in her life, she said, even peripherally. She had reverted to her maiden name ten years ago.

She loved her son Adam, but he had been a trial. "Parent to parent, Mr. Warden, there were times when I was in despair. Even when he was little, it was hard keeping Adam in school. Nobody likes school, I guess, but whatever it is that made the rest of us show up every day, sense of duty or fear of the consequences, whatever it is, Adam didn't feel it. He couldn't be bullied into it and he couldn't be shamed into it."

He had been in and out of psychiatric programs, apprenticeship programs, special learning facilities, and occasionally Juvenile Hall.

Not that Adam wasn't bright. "He reads constantly. Not just storybooks, either. And, frankly, it takes a certain amount of smarts to survive the way he has—on the street half the time. Adam is actually very clever."

When Ashlee talked about her son her expression was a mixture of pride, guilt, and apprehension, sometimes all three at once. Her large eyes darted from side to side as if she expected to be overheard. She played with her napkin, folding it and refolding it, finally tearing it into long strips that lay on the tabletop like aborted acts of origami.

"He ran away once when he was twelve, but that had nothing to do with this Copperhead thing. I swear I don't know what Adam imagines this Kuin is all about, apart from the business of destroying cities and making people's lives miserable. But it fascinates him. The way he watches the news nets is almost frightening." She dipped her head. "I'm reluctant to say it, but I think what Adam likes is basically just this *crushing* of things. I think he puts himself in Kuin's place. He wants to lift his foot and obliterate everything he hates. The talk about a new kind of world government is just set-dressing, in my opinion."

"Did he ever talk to you about Kaitlin or her group?"

Ashlee smiled sadly. "That's a question and a half. Did your Kaitlin ever talk to *you* about this stuff?"

"We talked. But no, she never mentioned anything political."

"That still puts you a step up from me. Adam has never confided in me about anything. Anything at all. Everything I know about my own son, I learned from observation. Excuse me, I think I need another coffee."

What she needed, I imagined, was another smoke. She paused at the counter, asked the clerk for a double-double, then ducked into the restroom for a while. She came out looking calmer. I think the counterman smelled tobacco when she picked up her coffee. He gave her a hard look, then rolled his eyes.

She sat down again, sighing. "No, Adam never talked about his meetings. Adam is seventeen, but like I said, he's not naive. He conducts his business pretty carefully. But, you know, I would overhear things once in a while. I knew he'd hooked up with one of the suburban Copperhead clubs, but for a while it seemed like that was almost a *good* thing. He was with people who had some, you know, background. Prospects. I guess in the back of my head was the idea that he would make friends and maybe that would lead to something, some opportunities, after all this time-travel shit blows over, excuse me. I thought he might meet a girl, or maybe somebody's dad would offer him a job."

I thought of Janice's plaintive, *What was I supposed to do? Lock her in the house?*

Janice had clearly not imagined her daughter in the company of an Adam Mills.

"I changed my mind when I walked in on one of his phone calls. He was talking about those people—I guess including your Kait, I'm sorry to say. And he was just vicious, contemptuous. He said the group was full of—" She lowered her head, ashamed. "Full of 'whitebread virgins.' "

She must have seen my reaction. Ashlee put her chin up, and her manner hardened. "I love my son, Mr. Warden. I don't have any illusions about the kind of person Adam is—or *will* be, unless he turns himself around. Adam has serious, serious problems. But he's my son, and I love him."

"I respect that," I said.

"I hope so."

"They're both missing. That's what we have to worry about now."

She frowned then, maybe reluctant to be included in the pronoun. Ashlee was accustomed to dealing with her own troubles in her own way; that was why she had bailed out of Regina Lee's meeting.

But then, so had I.

She said, "I would be very frankly pissed if you were trying to pick me up, Mr. Warden."

"That's not what this is about."

"Because I want to ask you for your phone number so we can keep in touch about Adam and Kaitlin. I don't have any hard information, but my guess is that their whole little group is attempting some kind of half-assed pilgrimage, Christ only knows where. So they're probably together. So we should keep in touch. I just don't want to be misunderstood."

I gave her my portable address. She gave me her home terminal.

She finished her coffee and said, "This is pretty much all bad news for you."

"Not all," I said.

She stood up. "Well, it was good meeting you." She turned and walked through the door into the street. I watched her through the window as she strode a half block between islands of lamplight, to a doorway adjoining a Chinese restaurant, where she fumbled with a key. An apartment over a restaurant. I pictured a threadbare sofa, maybe a cat. A rose in a wine bottle or a framed poster on the wall. The echoing absence of her son.

Ramone Dudley, the police lieutenant in charge of local missing persons, agreed to see me in his office the following afternoon. The meeting was brief.

Dudley was an obviously overworked desk cop who had delivered the same bad news too many times. "These kids," he said (clearly a homogenous mass, in Dudley's mind: *these kids*), "they have no future, and they know it. The thing is, it's true. The economy sucks, that's no secret. And what else do we have to offer them? Everything they hear about the future is all Kuin, Kuin, Kuin. Fucking Kuin. According to the fundies, Kuin is the Antichrist; all you can do is say your prayers and wait for the Rapture. Washington is drafting kids for some war we may never fight. And the Copperheads are saying maybe Kuin won't hurt us so bad if we bend over politely. That's not a real bouquet of options, when you think about it. Plus all that shit they hear in the music or learn in those encrypted chatrooms."

Plainly, Lieutenant Dudley blamed most of this on my generation. He must have met some inadequate parents in the course of his work. By the way he looked at me, he was pretty sure I was one of them.

I said, "About Kaitlin—"

He took a file from his desktop and read me the contents. There were no surprises. A total of eight youths, all involved in the junior arm of Whitman's social club, had failed to return home from a meeting. Friends and parents of the missing children had been extensively interviewed—"With the exception of yourself, Mr. Warden, and I was expecting you to turn up."

"Whit Delahunt told you about me," I guessed.

"He mentioned you briefly when we interviewed him, but no, not exactly. The call I got was from a retired fed named Morris Torrance."

Fast work. But then, Morris had always been diligent. "What did he tell you?"

"He asked me to give you as much cooperation as possible. This is it, as far as I'm concerned. I don't have a whole lot more to tell you, unless you have some specific questions. Oh, and he asked me one other thing."

"What's that?"

"He asked me to tell you to get in touch with him. He said he was sorry to hear about Kaitlin and he said he might be able to help you out."

Thirteen

Maybe I should have taken advantage of Regina Lee's communal therapy and admitted my fear for Kaitlin—fear, and the premonition of grief that drifted into consciousness whenever I closed my eyes. But that wasn't my style. I had learned at an early age to fake calm in the face of disaster. To keep my anxiety to myself, like a dirty secret.

But I thought about Kait constantly. In my mind she was still the Kaitlin of Chumphon, five years old and as fearless as she was curious. Children wear their natures like brightly-colored clothes; that's why they lie so transparently. Adulthood is the art of deceit. Because I had known Kaitlin as a child I had never lost sight of the vulnerable heart of her. Which made it all the more painful to imagine (or struggle not to imagine) where Kaitlin might be now, with whom. The most fundamental parental urge is the urge to nurture and protect. To grieve for a child is to admit ultimate impotence. You can't protect what goes into the ground. You can't tuck a blanket around a grave.

I spent much of every night awake, staring out the motel window and drinking, alternately, beer and diet cola (and peeing every half hour), until sleep broke over me like a glutinous wave. What dreams I had were chaotic and futile. Waking up to the brutal irony of spring, of sunlight in a bottomless blue sky, was like waking from a dream into a dream.

I had figured my contact with Ashlee Mills was a one-shot, but she called me on my pocket phone ten days after Kaitlin's disappearance. Her voice was businesslike and she came to the point quickly: "I arranged to meet someone," she said, "a man who might know something about Adam and Kaitlin, but I don't want to meet him alone."

"I'm free this afternoon," I said.

"He works nights. If you call what he does work. This might not be pretty."

"What is he, a pimp?"

"Uh-uh," she said. "He's a sort of a drug dealer."

I had spent much of the last week on the net, researching the phenomenon of "haj youth" and the Kuinist movement, tunneling into their hidden chatrooms.

There was, of course, no unified Kuinist movement. Lacking a flesh-and-blood Kuin, the "movement" was a patchwork of utopian ideologies and quasi-religious cults, each competing for the title. What they had in common was simply the act of veneration, the worship of the Chronoliths. For the hajists, any Chronolith was a holy object. Hajists attributed all sorts of powers to the physical proximity of a Kuin stone: enlightenment, healing, psychological transformation, epiphanies great and small. But unlike the pilgrims at Lourdes, for instance, the vast majority of hajists were young. It was, in the twentieth century term, a "youth movement." Like most such movements, it was as much style as substance. Very few Americans ever made a physical pilgrimage to a Chronolith site, but it was not uncommon to see a teenager with a Kuinist logo on his hat or shirt—most often the ubiquitous "K+" in a red or orange circle. (Or any of the subtler and supposedly secret signs: scarred nipples or earlobes, silver ankle bracelets, white headbands.)

The K+ symbol abounded in Ashlee's neighborhood, chalked or painted on walls and sidewalks. I pulled up outside the Chinese restaurant at the appointed time, and Ashlee scurried out of her apartment door and into the passenger seat. "It's good you have a cheap car," she said. "It won't attract attention."

"Where are we going?"

She gave me an address five blocks farther into the city, where the only surviving businesses were stockhouses, window-service fast-food outlets, and liquor stores.

"The guy's name," Ashlee said without preamble, "is Cheever Cox, and he's tied into pretty much all the trade you can't report on your IRS form. I know him because I used to buy tobacco from him." She said this in a carefully neutral tone but glanced at me for signs of disapproval. "Before I got my addict's license, I mean."

"What does he know about Kait and Adam?"

"Maybe nothing, but when I called him yesterday he said he'd heard about a cut-rate haj and some new rumor about Kuin and he didn't want to talk about it over an unencrypted line. Cheever's kind of paranoid that way."

"You think this is legitimate?"

"Tell you the truth? I don't really know."

She rolled down the window and lit a cigarette, almost defiantly, waiting for my reaction. Minnesota had some of the harshest tobacco laws in the country. But I was from out-of-state and old enough not to be shocked. I said, "Ashlee? Did you ever consider quitting?"

"Oh, please."

"I'm not passing judgment, I'm making conversation."

"I don't especially want to talk about it." She exhaled noisily. "There hasn't been a whole lot holding me together the last few years, Mr. Warden."

"Scott."

"Scott, then. It's not that I'm a weak person. But . . . did you ever smoke?"

"No." I had been spared the anti-abuse vaccines that were pushed on so many young people in those days (and the resultant risk of adult antibody disorders), but tobacco simply wasn't my vice.

"It's probably killing me, but I don't have much else." She seemed to struggle after a thought, then let it go. "It calms me down."

"I'm not condemning you for it. Actually, I always liked the smell of burning tobacco. At least from a distance."

She smiled wryly. "Uh-huh. You're a real degenerate, I can tell that about you."

"You miss California?"

"Do I miss *California*?" She rolled her eyes. "Is this a real conversation or are you just nervous about meeting Cheever? Because you don't have to be. He's a little shady but he's not a bad person."

"That's reassuring," I said.

"You'll see."

The address was a run-down semidetached wood-frame house. The porch light was out, probably permanently. The stairs sagged. Ashlee pulled open the rusty fly screen and rapped at the door.

Cheever Cox opened up when Ashlee identified herself. Cox was a bald man of about thirty-five, wearing Levis and a pale blue shirt with what looked like marinara sauce dribbled down the collar. "Hey, Ashlee," he barked, hugging her. He gave me a brief glance.

Ashlee introduced me and said, "It's about what we talked about on the phone."

The front room contained a faded sofa, two wooden folding chairs, and a coffee table with ashtray. Down the dim hallway I could see a corner of the kitchen. If Cox made a lot of money in the illicit drug trade, he wasn't spending it on decor. But maybe he had a country house.

He spotted the pack of cigarettes sticking out of Ashlee's shirt pocket. "Shit, Ashlee," he said, "you on a script too? Fucking government's taking away my business with those little pussy prescription sticks."

"I'll lose my script next year," Ashlee said, "if I'm not on a patch or a program. Worse, I'll lose my health insurance."

He grinned. "So maybe I'll see more of you then?"

"Not a chance." She glanced at me. "I'll get my teeth whitened and find a good job."

"Be a citizen," Cox said.

"Damn right."

"Marry your boyfriend, too?"

"He's not my boyfriend."

"Okay, Ash, I'm sorry, don't mind me. You want something? A little more than the druggist is willing to sell you?"

"I want to ask you some questions about Adam."

"Yeah, but that can't be all you want."

Cox made it obvious that he would have nothing to say unless Ashlee bought something from him. Business is business, he said.

"It's about my son, Cheever."

"I know, and I love you and Adam both, but Ashlee, it's *business.*"

So she paid him for a carton of what she called "loose smokes," which Cox fetched from the basement. She held the box in her lap. The box reeked.

Cox settled into his chair. "What it is," he told Ashlee, "is, I go into the squatters' buildings a lot, especially down on Franklin, or Lowertown, or the old Cargill warehouses, so I see these kids. And, you know, Adam hung with that crowd, too. It's not a big market for me because these kids don't have any money, basically. They're shoplifting food. But every once in a while one of 'em comes by some cash, I don't ask how, and they want a carton, two cartons, smokes and drinks and chemicals and so forth. A lot of times it was Adam who would come to me, because I knew him from when you and I did business on a more regular basis."

Ashlee lowered her eyes at this assertion but said nothing.

"Also, frankly, Adam has a little more on the ball than most of those people. They call themselves hajists or Kuinists but they're about as political as bricks. You know who does the real haj thing? Rich kids. Rich kids and celebs. They go to Israel or Egypt and burn their scented candles or whatever. Downtown, it's different. Most of these kids wouldn't go out of their way for Kuin if he was holding a coronation ball in their back yard. Well, Adam figured that out. That's why he was fooling around with the Copperhead clubs in Wayzata, Edina—looking for people who think the way he does but are maybe a little more gullible and a little more flush than the downtown crowd."

"Cheever," Ashlee said, "can you tell me if he's still in town?"

"I can't tell you a firm yes or no, but I doubt it. If he is, I haven't seen him. I talk to people, you know, I follow the links, I keep my ear to ground. There are always rumors. You remember Kirkwell?"

Last summer, a clinically paranoid retired butcher in Kirkwell, New Mexico, had announced that he was measuring increased background radiation at a dry spring outside the city limits—his own property, by coincidence. Probably he hoped to make the site a tourist attraction. He succeeded. By September, ten thousand destitute young hajists had camped there. The National Guard dropped food and water rations and exhorted the pilgrims to go home, but it was an outbreak of cholera that finally succeeded in clearing the property. The retired butcher promptly disappeared, leaving a number of class-action and public nuisance lawsuits in his wake.

"These rumors come and go," Cox said, "but the big one right now is Mexico. Ciudad Portillo. Adam was in this room three weeks ago and he was talking about it then—not that anybody paid much attention to him. That's why he hooked up with the suburban Copperheads, I think, because he wanted to go to Mexico and he thought that crowd could supply at least a little money, some transportation."

Ashlee said, "He went to *Mexico*?"

Cox held up his hands. "I can't tell you that for sure. But if I had to bet I'd say he was on the road and bound for the border, if he hasn't already crossed it."

Ashlee said nothing. She looked pensive and pale, almost beaten. Cox made a sympathetic sound. "That's the trouble," he said. "Stupid people do stupid things, but Adam is smart enough to do something *really* stupid."

We talked it around a little more, but Cox had said all he had to say. Finally Ashlee stood up and stepped toward the door.

Cox hugged her again.

"Come see me when your script runs out," he said.

I asked her on the drive back how she had known Adam was missing.

She said, "What do you mean?"

"It sounds like Adam was connected with squatter circles. If he wasn't living at home, how did you know he was missing?"

We pulled up at the curb. Ashlee said, "I'll show you."

She unlocked the street door and walked me up a narrow flight of stairs to her apartment. The apartment was laid out like any other railway flat: a big front room facing the street, two tiny bedrooms off a corridor, a square kitchen with a window over the rear alley. The apartment was stuffy; Ashlee said she preferred to keep the windows shut during the garbage strike. But it was neatly and sensibly furnished. It was the home of someone possessing taste and common sense, if not much capital.

"This door," Ashlee told me, "is Adam's room. He doesn't like people going in there, but he's not around to object."

In a sense, my first real contact with Adam was this glimpse of his room. I suppose I expected the worst: pornography, graffiti, maybe a shotgun buried in the laundry hamper.

But Adam's room was nothing like that. It was more than orderly, it was icily neat. The bed was made. The closet door was open and the number of bare hangers suggested that Adam had packed for a long trip, but what remained of his wardrobe was neatly arrayed. The bookshelves were makeshift brick-and-board arrangements but the books were upright and in alphabetical order, not by author but by title.

Books tell you a lot about the people who choose and read them. Adam clearly leaned toward the more technical sort of nonfiction—electronics manuals, textbooks (including organic chemistry and American history), *Fundamentals of Computation*, plus random biographies (Picasso, Lincoln, Mao Zedong), *Famous Trials of the Twentieth Century, How to Repair Almost Anything, Ten Steps to a More Efficient Fuel Cell.* A child's astronomy book and a spotter's guide to manned satellite orbits. *Ice and Fire: The Untold Story of the Lunar Base Tragedy.* And, of course, books about Kuin. Some of these were mainstream works, including McNeil and Cassel's *Asia Under Siege*; most were gaudy fringe publications with titles like *End of Days* and *Fifth Horseman.*

There were no photographs of living human beings visible, but the walls were papered with magazine shots of various Chronoliths. (Briefly, and uncomfortably, I was reminded of Sue Chopra's office in Baltimore.)

Ashlee said, "Does it look like he never comes home? This is Adam's ground zero. Maybe he didn't sleep here every night, but he was here for a good eight or ten hours out of every twenty-four. Always."

She closed the door.

"Funny," she said, "I always thought of myself as making a home for Adam. But that's not how it worked. He made his own home. It just happened to be inside mine."

• • •

She fixed coffee and we talked a while longer, sitting on Ashlee's long sofa with the sound of street traffic coming through the closed but single-glazed windows. There was something deeply comforting about the moment—Ashlee moving in the kitchen, absentmindedly smoothing her bristly hair with her hand—something almost *viscerally* comforting, a shadow of the kind of domesticity I had misplaced more than a decade ago. I was grateful to her for that.

But the moment couldn't last. She asked me about Kaitlin and I told her something (not everything) about Chumphon and the way I had spent the last ten years. She was impressed that I had seen the Jerusalem arrival, not because she felt any reverence for Kuin but because it meant I had moved, if only peripherally, among the kind of people she imagined were relatively rich and vaguely famous. "At least you were doing something," she said, "not just spinning your wheels."

I told her she had obviously done more than spin her wheels: It couldn't have been easy for a single woman to raise a child during the economic crisis.

"They call it spinning your wheels," she said, "when you can't get traction. And I guess that's how I feel about Adam. I tried to help him, but I couldn't get traction." She paused and then turned to face me, her expression less guarded than it had been. "Suppose they *did* go to Mexico—Adam and Kaitlin and all that group. What do we do?"

"I don't know," I said. "I have to talk to some people."

"Would you follow Kaitlin all the way to Portillo?"

"If I thought I could help her. If I thought it would do any good."

"But you're not sure."

"No. I'm not sure."

My pocket phone rang. It was set to take messages, but I checked the display to see who was calling. It might have been Janice saying Kait had come home, that the whole thing was a stupid misunderstanding. Or it might have been Ramone Dudley calling to tell me the police had found Kait's body.

It was neither. According to the text display, the call was from Sue Chopra. She had tracked down my private terminal address (despite the fact that I had changed it when I left Baltimore), and she wanted me to reply as soon as possible.

"I should take this in private," I told Ashlee.

She walked me down the stairs and out to the car. I took her hand. It was late, and the street was empty. The streetlights were the old-fashioned mercury vapor kind, and they put amber highlights in Ashlee's short blond hair. Her hand was warm.

"If you find out something," she said, "you have to tell me. Promise me that."

I promised.

"Call me, Scott."

I believe she genuinely wanted me to call her. I believe she doubted that I would.

"First of all," Sue said, leaning into the lens so that her face filled the motel terminal's phone window like a myopic brown moon, "I want you to know I'm not pissed about the way you left town. I understand what that was all about, and if you chose not to confide in me, I guess I have myself to blame. Although—I don't know why it is, Scotty, you always expect the worst of people. Did it even occur to you we might want to *help*?"

"You know about Kait," I said.

"We looked into the situation, yeah."

"You talked to the police."

"I know you're going to do what you have to do, but I want to make sure you don't feel like a fugitive." She added, more plaintively, "I would still like to talk to you once in a while. As far as I'm concerned, you still work here. Ray is a good foil for the math work, and Morris tries hard to understand what we're doing, but I need someone who's bright enough to pay attention but doesn't have any preconceived ideas." She lowered her eyes and added, "Or maybe that's just an excuse. Maybe I just need somebody to talk to."

This was, among other things, her way of apologizing for all the invasive prodding of the last few years. But I had never blamed Sue for that. It might have been her ideas about tau turbulence that put me in a vulnerable position, but she had been careful to build a wall between me and the federal juggernaut. The juggernaut had lately turned its attention elsewhere; Sue still wanted to be my friend.

She said, "I'm so unhappy about what happened with Kaitlin."

"The only thing I can tell you about Kait is that she hasn't come home yet. I'd as soon not dwell on it. So distract me. Gossip. Has Ray found a girlfriend? Have you?"

"Are you drinking, Scotty?"

"Yes, but not enough to justify the question."

She smiled sadly. "All right. Ray is still wandering in the wilderness. Me, I'm seeing this woman I met at a bar. She's very sweet. She has red hair and collects Dresden china and tropical fish. But it's not serious."

Of course not. Sue conducted her love affairs almost at a distance, deferentially and with the expectation of disappointment.

Her real romance was with her work, which was what she preferred to talk about. "The thing is, Scotty, we've had a little bit of a breakthrough. That's what's obsessing everybody right now. Most of this is classified, but since there are rumors all over the net I can tell you at least a little bit about it."

She told me probably more than she should have, but much of it went over my head. The gist was that someone at MIT had succeeded in conjuring negative-tau particles out of the vacuum (which is in any case a seething cauldron of what physicists call "virtual" particles) and stabilizing them long enough to demonstrate the effect. These were hadrons with, essentially, negative duration. They carved holes, if you like, into the past—about a millisecond of the past, not Kuin's ponderous twenty years and three months, but in principle it was the same phenomenon.

"We're very close," Sue said, "to understanding exactly what it is Kuin is doing. And even Kuin might not have figured all the angles. Given enough time, we can create whole new technologies. I mean, star travel, Scotty: that's a real possibility!"

"Does it matter?"

"Of course it matters! We're talking about a potential new era in the history of the fucking species—*yes* it matters!"

"Kuin has already put his fingerprints on half the world, Sue. I would hate to see him extend his reach beyond the surface of the planet."

"Well, but this is the key to *that*, too. If we can figure out how a Chronolith works, we can interfere with it. With the right application we might be able to make a Chronolith simply *go away*."

"And achieve what?" The last few days had pumped up my cynicism. "It's a little late for that, don't you think?"

"No," she said, "I don't. Remember, it isn't Kuin we have to be afraid of. It's not even the Chronoliths. *Feedback*, Scotty, that's the key. The real problem here is the perception of Kuin's invincibility, which rests on the invincibility of his monuments. Destroy one, and you destroy the myth. Suddenly he's not a godlike force anymore, he's just another would-be Hitler or Stalin."

Still, I suggested, it might be too late for that.

"Not if we can demonstrate his weakness."

"Can you?"

She paused. Her smile faltered. "Well, maybe. Maybe soon," she said.

But not soon enough for Kait, who was probably in Mexico, imbued with her own notions of Kuin's invincibility and promise. I reminded Sue that I had things to do. She said, "I'm sorry if I kept you up, Scotty, but I really do think it's important for us to keep in touch."

Because, of course, she had not abandoned her own faux-Jungian idea that our futures were intertwined—that Kuin, among other things, had imposed on us a fate.

"Anyway, that's the real reason I called," she said. "I told somebody about your problem. And he wants to help you."

"Not Morris," I said. "I like Morris well enough, but even Morris will tell you he's not an experienced field agent."

"No, not Morris, although he'd love to help. No, this is someone with a whole different kind of experience."

I should have seen it coming. It was Sue, after all, who had looked most deeply into my past, particularly the time at Chumphon. But I was blindsided all the same.

"Maybe you remember him," she said. "His name is Hitch Paley."

Fourteen

Sometime during that week—before Hitch arrived, before events began to tumble out of control—Ashlee said, in the middle of a phone conversation, "You know the Charles Dickens story, *A Christmas Carol*?"

"What about it?"

"I was thinking about Kuin and the Chronoliths and all that. You know in Dickens where Scrooge goes into the future and sees his own funeral? And he says to the ghost, 'Are these the shades of things that *must* be, or things that *may* be?' Or something like that?"

"Right," I said.

"So the Chronoliths, Scott, are they *must* be or *may* be?"

I told her no one was certain about that. But if I understood Sue correctly, the events marked by the already existing Chronoliths were *must-bes* in one form or another. There was no bright alternative future in which we stopped Kuin before his conquests and made the Chronoliths into harmless free-floating paradoxes. Kuin *would* conquer Chumphon, Thailand, Vietnam, Southeast Asia; time might be fluid, but the monuments themselves were immutable and fundamental.

Then why not despair? I suppose Sue's answer would be that the battle wasn't finished. Much of the civilized world was still free of Chronoliths, which suggested that Kuin's conquests were a step-like process with gains and reversals. There had not yet been a Chronolith on North American soil. Maybe there never would be, if we did the right thing. Whatever the right thing was.

Sue had broached to me the idea of "negative feedback." If what Kuin was doing with the Chronoliths represented a kind of positive feedback—a signal reinforced and amplified through time and human expectation—then the solution might be the opposite. A Chronolith that appeared and was subsequently destroyed would cast doubt on the process; the cancerous impression of Kuin's invincibility would be, if not shattered, at least weakened.

He might take half the Earth, but not *our* half.

That was Sue Chopra's faith. I hoped she was right. I was prepared to act on that assumption.

In all honesty, however, I cannot say that I believed it.

Well, then, here was Hitch Paley, stepping out of a battered Sony compact (which by all rights should have been a motorbike) into the motel parking lot. We had agreed to meet at nine this morning. He was fifteen minutes late. In a sense, ten years late.

He hadn't changed much. I recognized him immediately, even from a dozen yards away under the shade of the coffee shop awning. I was delighted and I was afraid.

He wore a full beard and a dung-green leather jacket. He had put on a little weight, which only served to emphasize his broad nose, his high cheekbones, the Neanderthal slope of his skull. He spotted me, walked bandy-legged across the sunny space between us, and put out his huge right hand.

"Hey, buddy," he said. "You got that package I asked you to pick up?"

I muttered something about the package; he grinned and slapped me on the back and said, "I'm just shitting you, Scotty; we'll talk about that later." We went into the coffee shop and occupied a booth.

Of course Sue Chopra had known about Hitch. All my efforts on his behalf—to avoid implicating him during the polygraph interview, for instance—had been obvious and futile. Hitch was one of Sue's so-called primary observers, and he must have figured in her connect-the-dots project from the very beginning. Hitch had been deep into the tau turbulence, certainly as deep as I had been.

I had assumed Hitch would also be unfindable, but he had probably hung around Chumphon a little longer than he might have had he understood just how closely witnesses were being scrutinized—long enough for the FBI to target his internet signature or even plant a locator on him. In any case, they had found him.

They had found him, and Sue had offered him the alternative of prompt arrest or a job. Hitch had made the wise choice.

"It's not exactly an office job," he said. "Good pay, travel, no strings. Supposedly a clean criminal record at the end of it, though the end is nowhere in sight. First thing they did was send me around the Pacific Rim hunting rumors about Kuin, not that anything substantial came of it. But I been busy, Scotty. Scouting touchdown sites in, you know, Ankara, Istanbul, doing little unofficial things here and there, talking to Kuinists—lately, talking to the homegrown kind. Copperheads and hajists."

"You're a spy?"

He gave me a sour look. "Right, I'm a spy. I drink martinis and play a lot of baccarat."

"But you know about the haj thing."

"I know more about the 'haj thing' than most people. I've been inside it. And I will do whatever I can to help you find Kait."

I sat back in the booth, wondering if this was what I wanted. If this was wise.

"You know," Hitch said, "when I think of Kaitlin, I still think of her at Chumphon. The way she'd run down the tide line in that pink one-piece Janice liked to dress her in, leaving these footprints in the sand like little bitty bird footprints, heel-and-toe. We should have taken better care of her, Scotty."

He said "we" to be friendly. He was talking about me.

Hitch did not reminisce much, nor did he waste time. He had already gotten the details of the situation from Ramone Dudley, and I added what little I had personally learned while we stared at the coffee shop menus.

He said, "Mexico is a good bet. But we have to know more than we do before we come to any conclusions."

He suggested another talk with Whit Delahunt. I agreed, on the condition that we not alarm Janice unduly. "And we should talk to Ashlee Mills, too. If she's home, we could pick her up on the way to see Whit."

"Not good," Hitch said, "to get too many people involved here."

"Ashlee's as involved as I am. She's been more helpful than the police, actually."

"You vouch for her, Scotty?"

"Yes."

"Okay." He looked at me critically. "You haven't been eating or sleeping much, it looks like."

"It shows?"

"Maybe you ought to try the steak and eggs."

"I'm not hungry."

"Steak and eggs, Scotty. For Kait's sake, let's say."

I didn't want the food, but it looked good when the waitress delivered it. I had surprisingly little trouble emptying the plate.

"Feel better?" Hitch asked.

"What I feel is the hardening of my arteries."

"Bullshit. You need the protein. We have some work ahead of us, and not just today."

I heard myself say, "Can we really get her back?"

"We'll get her back. Count on it."

Ashlee did a double take when she saw Hitch Paley for the first time, then shot me a look: You have friends like *this?*

Which was fair enough. Hitch still looked like a small-time criminal—he could have passed for a drug dealer *à la* Cheever Cox, or maybe the kind of bulky individual who collects on bad debts. I sketched out some of our past and repeated some of what Hitch had told me. Ashlee nodded but clearly continued to suspect that Hitch was something more than Sue Chopra's ears on the underworld.

She took me aside and said, "Can he help us find Kait and Adam? That's all I really need to know."

"I think he can."

"Then let's go see this Whitman Delahunt."

I drove. The afternoon air was gently breezy, the sky raked with high cloud. Hitch was silent in the car. Ashlee hummed a tune I recognized as an old Lux Ebone song, something sad. Something from the time when songs still mattered, when everyone knew the same songs. This year's popular songs all sounded like marching music to me: drums and cymbals and trumpet notes drowning in their own echoes. But I suppose every decade gets the music it deserves.

Hitch had spotted the nicotine stains on Ashlee's fingers. "You can go ahead and smoke," he said, "I don't give a fuck."

• • •

The house where Whit and Janice lived had not aged especially gracefully, nor had the neighborhood it inhabited, but both were still well above the national average. People here could afford to have their trash hauled away, even during the collectors' strike. The lawns were green. Here and there, rust-speckled landscape robots crawled among the hedges like sluggish armadillos. If you squinted a little, it looked like the last ten years hadn't happened.

Whitmam answered the door and recoiled when he saw me. He didn't like the looks of Hitch or Ashlee, either. His expression turned blank and he said, "Janice is upstairs, Scott. Do you want me to call her?"

"We just want to ask you a couple of questions," I said. "Janice doesn't need to be involved."

He clearly didn't want to invite us in, but he may also have been reluctant to discuss his Copperhead politics in front of any passing neighbors. We stepped into the cool shade of the house. I introduced Hitch and Ashlee without being specific about why I had brought them. When we were away from the door, Hitch took the initiative. He said, "Scotty told me about the club you belong to, Mr. Delahunt. What we need now is a list of the other adult members."

"I already gave that to the police."

"Yeah, but we need it too."

"You have no right to make such a demand."

"No," Hitch said, "and you're not obliged to give it to us, but it will help us find Kaitlin."

"I doubt that." Whit turned to me. "I could have talked to the police about you, Scott. I wish I had."

"It's okay," I said, "I talked to them myself."

"You'll be talking to them again if you persist in—"

"In what," Hitch interrupted, "trying to save your daughter from this mess she got herself into?"

Whit looked like he wanted to stamp his foot. "I don't even *know* you! What do you have to do with Kaitlin?"

Hitch smiled faintly. "She used to have a scar under her left knee where she fell on a broken bottle outside the Haat Thai. Does she still have that scar, Mr. Delahunt?"

Whit opened his mouth to answer, but he was interrupted: "Yes."

Janice's voice. It came from the stairway. She had been listening. She came the rest of the way down, regal in her grief. "It's still there. But it's mostly faded. Hi, Hitch."

This time Hitch's smile was genuine. "Janice," he said.

"You're helping Scott look for Kaitlin?"

He said he was.

"That's good, then. Whit, would you give these people the information they want?"

"That's absurd. They can't come here and make this kind of demand."

"It sounded more like a request. But they might help Kait, and that's what matters, isn't it?"

Whit choked back a protest. There was a ferocity hidden in Janice's voice, an old and potent anger. Maybe Hitch and Ashlee didn't hear it, but I did. And so did Whit.

It took a while, but he gave us a mostly-legible handwritten list of names, addresses, terminal numbers.

"Just keep my name out of it," he muttered.

Hitch gave Janice a big hug and Janice returned it. She had never much cared for Hitch Paley, probably for good reason, but the fact that he was here and searching for Kait must have redeemed him in her eyes. She took my hand as we were leaving and said, "Thank you, Scott. I mean it. I'm sorry about what I said a few days ago."

"Don't be."

"The police are still telling us Kait's in town. But she's not, is she?"

"Probably not."

"God, Scott, it's just so—" She couldn't find a word for it. She put her hand to her mouth. "Be careful," she said. "I mean, *find* her, but . . . you be careful."

I promised her I would.

When we left the house Hitch said, "Does Janice know she's married to an asshole?"

"She's beginning to suspect," I said.

We went to Ashlee's for an evening meal and to plot strategy.

I helped Ash in the kitchen while Hitch used his pocket terminal to make a few calls. Ashlee put together a rice and chicken dish she called "poverty pilaf," cubing the raw chicken neatly with a cheap steel cleaver. She asked me how long I'd been married to Janice.

"About five years," I said. "We were both very young."

"So you've been divorced a long time."

"It doesn't seem so long sometimes."

"She strikes me as a very together person."

"Together if not always very flexible. This has been hard on her."

"She's pretty lucky, living the life she does. She ought to appreciate that."

"I don't think she feels very lucky right now."

"No, I didn't mean—"

"I understand, Ashlee."

"Putting my fucking foot in it again." She brushed her hair out of her eyes.

"Can I chop those carrots for you?"

She seasoned the pilaf, meticulously and sensibly. We rejoined Hitch while it baked.

Hitch had rested his big booted feet on Ashlee's coffee table. "Here's what we have," he said. "This is from Whitman and a couple of other sources including the cop, Ramone Dudley. Whit's bullshit Copperhead club has twenty-eight regular dues-paying members, and ten of them are upper management from the company he works at, so maybe he's right about joining for career reasons. Twenty-eight adults, of whom eighteen are single or childless couples. Ten members have kids of various ages but only nine actually introduced their offspring to the Youth Group. Including a pair of sibs, that's ten kids plus six outsiders like Adam who applied independently. But there was a core group of eight who were *deeply* involved, including Kait and Adam. They're the ones who disappeared."

"Okay," I said.

"So let's assume they left town. They would have been too conspicuous on a plane or a bus, given that they're traveling together. I doubt the suburban contingent would have agreed to hitchhike, considering the number of fucked-up adults already on the road. So that leaves private transportation. And probably something fairly big. You can stuff eight people into a landau, but not without attracting attention and making everybody grouchy."

"This is pretty conjectural," I said.

"Okay, but follow me for a minute. If they're driving, *what* are they driving?"

Ashlee said, "Some of these kids must own cars."

"Right. And Ramone Dudley looked into that. Four of the eight *do* have vehicles registered to their names, but the vehicles are all accounted for. None of the parents reported a stolen car, and in fact pretty much every auto theft in the city during the time these kids took off was either clearly professional or a joyride that ended with the vehicle trashed or burned. Stealing a car isn't as easy as it used to be. Even if you get past the personalized locks, every car assembled or imported in the last ten years routinely broadcasts its serial number and GPS coordinates. Mostly people use it to find their car in a parking lot, but it also complicates auto theft considerably. A modern car thief is a technician with a lot of different cracking skills, not a kid out of high school."

"So they didn't use one of their own cars and they didn't steal one," Ashlee said. "Great. That leaves nothing. Maybe they *are* still in town."

"That's what Ramone Dudley thinks, but it doesn't make any

sense. These kids are pretty obviously on a haj. So I asked Dudley to check the four cars they own, a second time. So he did."

"Ah—he found something?"

"Nope. Nothing's changed. Three of the vehicles are still exactly where they've been parked for the last week. Only one's been moved at all, and only for round trips to the local grocery pickup, not more than twenty miles on the odometer since the disappearance. The kid left a set of keys with his mom."

"So we're no farther ahead."

"Except for one thing. This mom who's driving her kid's car to the store. On Whit's list she's Eleanor Helvig, member in good standing of the Copperhead club along with her husband Jeffrey. Jeffrey is a junior VP at Clarion Pharmaceuticals, a couple of levels above Whit. Jeff's making pretty good money these days and there are three vehicles registered to the family: his, his wife's, and his kid's. *Nice* cars, too. A couple of Daimlers and a secondhand Edison for Jeff Jr."

"So?"

"So why is the wife driving the Edison for groceries, when her Daimler's a big utility vehicle with lots of room in the back?"

Ashlee said, "Could be all kinds of reasons."

"Could be . . . but I think we should ask her, don't you?"

Dinner was excellent—I told Ashlee so—but we couldn't stay to savor it. Ashlee elected to stay home while Hitch and I did the leg work, on the condition that we would call her as soon as we learned anything.

In the car I said, "About that package . . ."

"Right, the package. Forget about it, Scotty."

"I'm not going to forget an old debt. You fronted me the cash to leave Thailand. All I owed you was a favor, and it didn't happen."

"Yeah, but you *tried*, right?"

"I went to the place you told me about."

"Easy's?" Hitch was grinning now, the kind of grin that used to make me deeply uncomfortable (and was having that effect again).

I said, "I went to Easy's, but—"

"You mentioned my name to the guy there?"

"Yeah—"

"Old guy, gray-haired, kinda tall, coffee-colored?"

"Sounds like the man. But there was no package, Hitch."

"What, he told you that?"

"Uh-huh."

"Did he tell you that in a *gentle* way?"

"Far from it."

"Got a little irritated, did he?"

"Practically reached for a gun."

Hitch was nodding. "Good . . . good."

"Good? So the package was late, or what?"

"No. Scotty, there never *was* any package."

"The one you told me to pick up for you—?"

"No such object. Sorry."

I said, "But the money you gave me—"

"Mainly, no offense, but I thought you'd be safer back in Minneapolis. I mean, there you were, stuck on the beach, Janice and Kaitlin gone, and you were starting to drink pretty heavy, and Chumphon wasn't a good place to be a drunk American, especially with all the press guys getting rolled on a regular basis. So I took pity on you. I gave you the money. I had it to spare: Business was good. But I didn't think you'd take it as a gift and I didn't want to call it a loan because I didn't want you trying to find me and pay it back like a good scout. Which, admit it, you *would* have. So I made up this 'package' thing."

"You made it *up*?"

"I'm sorry, Scotty, I guess you thought you were a drug mule or something, but that kinda appealed to my sense of humor, too.

Knowing your whole college-educated clean-cut image of yourself, I mean. I thought a little moral dilemma might put some variety into your life."

"No," I said, "this is bullshit. The guy at Easy's recognized your name . . . and you just described him to me."

I was driving into the sunset and the lights on the dash were just starting to brighten. The air coming in the window was cool and relatively sweet. Hitch took his time answering.

Then he said, "Let me tell you a little story, Scotty. When I was a kid I lived in Roxbury with my mom and my little sister. We were poor, but that was back when the relief money was enough to get you by if you were careful about things. It wasn't especially bad for me, or at least I didn't know any better than to be happy with what I had, plus maybe a little shoplifting on the side. But my mom was a lonely woman, and when I was sixteen she married this tough old piece of shit named Easy G. Tobin. Easy ran a mail pickup and sold coke and meth out the back door. I will say for Easy that he never actually hit her—or me or my sister, either. He wasn't a monster. He kept his drug business away from the house, too. But he was mean. He *talked* mean. He was smart enough that he never had to raise his voice, he could cut you down with just a few words, because he had the talent for knowing what you hated about yourself. He did that to me and he did that to my sister, but we were the minor leagues. Mainly he did it to my mom, and by the time I was ready to leave home a couple years later I had seen more of her tears than I cared to. She wanted to get rid of him but she didn't know how, and Easy had a couple of other ladies on the side. So me and a few of my friends, we followed Easy to one of his ladyfriends' houses and we went in there and punished him a little bit. We didn't, you know, beat him senseless, but we made him scared and we kicked him around some and we told him to get his ass out of my mom's house or we'd do worse than that. He said that was okay with him, he was sick of me and my sister and he had used up my mom—his words—and he meant to leave anyhow, and I said that was fine as long he did it, and I would be keeping my eye on him. He said, 'I'll forget your name in a week, you little shit,' and I said he'd hear from me now and then and he'd better *not* forget my name because I wouldn't forget his. Well, we left it at that. But I made it a point for some years to see that he *did* come across my name, at least now and then, every once in a while. A card, a phone call, like a negative Hallmark moment. Just to keep him on his toes. I guess he remembered me, huh, Scotty?"

I said, "He could have killed me."

"Yeah, but I didn't think it was likely. Besides, that was a fair piece of change I gave you. I figured you understood it might entail a little bit of risk."

"God damn," I said faintly.

"And, see? This way, you don't have to thank me."

We were lucky enough to find Mrs. Jeffrey Helvig home alone.

She came to the door in casual clothes, wary as soon as she saw us in the porch light. We told her it was about her son, Jeff Jr. She told us she had already talked to the police and we certainly didn't look like police to her, so who were we and what did we *really* want?

I showed her enough ID to establish that I was Kaitlin's father. She knew Janice and Whit, though not very well, and had met Kait on more than one occasion. When I made it clear that I wanted to talk about Kaitlin she relented and asked us in, though she was clearly not happy about it.

The house was meticulously clean. Eleanor Helvig was fond of cork coasters and lace antimacassars. A dust precipitator hummed in one corner of the living room. She stood conspicuously next to the home security panel, where a touch of her finger would narrowcast an alarm and a camera view to the local police. We were probably already being recorded. She was not afraid of us, I thought, but she was deeply wary.

She said, "I know what you're going through, Mr. Warden. I'm going through it myself. You understand if I'm not anxious to talk about Jeff's disappearance yet again."

She was defending herself against some accusation not yet made. I thought about that. Her husband was a Copperhead—a true believer, according to Whit. She had accompanied him to most but not all of the meetings. She would probably echo his opinions but she might not be deeply or genuinely convinced of them. I hoped not.

I said, "Would it surprise you, Mrs. Helvig, if I told you it looks like your son and his friends are on a haj?"

She blinked. "It would offend me, certainly. Using that word in that way is an insult to the Muslim faith, not to mention a great many sincere young people."

"Sincere young people like Jeff?"

"I hope Jeff is sincere, but I won't accept a facile explanation of what's happened to him. I should tell you honestly that I'm skeptical of absentee fathers who rediscover their children in times of crisis. But that's the kind of society we live in, isn't it? People who think of parenthood as a genetic merger, not a sacred bond."

Hitch said, "You think Kuin will make that better?"

She stared back at him defiantly. "I believe he could hardly make it worse."

"Do you know what a haj *is*, Mrs. Helvig?"

"I told you, I don't like that word—"

"But a lot of people use it. Including a lot of idealistic children. I've seen a few. You're right, it's a rough world we live in, and it's hard on the children in particular. I've seen them. I've seen haj kids butchered by the side of the road. Children, Mrs. Helvig, raped and killed. They're young and they may be idealistic, but they're also very naive about what it takes to survive outside of suburban Minneapolis."

Eleanor Helvig blanched. (I believe I did, too.) She said to Hitch, "Who are you?"

"A friend of Kaitlin. Did you ever meet Kait, Mrs. Helvig?"

"She came by the house once or twice, I think . . ."

"I'm sure your Jeff is a strong young man, but what about Kaitlin? How do you think she'll do out there, Mrs. Helvig?"

"I don't—"

"Out there on the road, I mean, with all the homeless men and soldiers. Because if these kids *did* go off on a haj, they'd be safer in a car. Even Jeff."

"Jeff can take care of himself," Eleanor Helvig whispered.

"You wouldn't want him hitchhiking, would you?"

"Of course not—"

"Where's your husband's car, Mrs. Helvig?"

"He took it to work. He's not home yet, but—"

"And Jeff's car?"

"In the garage."

"And yours?"

She hesitated just long enough to confirm Hitch's suspicions. "In for repairs."

"At what garage, exactly?"

She didn't answer.

"We don't have to discuss this," Hitch said, "with the police."

"He's *safer* in the car. You said so yourself."

She was whispering now.

"I'm sure you're right."

"Jeff Jr. didn't talk about the . . . pilgrimage, but when he asked for the car I guess I should have suspected. His father said we ought not to tell the police. It would only make Jeff a criminal. Or us, for abetting him. He'll be back, though. I know he will."

"You could help us—" Hitch began.

"You see how upside-down everything is? Can you *blame* the children?"

"Give us your license and the car's GPS signature. We won't bring the police into it."

She reached absently for her purse, then hesitated. "If you do find them, will you be nice to Jeff?"

We promised we would.

Hitch talked to Morris Torrance, who traced the car to El Paso. The GPS package was sitting in a local recycler's yard; the rest of the car was missing, probably sold or bartered for safe passage across the border. "They're bound for Portillo," Hitch said, "almost certainly."

"So we go there," I said.

He nodded. "Morris is arranging the flight. We need to leave as soon as possible."

I thought about that. "It's not just a rumor, is it? Portillo, I mean. The Chronolith."

"No," he said flatly. "It's not just a rumor. We need to be there soon."

Fifteen

At the exit into Portillo we were turned away by soldiers who told us the town was already uninhabitable, full of Americans squatting like dogs on the street, a disgrace. As if to confirm this, they waved through a convoy of Red Cross relief trucks while we waited.

Hitch didn't argue with the soldiers but drove a couple of miles farther south along the cracked and potholed highway. He said there was another way into Portillo, not much more than a goat track but passable enough in the battered van we had rented at the airport. "The back roads are safer anyway," he said. "Long as we don't stop." Hitch had always preferred back roads.

"Why *here*?" Ashlee wondered, looking out the window into a blank Sonoran landscape, agaves and yellow scrub grass and the occasional struggling cattle ranch.

The Kuin recession had been hard on Mexico, rolling back the gains of the Gonsalvez administration and restoring the venerable and corrupt Partido Revolucionario Institucional to power. Rural poverty had reached pre-millennial levels. Mexico City was simultaneously the most densely populated city on the continent and the most polluted and crime-ridden. Portillo, contrarily, was a minor town without any known strategic or military significance, one more dusty village drained of prosperity and left to die.

"There are more Chronoliths outside urban centers than in them," I told Ashlee. "Touchdown points seem almost random, excepting the large-scale markers like Bangkok or Jerusalem. Nobody knows why. Maybe it's easier to build a Chronolith out where there's some free space. Or maybe the smaller monuments are erected before the cities fall to the Kuinists."

We had a cooler full of bottled water and a couple of boxes of camp food. More than enough to last us. Sue Chopra, back in Baltimore, was still correlating data from her unofficial network of informants and from the latest generation of surveillance satellites. The news about Portillo hadn't been made public. Officials feared it would only attract more pilgrims. But Internet rumors had done that quite efficiently despite the official veil of silence.

We had food and water for five days at least, which was more than enough because, according to Sue's best estimate, we were less than fifty hours away from touchdown.

The "goat track" was a rut through rocky chaparral, crowned by the endless turquoise sky. We were still a dozen miles outside of town when we saw the first corpse.

Ashlee insisted on stopping, though it was obvious there was nothing we could do. She wanted to be sure. The body, she said, was about Adam's size.

But this young man dressed in a dirty white hemp shirt and yellow Kevlar pants had been dead quite a while. His shoes had been stolen, plus his watch and terminal, and surely his wallet, though we didn't check. His skull had been fractured by some blunt instrument. The body was swollen with decomposition and had evidently attracted a number of predators, though only the ants were currently visible, commuting lazily up his sun-dried right arm.

"Most likely we'll see more of this kind of thing," Hitch said, looking from the corpse to the horizon. "There are more thieves than flies in this part of the country, at least since the PRI canceled the last election. A couple thousand obviously gullible Americans in one place is a magnet for every homicidal asshole south of Juarez, and they're way too hungry to be scrupulous."

I suppose he could have said this more gently, but what would be the point? The evidence lay on the sandy margin of the road, stinking.

I looked at Ashlee. Ashlee regarded the dead young American. Her face was pale, and her eyes glittered with dismay.

Ashlee had argued that she ought to come with us, and in the end I had agreed. I might be able to rescue Kaitlin from this debacle, but I had no leverage with Adam Mills. Even if I could find him, Ashlee said, I wouldn't be able to argue him out of the haj. Maybe no one could, including herself, but she needed to try.

Of course it was dangerous, brutally dangerous, but Ashlee was determined enough to attempt the trip with or without us. And I understood the way she felt. Sometimes the conscience makes demands that are non-negotiable. Courage has nothing to do with it. We weren't here because we were brave. We were here because we had to be here.

But the dead American was a demonstration of every truth we would have preferred to evade. The truth that our children had come to a place where things like this happened. That it might as easily have been Adam or Kaitlin discarded by the side of the road. That not every child in jeopardy can be saved.

Hitch climbed behind the wheel of the van. I sat in the back with Ash. She put her head against my shoulder, showing fatigue for the first time since we'd left the United States.

There was more evidence that we weren't the only Americans to have taken this route into Portillo. We passed a sedan that had ridden up an embankment and broken an axle and been abandoned in place. A rust-eaten Edison with Oregon plates scooted recklessly around us, billowing clouds of alkaline dust into the afternoon air. And then, at last, we topped a rise, and the village of Portillo lay before us, dome tents clustered on the access roads like insect eggs. The main road through Portillo was lined with adobe garages, trash heaps generated by the haj, poverty housing, and a nearly impassable maze of American cars. The town itself, at least from this distance, was a smudge of colonial architecture bookended by a couple of franchise motels and service stations. All of it belonged now, by default, to the Kuinists. Haj youth of all kinds had gathered here, most with inadequate supplies and survival skills. The town's permanent residents had largely abandoned their homes and left for the city, Hitch said; those who remained were the infirm or the elderly, thieves or water-sellers, opportunists or overwhelmed members of the local constabulary. There was very little food outside of the supply tents set up by international relief agencies. The army blockade was turning away vendors, hoping hunger would disperse the pilgrimage.

Ashlee gazed at this dust-bleached Mecca with obvious despair. "Even if they're here," she said, "how do we find them?"

"You let me do some leg work," Hitch said, "that's how. But first we have to get a little closer."

We drove across rocky soil to a stretch of cracked tarmac. The stench of the haj came through the windows with the subtlety of a clenched fist, and Ashlee lit a cigarette, mostly to cover the smell.

Hitch parked us behind a fire-blackened adobe shack roughly half a mile out of town. The van was hidden from the main road by a stand of dry jacarandas and stacks of excrement-encrusted chicken coops.

Hitch had bought weapons after we crossed the border and he insisted on showing Ashlee and me how to use them. Not that we resisted. I had never discharged a weapon in my life—I had grown up in a gun-shy decade and had learned a civilized loathing of handguns—but Hitch left me a pistol with a full clip and made sure I knew how to disengage the safety mechanism and hold the weapon so that I wouldn't break my wrist if I fired it.

The idea was that Ashlee and I would stay with the van, guarding our food, water, and transportation, while Hitch went into Portillo to locate Adam's haj group and broker a meeting. Ashlee wanted to head directly into town—and I understood the need—but Hitch was adamant. The van was our major asset and needed protection; we would be useless to Kaitlin or Adam without the vehicle.

Hitch took a weapon of his own and walked toward town. I watched him vanish into the dusk. Then I locked the van's doors and joined Ashlee in the front seat, where she had fixed us a meal of trail bars and apples and tepid instant coffee from a thermos. We ate silently while the light drained from the sky. Stars came out, bright and sharp even through the smoke haze and the dusty windshield.

Ashlee put her head against me. Neither of us had bathed since we entered the country, and that fact was conspicuously obvious, but it didn't matter. The warmth mattered, the contact mattered. I said, "We'll need to sleep in shifts."

"You think it's that dangerous here?"

"Yes, I do."

"I don't believe I *can* sleep."

But she was fighting a yawn as she said it.

"Crawl into the back," I said. "Cover up with the blanket and close your eyes for a while."

She nodded and stretched out on one of the rear benches. I sat at the wheel with the pistol next to me, feeling lonely and futile and foolish, as the day's heat leached away.

It was possible even at this distance to hear the night sounds of Portillo. It was one sound, really, a white rush of noise compounded of human voices, reproduced music, crackling fires, laughter, screams. It occurred to me that this was the millenarian madness we had escaped at the turn of the century, hundreds of hajists cashing in on the moral carte blanche of a guaranteed end-of-the-world. Redeemer or destroyer, Kuin owned tomorrow and the day after tomorrow, all the tomorrows, at least in the minds of the hajists. And at least on this occasion they wouldn't be disappointed: The Chronolith would arrive as predicted; Kuin would put his mark on North American soil. Probably a great number of these same hajists would be killed by the cold shock or the concussion, but if they knew that, and in all likelihood they did, they didn't care. It was a lottery, after all. Great prizes, grave risks. Kuin would reward the faithful . . . or at least the survivors among them.

I couldn't help wondering how much of this madness Kait had bought into. Kaitlin was imaginative, and she had been a solitary child. Imaginative and naive: not a good combination, not in this world.

Did Kait genuinely believe in Kuin? In some version of Kuin she had conjured out of her own longing and insecurity? Or was this all just an adventure, a melodramatic lunge out of the cloistered household of Whitman Delahunt?

The fact was, she might not be glad to see me. But I would take her out of this nightmarish place if I had to do it by main force. I couldn't make Kaitlin love me, but I could save her life. And that, for now, would be enough.

The night dragged. The roar of Portillo ebbed and rose in an elusive stochastic rhythm, like waves on a beach. There was a cricket in the wild sage east of the van adding his own distinct voice to the cacophony. I drank more of Ashlee's coffee and left the van briefly to relieve myself, stepping around a rusted axle and drivetrain that lurked in the high weeds like an animal trap. Ashlee stirred and muttered in her sleep when I closed the door again.

There was a little traffic on the road, mainly hajists joyriding, hooting from the windows of their cars. Nobody spotted us; nobody stopped. I was beginning to doze in place when Ashlee tapped me on the shoulder. The dash clock said 2:30.

"My turn," she said.

I didn't argue. I showed her where I'd left the pistol and I stretched out on the back bench. The blanket was warm with her body heat. I slept as soon as I closed my eyes.

"Scott?"

She shook me gently but urgently.

"Scott!"

I sat up to find Ashlee leaning over the driver's seat, rocking my shoulder with her hand. She whispered, "There are people outside. *Listen!*"

She turned forward and slumped down, keeping her head out of sight. The darkness was not absolute. A half moon had risen. There was, for a long moment, utter silence. Then, not very far away, a woman's terrified moan, followed by stifled laughter.

I said, "Ashlee—"

"They came by a minute ago. A car on the road. They pulled up and stopped and there was a little, uh, yelling. And then—I couldn't really see this until I turned the side mirror, and even then the tree was in the way, but it looked like somebody fell out of the car and ran into the field. I think a woman. And two guys ran out after her."

I thought about this. "What time is it?"

"Just four."

"Give me the pistol, Ash."

She seemed reluctant to hand it over. "What should we do?"

"What we'll do is, I'll take the pistol and get out of the van.

When I signal, you turn on the high beams and start the engine. I'll try to stay in sight."

"What if something happens to you?"

"Then you pull out of here fast as you can. If something happens to me, that means they've got the gun. Don't hang around, Ash, all right?"

"So where would I *go*?"

It was a reasonable question. Into Portillo? Back toward the relief camps, the roadblock? I wasn't sure what to tell her.

But then the woman outside screamed again, and I couldn't help thinking that it might be Kaitlin out there. It didn't sound like Kaitlin's voice. But I hadn't heard Kait scream since she was a toddler.

I told Ashlee I'd be careful but if anything happened the important thing was for her to get away—maybe hide the van closer to town and keep an eye out for Hitch come morning.

I left the vehicle and eased the door shut behind me. When I was a few feet away I signaled for her to hit the lights.

The van's high beams sprang out of the starry night like military searchlights, and in the stillness the engine roared like some throaty wild animal. The woman and her two assailants froze in the glare, not more than ten yards distant.

All three were young, possibly Adam's age. The men were engaged in an act of forcible intercourse. The woman was on her back in the weeds, one man pinning her shoulders while the other parted her legs. She had turned her face away from the light, while the men had raised their heads like prairie dogs sensing a predator.

They seemed not to be armed, which made me feel a little giddy with the weight of the pistol in my hand.

I raised the weapon toward their dumbfounded faces. I would have ordered them to get away from her—that was the plan—but I was nervous, and my finger twitched on the trigger and the pistol went off unexpectedly.

I nearly dropped it. I don't know where the bullet went . . . it didn't hit anyone. But it scared them very effectively. I was still half-blind from the muzzle flash but I tracked the would-be rapists as they ran for their car. I wondered if I should fire again, but I was afraid that might happen whether I wanted it to or not. (Hitch told me later the gun had been modified for low trigger resistance and had probably been used for criminal purposes before we got hold of it.)

The two men leaped into their automobile with a startling economy of motion. If there had been weapons in the car I might have been in trouble—that occurred to me, belatedly—but if they had them they didn't use them. The car came alive and roared off toward town, spraying gravel against the stacked chicken coops.

Which left only the girl.

I turned back to her, remembering to keep the muzzle of the gun toward the ground this time. My right wrist still ached with the shock of the unexpected recoil.

The girl had stood up in the blaze of the headlights and was already buttoning a pair of torn Levis. She looked at me with an expression I could not quite fathom—mostly fear, I think; partly shame. She was young. Her face was smudged and tear-stained. She was so thin she looked almost anorexic, and there was a long clotting scratch across her left breast.

I cleared my throat and said, "They're gone—you're safe now."

Maybe she didn't speak English. More likely, she didn't believe me. She turned and ran into the high weeds parallel to the road, exactly like a frightened animal.

I took a few steps but didn't follow her. The night was too dark, and I didn't want to leave Ashlee alone.

I hoped the girl would be safe, unlikely as that seemed.

Sleep, after that, was out of the question. I joined Ashlee up front and we sat together, vigilant and pumped with adrenaline. Ash put a cigarette between her lips and ignited the tip with a tiny propane lighter. We didn't talk about the assault we had both witnessed, but a short time later, when the eastern sky began to show a faint blue, Ashlee said this:

"You have to not ask her. Kaitlin, I mean."

"Ask her what?"

But it was a stupid question.

"Probably you don't need this advice. It's not like I'm a model parent or anything. But when you get Kaitlin back, don't interrogate her. Maybe she'll talk to you or maybe she won't, but let her make that decision for herself."

I said, "If she needs help—"

"If she needs help, she'll ask for it."

I left that alone. I didn't want to speculate about what might or might not have happened to Kait. Ashlee had said what she meant to say and she turned back to the window, leaving me to wonder what had prompted her advice, what she herself might once have endured and refused to confess.

We dozed while the sun began to make the world warm. Hitch tapped on the window glass a little later, startling us out of sleep. Ashlee reached for the pistol but I caught her wrist.

I rolled the window down.

"Impressive guarding," Hitch said. "I could have killed both of you."

"Did you find them?"

"Kaitlin's there. Adam, too. You want to feed me? We have a good deal of work ahead of us."

Sixteen

We entered the village of Portillo slowly, crawling the van through foot traffic, down a single lane between parked or abandoned hajist vehicles. By morning light the main road was as crowded as a carnival midway and resembled one, though the crowds were subdued in the aftermath of the night. Pilgrims walked dazedly and aimlessly or slept on bedrolls under the town's tattered awnings, safer in the daylight than in the dark. Water-sellers trawled the crowd with plastic gallon jugs slung over their shoulders. Kuinist flags and symbols had been draped from the upper windows of buildings. Local sanitary facilities had been overwhelmed and the smell of the trench latrines was pervasive and awful. Most of these people had arrived within the last three days, but there were already cases of dysentery, Hitch said, showing up at the relief tents.

Adam and company were camped west of the main drag. During the night Hitch had spoken briefly to Adam and not at all to Kait, though he had confirmed her presence. Adam had agreed to speak to Ashlee but had been reluctant to grant permission for Kait to see me. Adam was clearly in charge and speaking on behalf of the others, which information made Ashlee hang her head and mutter to herself.

Also present, at least on the outskirts of Portillo, were members of the press, riding bullet-resistant uplinked recording trucks with polarized windows. I had mixed feelings about that. In Sue's interpretation of the Chronoliths and their metacausality, the press acted as an important amplifier in the feedback loop. It was precisely the globally broadcast image of these objects that served to burn the impression of Kuin's invincibility into the collective imagination.

But what was the alternative? Repression, denial? That was the genius of Kuin's monuments: They were grotesquely obvious, impossible to ignore.

"We get there," Hitch said, "you let me do a little talking, then we'll see what happens."

"Not much of a plan," I said.

"As much of a plan as we've got."

We parked the van as close as possible to the cluster of tents where Adam and his friends had camped alongside dozens of others. The tents were almost ridiculously gaudy in this dry place, blue and red and yellow nylon mushrooming out of the packed earth of a masonry yard parking lot. Ashlee began to crane her head anxiously, looking for Adam. Of Kaitlin there was no sign.

"Stay here," Hitch said. "I'll negotiate us in."

"Negotiate?" Ash asked, faintly indignant.

Hitch gave her a cautionary look and closed the door behind him.

He walked a few paces to an octagonal shelter of photosensitive silver mylar and called out something inaudible. Within moments the flap opened and Adam Mills stepped out. I knew it was Adam by the sound of Ashlee's indrawn breath.

He was dressed in dust-caked khakis but seemed essentially healthy. He was skinny but tall, almost as tall as Hitch, a black backpack looped over his shoulders. He didn't even glance at the van, just waited for Hitch to speak his piece. I couldn't see his face in any great detail at this distance, but he was evidently relaxed, not frightened.

Ashlee reached for the door but I pulled her hand away. "Give it a minute."

Hitch talked. Adam talked. Finally Hitch pulled a roll of bills out of his back pocket and counted them into Adam's palm.

Ashlee said, "What's that, a *bribe*? He's *bribing* Adam?"

I said it looked that way.

"For what? For you to see Kait? Me to see *him*?"

"I don't know, Ash."

"God, that's so—" She lacked a word for her contempt.

"It's strange times," I said. "Strange things happen."

She slumped back in her seat, humiliated, and was silent until Hitch beckoned us out. I set the van's security protocols, unlikely as that was to afford us any real protection. Outside, the air was dry and the stench was overwhelming. A few yards away a young man in once-white trousers was shoveling loose earth into a ditch latrine.

Ashlee approached Adam tentatively. I don't know, but I suspect, that she was reluctant to face him now that the longed-for moment had finally arrived . . . reluctant to face the futility of the meeting, the fact of his resistance. She put her hand on his shoulder and looked into his eyes. Adam gazed back impassively. He was young, but he wasn't a child. He gave no ground, only waited for Ashlee to speak, which I suppose was what he had been paid to do.

The two of them walked a few paces away down a trail between the tents. Hitch said to me, "It's a fucking lost cause. She just doesn't know it."

"What about Kait?"

He gestured at a small sun-yellow tent.

I found myself thinking of the Cairo arrival of three years ago. Sue Chopra had obtained video recordings of the event from a dozen different angles, in all its phases—the calm before the manifestation, the cold shock and the thermal winds, a column of ice and dust boiling into a dry blue sky, and finally the Chronolith itself, glaringly bright, embedded in the sprawl of suburban Cairo like a sword driven into a rock.

(And who will pull this sword from the stone? The pure of heart, perhaps. Absent parents and failed husbands need not apply.)

I suppose it was the incongruity I had found so striking about Cairo: the tremulous waves of desert heat; the ice. The layers of mismatched history, office towers erected over the rubble of a thousand-year autarchy, and this newest of monuments, Kuin ponderous and remote as a pharaoh on his frigid throne.

I don't know why the image came to me so vividly. Perhaps because this dry Sonoran village was about to receive its own throne of ice, and maybe there was already the faintest chill in the air, a shiver of premonition, the bitter smell of the future.

"Kaitlin?" I said.

A vagrant wind lifted the flap of the tent. I squatted and put my head inside.

Kait was alone, uncurling from a nest of dirty blankets. She blinked in the yellow nimbus of sun through nylon. Her face was thin. Her eyes were banded with fatigue.

She looked older than I remembered her, and I told myself that was because of what she must have endured on this haj, the hunger and the anxiety, but the fact was that she had slipped away from me, grown out of my mental image of her well before she left Minneapolis.

She looked at me a long time, her expression evolving through incredulity, suspicion, gratitude, relief, guilt. She said, "Daddy?"

It was all I could manage just to say her name. Which was probably for the best. It was all I needed to say.

She came out of the blankets and into my arms. I saw the bruises on her wrists, the deep cut that ran from her shoulder almost to her elbow in a track of clotted brown blood. But I did not ask her about these things, and I understood the wisdom of Ashlee's advice: I couldn't un-wound her. I could only hold her.

"I'm here to take you home," I said.

She wouldn't meet my eyes but she said, almost inaudibly, "Thank you."

Another breeze kicked up the flap of the tent, and Kaitlin shivered. I told her to get dressed quick as she could. She pulled on a pair of ragged denims and a cheap serape.

And I shivered myself, and it occurred to me that the air was a little too cold for this sun-hammered morning—unnaturally cold.

Outside, Hitch was calling my name.

"Get her into the van," he told me, "and you best be quick about it. This wasn't part of the deal—I bargained for you to talk, not to take her away." He turned his face into the wind. "I get the feeling things are happening a little faster than we planned."

Kaitlin tumbled onto one of the van's back benches and wrapped a loose blanket around herself. I told her to keep her head down, just a little while. Hitch locked the door and went to corral Ashlee.

Kait sniffled, and not just because she was close to tears. She had caught something, she said, a flu or possibly one of the intestinal diseases that were circulating through Portillo as the crowds grew thirstier and the water sellers less scrupulous. Her eyes were filmed and a little vague. She coughed into her fist.

Outside, tents and canvas shelters clapped in the stiffening wind. Hajists began to crawl out, evicted by the noisy weather, dozens of bewildered pilgrims in Kuinist gear and torn clothing shading their eyes and wondering—beginning to wonder—whether this gale might mark the beginning of a sacred event, a Chronolith announcing itself in the dropping temperature and the peaking breeze.

And maybe it was. The Kuin of Jerusalem had appeared more decisively than this and with less warning, but it was a fact that Chronolith arrivals varied from place to place (and time to time) in their intensity, duration, and destructiveness. Sue Chopra's calculations were based on somewhat problematic satellite data and could have been skewed by several hours or more.

In other words, we might be in mortal danger.

A gust rocked the van and provoked Kaitlin's attention. She pressed her face against the side window, gaped at scalloped clouds of Sonoran dust suddenly billowing inward from the desert. "Daddy, is this—?"

I said, "I don't know."

I looked for Ash, but she was hidden by the increasingly anxious crowd of hajists. I wondered how far west of central Portillo we were, but that was impossible to estimate . . . a mile, say, at best. And there was no telling precisely where the Chronolith would appear, no way of calculating the perimeter of the danger zone.

I told Kait to stay under the blanket.

The crowd began to move then, almost as if the hajists had reached an unspoken consensus, out of this dirt-pack lot toward the connecting streets, toward town. I caught sight of Hitch's coiled black beard, then Hitch himself, and Ashlee, and Adam.

Hitch appeared to be arguing with Ashlee, and Ash was arguing with her son, her hands on Adam's arms as if she were begging him. Adam stood resolutely still, enduring the embrace, while the wind whipped his blond hair in front of his eyes. If the haj had been hard on him, he didn't show it. He looked impassively from his mother's face to the darkening sky. He retrieved what looked like a rolled thermal jacket from his backpack.

I don't know what Ashlee said to Adam—she has never discussed this with me—but it was obvious even at this distance that Adam wouldn't be coming back with us. A lifetime of frustration was written into the body language of that encounter. What Ashlee couldn't admit—tugging at her son, pleading with him—was that Adam simply didn't care what she wanted; that he hadn't cared for a long time; that he might have been born unable to care. She was simply a distraction from the deeply interesting event that had apparently begun, the physical manifestation of Kuin, of the idea or the mythology in which he had invested all his loyalty.

Now Hitch was pulling at Ashlee, trying to bring her back to the van, his face screwed up against the abrasive wind but his gestures nearly frantic. Ashlee ignored him as long she could, until Adam broke away from her and only Hitch's support kept her from falling to her knees.

She looked up at her son and said one more thing. I think it was his name, just as I had called Kaitlin's name. I'm not sure, since the roar of the wind and the noise of the crowd had grown much louder very quickly, but I believe it was Ashlee's keening of her son's name that cut through the thickening air.

I got behind the wheel of the van. Kaitlin moaned into her blanket.

Hitch dragged Ashlee to the vehicle and pushed her inside, then climbed into the shotgun seat. I found I had already started the engine.

"Just fucking drive," Hitch said.

But it was almost impossible to make rapid progress against the tide of hajists. If Adam had camped any closer to Portillo we would have been locked in. As it was, we were able to crawl toward the margin of the road and make slow but steady progress westward, the press of pilgrims thinning as we retreated.

But the sky had grown very dark, and it was cold now, and dust scored the windshield and cut visibility to a few feet.

I had no idea where this road might lead. This wasn't the direction we had come. I asked Hitch but he said he didn't know; the map was stashed in back somewhere, and anyway it didn't matter; our options had come down to one.

The duststorm glazed the windshield into opacity and was, by the sound of it, also fouling the engine. I closed the windows and cranked up the vehicle's heater until we were all sweating. Our dirt track dead-ended at a wooden bridge over a shallow, dry creek bed. The bridge was splintered, rocking in the intensifying wind, and would clearly not support the weight of the van. Hitch said, "Drive down that embankment, Scotty. At least put a little dirt between us and Portillo."

"Pretty steep grade."

"You have a better idea?"

So I turned off the road, drove over brittle scrub grasses and down the berm. The van braked itself sporadically and the dash lit up with function alarms, and I believe we would have overbalanced if not for my iron grip on the steering wheel—which was a matter of instinct, not skill. Hitch and Ashlee were silent, but Kaitlin let out a little sound, about the same pitch as the wind. We had just reached the flat and stony basin when an uprooted acacia flew overhead like a stiff black bird. Even Hitch gasped when he saw that.

"Cold," Kaitlin moaned.

Ashlee unfolded the last of the blankets, gave two of them to Kait and tossed one up to us. The air inside reeked of hot heater coils, but the temperature had risen only marginally. I had seen the thermal shock in Jerusalem, from a distance, but I hadn't guessed just how painful it would be, a sudden numbing cold that radiated inward from the extremities to the heart.

Stolen energy, drained from the immediate environment by whatever force it was that could unwind a massive object through time. A fresh wind howled above the arroyo and the sky turned the color of fish scales. We had packed thermally-adaptive body gear, and we broke this out; Ashlee helped Kait into a jacket a size too big for her.

A dire thought occurred to me, and I reached for the handle of the door.

"Scotty?" Hitch inquired.

"I need to drain the radiator," I said. "If that water freezes, we lose our transportation."

We had been wise enough to carry our drinking water in flexible bags which would expand as necessary. We had also dumped anti-freeze into the van's radiator. But we hadn't anticipated being this close to the arrival. A serious flash-freeze would probably demolish the engine's coolant system and strand us here.

"May not be time."

"So wish me luck. And hand me the tool box."

I let myself out into the gale. Wind slammed the door behind me. The wind came up the arroyo from the south, feeding the steep thermoclines of the arriving Chronolith. The air was choked with dust and sand. I had to shield my eyes with my hand in order to open them even a slit. I navigated to the front of the van by touch.

The vehicle had come down at a steep angle into a sandy ridge, and the front of it was entrenched up to the bumper. There was a burst of auroral light overhead as I scooped out a space with my hands. The thermal jacket was keeping my core temperature up—at least so far—but my breath turned to frost with every exhalation and my fingers were clumsy and fiery-numb. Too late to go back for gloves. I managed to open the tool box and fumble out a wrench.

The radiator system was designed to be drained from beneath by loosening a valve nut. I clasped the nut with the wrench but it refused to turn.

Leverage, I thought, bracing my feet against the tire, leaning into the angle of the wrench like a sculler leaning into an oar. The noise of the wind was overpowering, but under it there was another sound, the thunderclap of the arrival, then the shockwave through the ground, a hard mule-kick from below.

The valve nut popped, and I sprawled into the sand.

A trickle of water ran out and instantly froze against the ground—enough to relieve the pressure inside the radiator, though stray ice could still crack any number of vital systems, if we were unlucky.

I tried to stand and found that I couldn't.

Instead I rolled into the meager shelter created by the angle of the van against the earth. My head was suddenly too heavy to hold erect, and I put my numbed hands between my thighs and curled into the meager warmth of my thermal jacket and promptly lost consciousness.

When I opened my eyes again the air was still and I was back inside the van.

Sunlight burned on the scrim of ice that had formed on the windshield. The heater was pumping out steamy warm air.

I sat up, shivering. Ashlee was already awake, chafing Kaitlin's hands between her own, and that sight worried me; but Ashlee said at once, "She's all right. She's breathing."

Hitch Paley had dragged me inside after the worst of the thermal shock had passed. Currently he was outside replacing the valve nut I had loosened. He stood, peered in through the fogged window, and gave me a thumbs-up when he saw that I was awake.

"I think we'll be okay," Ashlee said. Her voice was raw, and I realized that my own throat was sore when I swallowed, no doubt from the briefly supercooled air we had all inhaled. Lungs a little achy, too, and fingers and toes still bereft, at their tips, of sensation. Some crusted blood on the palm of my right hand where the freezing wrench had taken away a layer of skin. But Ashlee was right. We had survived.

Kait moaned again. "We'll keep her covered up," Ash said. "But she's already sick, Scott. We need to worry about pneumonia."

"We need to get her back to civilization." And up that embankment again, to begin with. Not a sure thing.

When I felt able, I opened the driver's-side door and climbed out. The air was relatively warm again, and surprisingly fresh, save for a haze of dust that was settling everywhere like fine snow. Prevailing winds had carried the ice fog off to the east.

Frost steamed off the rocks and sand of the creek bed. I climbed to the top of the embankment and looked back at the town—what remained of it.

The Kuin of Portillo was still shrouded in ice, but it was clearly a large monument. The figure of Kuin was standing, one arm upraised in a beckoning gesture.

The town of Portillo lay at his immense feet, dim in the mist but obviously devastated.

The radius of the thermal shock was enormous. All but a few of the hajists must have died, it seemed to me, though I did see some vehicles moving at the perimeter of the town, probably Red Cross mobile stations.

Ashlee came up the slope behind me, panting. Her breath halted briefly when she saw the scope of the destruction. Her lips trembled. Her face was brown with dust, rivered with tears.

"But he might have got away," she whispered: meaning, of course, Adam.

I said that was possible.

Privately, I doubted it.

Seventeen

By means of a connecting series of dirt roads and cattle tracks we managed to skirt the steaming ruins of Portillo and connect at last with the main road.

The dead—no doubt massive numbers of them—remained in town, but we passed clusters of refugees along the highway. Many were limping, crippled by frostbite. Some had been blinded by ice crystals. Some had sustained injuries from falling masonry or other shockwave events. All sense of threat had vanished from them, and Ashlee twice insisted on stopping to distribute our few blankets and a little food, and to ask about Adam.

But none of these young people had heard of him, and they had more pressing concerns. They begged us to relay messages, call parents or spouses or family in L.A., in Dallas, in Seattle. . . . The parade of misery was overwhelming, and at length even Ashlee had to turn away from it, though she continued to scan the refugees for any sign of Adam until we were farther north than even a healthy hajist could had walked. The sight of relief trucks and military ambulances streaming toward Portillo eased her conscience but not her fears. She lapsed into her seat, stirring only to tend to Kaitlin now and then.

My fears for Kait deepened during the drive. She was sicker than I had realized, and her exposure to the thermal shock had made matters worse. Ashlee took Kait's temperature with the thermometer from the first-aid kit, then frowned and fed her a couple of antipyretic capsules and a long drink of water. We were forced to stop several times for Kaitlin to lope away from the van and relieve her bowels, and each time she stumbled back she was visibly weaker and unspeakably humiliated.

We needed to get her into a reputable hospital. Hitch placed a call to Sue Chopra and reassured her that we had survived, though Kait was ill. Sue recommended crossing the border, if possible, before admitting Kait for medical care, since young Americans in-country without papers were currently being jailed. The Nogales border crossing was swamped—there had been a rumor, this one false, of an impending arrival in that city—but Sue said she would arrange for someone from the consulate to escort us through. A hospital room would be waiting in Tucson.

Ashlee administered a broad-spectrum antibiotic from our medical kit and Kait slept fitfully through the hot afternoon. Hitch and I exchanged driving duties.

I thought about Ashlee. Ashlee had just lost her son, or believed she had. It was remarkable that she was able to care for Kaitlin at all—moving under the weight of her grief with great deliberation. And Kait responded to this kindness instinctively. She was at ease with her head in Ashlee's lap.

It occurred to me that I loved them both.

• • •

I obeyed Ashlee's injunction: I did not, then or later, ask Kaitlin what had happened to her during the haj.

Maybe I should qualify that. There was a time, as I sat with Kait in her hospital room in Tucson waiting for the doctor to come back with her bloodwork, when I couldn't restrain myself. I didn't ask her directly what had happened in Portillo; only why she had gone there—what had made her leave home and ally herself with the likes of Adam Mills.

She turned her head away from me in acute embarrassment. Her hair fell across the crisp white pillow, and I saw the suture line of her long-healed cochlear surgery, a very faint, pale seam along the descending line of her throat.

"I just wanted things to be different," she said.

Ashlee stayed with me in Tucson while Kait recovered.

We rented a motel room and lived together chastely for a week. Ashlee's grief was intensely private, often almost invisible. There were days when she seemed almost herself, days when she would smile when I came in the door with a bag of take-out Mexican or Chinese food. In some part, she may have harbored the hope that Adam had survived (though she refused to discuss the possibility or tolerate the mention of Adam's name).

But she was subdued, quiet. She slept during the sweltering afternoons and was restless at night, often sitting in front of the ancient cable-linked video panel long after I had gone to bed.

Nevertheless, we had come together in an important way. Our futures had commingled.

We didn't talk about any of this. All our conversation was pointedly trivial. Except once, when I was leaving the room for a run to the all-night convenience store down the block. I asked her if she wanted anything.

"I want a cigarette," she said tightly. "I want my son back."

• • •

Kait remained in the hospital for most of another week, regaining her strength and enduring a fresh set of tests. I visited daily, though I kept the visits brief—she seemed to prefer it that way.

During my last visit before her release, Kaitlin and her doctor shared some bad news with me.

I didn't want to trouble Ashlee with this—at least, not yet. When I came back to the hotel room I found Ash somewhat recovered, more talkative. I took her out to dinner, though not very far out: the motel restaurant. It served us sirloin tips and coffee. The framed faux-Navajo prints and cattle-skull decor were reassuringly classless.

Ashlee talked (suddenly she seemed to need to talk) about her childhood, the time before she married Tucker Kellog, memories consisting not of narratives but of snapshots she had fixed in her mind. A dry, windy day in San Diego, shopping with her mother for linens. A school trip to a petting zoo. Her first year in Minneapolis, how astonished she had been by the winter storms, her commute to work blockaded by snowdrifts and windrows. Old shows she used to watch, some of which I had also seen: *Someday, Blue Horizon, Next Week's Family.*

Over dessert she said, "I talked to the Red Cross. They're still down in Portillo, taking names—counting the dead. If Adam survived, he didn't register with any of the relief agencies. On the other hand, if he's dead—" She said this with a studied nonchalance, obviously fake. "Well, they haven't identified his body, and they're very good at that. I let them call up his genome profile from his medical records. No match. So I don't know if he's alive or dead. But I realized something else."

Her eyes glittered. I said, "We don't have to talk about this."

"No, Scott, it's okay. What I realized is that, alive or dead, I've lost him. Maybe I'll see him again, maybe I won't, but that's up to him, if he's alive, I mean. That's what he tried to tell me in Portillo.

Not that he hates me. But that he's not mine in any meaningful way anymore. He belongs to himself. I think he always did."

She was silent for a while, then she drank the last of her coffee and turned away the waitress who offered more.

"He gave me something."

I said, "Adam did?"

"Yes. In Portillo. He said I could remember him by it. Here, look."

She had folded the gift into a handkerchief inside her purse. She unwrapped it and pushed it across the table.

It was a necklace, a cheap chain with a pendant. The pendant looked like a lump of pitted black plastic drilled to take an eyelet. It was almost defiantly ugly.

"He said he got it from a vendor in Portillo. It's a kind of sacred object. The stone isn't a stone, it's—"

"An arrival relic."

"Yes, that's what Adam called it."

The arrival of a Chronolith creates odd debris. The steep temperature and pressure gradients near the touchdown site will freeze, crack, warp and otherwise mangle ordinary materials. Souvenir-hunters sell such items to the gullible and they are seldom authentic.

"It's from Jerusalem," Ashlee added. "Supposedly."

If that was true, this misshapen lump might once have been something useful: a doorknob, a paperweight, a pen, a comb.

I said, "I hope it isn't."

Ashlee looked crestfallen. "I thought you'd be interested. You were there, in Jerusalem, when it happened. Sort of a coincidence."

"I don't like those kinds of coincidences."

I told her about Sue's notion of tau turbulence. I said I had been in the turbulence too often, that it had affected my life (if "affected" is the word for an acausal connection) in ways I didn't like.

Ashlee was dismayed. She mouthed the words, *tau turbulence.* "Can you catch it," she asked, "from a thing like this?"

"I doubt it. It's not a disease, Ash. It's not contagious. I just don't care to be reminded."

She folded the necklace into its handkerchief and put the bundle into her purse again.

We went back to the room. Ashlee turned on the video panel but ignored it. I read a book. After a while she came to the bed and kissed me—not for the first time, but harder than she'd kissed me for a while.

It was good to have her back in my arms, good to fold myself around her small, lithe body.

Later on, I drew open the curtains and we lay invisible in the dark watching cars pass on the highway, headlights like parade torches, taillights like floating embers. Ashlee asked me how the visit with Kait had gone.

"She's better," I said. "Janice is flying in tomorrow to take her home."

"Has she talked about the haj?"

"Very little."

"She's been through a lot."

"There was some scarring," I said.

"I'll bet."

"No. I mean, I talked to her doctor, too. There was a secondary infection, a uterine infection. Something she picked up in Portillo. It's cured, but there was scarring. Kait can't have children, not naturally, not without hiring a host. She's infertile."

Ashlee pulled away from me and stared out at the darkness and the highway. She groped at the side table for a cigarette.

"I'm sorry," she said. There was a strained note in her voice.

"She's alive. That's what matters."

(In fact Kait had been silent while the doctor gave me the bad news. She had watched me from her bed, unblinking, no doubt trying to divine my reaction from my face, wanting to know whether I would withdraw my sympathy and leave her stranded under those blank white hospital sheets.)

"I know how she feels," Ashlee said.

"You're trembling."

"I know how she feels, Scott, because they told me the same thing after Adam was born. There were complications. I can't have any more babies."

More traffic came down the highway, rolling bars of light over the textured ceiling of the room. We sat in shadow, looking at each other like lost children, and then we came into each other's arms again.

In the morning we packed for the trip back to Minneapolis. Ashlee left the room briefly while I was shaving.

She didn't think I saw her when she stepped out the door.

I watched from the window as she crossed the parking lot, dodged the rear bumper of a floral delivery van, fished a folded handkerchief out of her purse, kissed the crumpled package and then tossed it into an open Dumpster.

I returned the favor later that day: I called Sue Chopra and told her I didn't work for her anymore.

PART THREE

Turbulence

Eighteen

Time has an arrow, Sue Chopra once told me. It flies in one direction. Combine fire and firewood, you get ashes. Combine fire and ashes, you don't get firewood.

Morality has an arrow, too. For example: Run a film of the Second World War backward and you invert its moral logic. The Allies sign a peace agreement with Japan and promptly bomb Hiroshima and Nagasaki. Nazis extract bullets from the heads of emaciated Jews and nurse them back to health.

The problem with tau turbulence, Sue said, is that it mingles these paradoxes into daily experience.

In the vicinity of a Chronolith, a saint might be a very dangerous man. A sinner is probably more useful.

Seven years after Portillo, with the military monopolizing the output of the communication and computation industries, a secondhand processor substrate of decent consumer quality would draw as much as two hundred dollars on the open market. A Marquis Instruments strat board of 2025 vintage outperformed its modern consumer equivalents in both speed and reliability; ounce for ounce, it was worth more than gold bullion. I had five of them in the trunk of my car.

I drove myself and my strat boards and my collection of surplus connectors, screens, dishes, codems, and outboard accessories to the open market at Nicollet Mall. It was a bright and pleasant summer morning, and even the empty windows of the Halprin Tower—abandoned in mid-construction when its financial backing collapsed last January—seemed cheerful, up there in the relatively clean air.

A homeless man had unrolled his blanket in the spot by the fountain that was my customary location, but he didn't object when I asked him to move along. He understood the drill. Market niches were jealously guarded, vendor seniority scrupulously respected. Many of the Nicollet vendors had been here since the beginning of the economic contraction, when local police had been known to enforce the anti-peddling laws at gunpoint. That kind of hardship breeds solidarity. We all knew one another, and though conflicts were hardly unusual, vendors as a rule honored and would protect one another's spaces. Veterans of long standing held the best spots; newcomers took the dregs and often had to wait months or years for a vacancy to come up.

I was somewhere between the veterans and the newbies. The fountain spot was away from the prime aisles but spacious enough that I could park the car and unload my folding table and stock without having to use a handcart . . . as long as I got there early and set up before the crowds began to gather.

This morning I was a little late. The vendor next to me, a man named Duplessy who sold and tailored used clothing, had already set up shop. He strolled over as I was unpacking my goods.

He eyed the fresh merchandise. "Whoa, strat boards," he said. "Are they authentic?"

"Yup."

"Looks like quality. Are you hooked up with a supplier?"

"Just got lucky." In fact I had bought the boards from an amateur office-furniture and lighting-fixture liquidator who had no idea of their resale value. It was a one-shot deal, alas.

"You want to trade something for one of those? I could put you in a nice formal suit."

"What would I want with a suit, Dupe?"

He shrugged. "Just asking. Hope we get some customers today. In spite of the parade."

I frowned. "Another parade?" I should have paid attention to the news.

"Another A&P parade. All flags and assholes, no confetti. No clowns . . . in the narrow sense of the word."

Adapt and Prosper was a hard-core Kuinist faction, despite their occasional conciliatory rhetoric, and every time they carried their blue-and-red banner through the Twin Cities there were bound to be counter-demonstrations and some photogenic head-knocking. On parade days, noncombatants tended to stay out of the streets. I guessed the Copperheads still had a right to voice their opinions. Nobody had repealed the Constitution. But it was a pity they had to pick a day like this—blue sky and a cool breeze, perfect shopping weather.

I watched Dupe's goods for him while he ran off to grab breakfast from a cart. By the time he got back I had sold one of my boards to another vendor, and by lunch, though crowds were light, two more had gone, all at premium prices. I had made a decent profit on the day and as the streets emptied around one o'clock I packed up again. "Afraid of a little old street fight?" Dupe called out from his heaped mounds of cotton and denim.

"Afraid of the traffic." Police roadblocks were sure to be going up all over the urban core. Already, as the crowds thinned, I had seen grim young men with A&P armbands or K+ tattoos gathering on the sidewalks.

What worried me, though, was not the traffic or the threat of violence so much as the lean and bearded man who had twice cruised past my table and was still hovering nearby, looking away with patently fake indifference whenever I glanced in his direction. I had met my share of shy or undecided customers, but this gentleman had given the goods a cursory and superficial look and seemed more interested in repeatedly checking his watch. He was probably an innocent twitch, but he made me nervous.

I had learned to trust these instincts.

I managed to get out of the downtown core before any serious trouble started. Pro-K and anti-K scuffles had become almost routine lately and the police had learned how to manage them. But the residue of the pacification gas (which smells like a combination of moist cat litter and fermented garlic) would linger for days, and it cost the city a small fortune to scrape the oxidizing lumps of barrier foam off the streets.

A lot of things had changed in the seven years since the arrival of the Portillo Chronolith.

Count those years: seven of them, the nervous prewar years, pessimistic years. Years when nothing seemed to go right for the country, even setting aside the economic crisis, the Kuinist youth movement, the bad news from abroad. The Mississippi-Atchafalaya disaster dragged on. Past Baton Rouge, the Mississippi had settled in its new course to the sea. Industry and shipping had been devastated, whole towns drowned or left without drinking water. There was nothing sinister about this, only nature winning a round over the Corps of Engineers. Sedimentation changes river gradients and gravity does the rest. But it seemed, in those days, oddly symbolic.

The contrast was inescapable: Kuin had mastered time itself, while we were crippled by water.

Seven years ago, I couldn't have pictured myself as a glorified scrap dealer. Today I felt fortunate to be in that position. I usually cleared enough money in any given month to pay the rent and put food on the table. A great many people weren't so lucky. Many had been forced into the dole lines and the soup kitchens, ripe recruiting grounds for the P-K and A-K street armies.

I tried to phone Janice from the car. After a few false starts I got a connection, at some ridiculously diminished baud rate that made her sound as if she was shouting through a toilet-paper roll. I told her I wanted to take Kait and David out for dinner.

"It's David's last night," Janice said.

"I know. That's why we want to see them. I know it's short notice, but I wasn't sure I'd be finished downtown in time." Or whether I would have the cash to fund even a home-cooked meal for four, but I didn't say that to Janice. The Marquis boards had subsidized this little luxury.

"All right," she said, "but don't bring them back too late. David gets an early start tomorrow."

David had received his draft notice in June and was off to basic training at a Uniforces camp in Arkansas. He and Kaitlin had been married for just six months, but the draft board didn't care. The Chinese intervention was eating up ground troops by the boatload.

"Tell Kait I'll be there by five," I said, as the phone link crackled and then evaporated. Then I called Ashlee and told her we'd have guests for dinner. I volunteered to do the shopping.

"I wish we could afford meat," she said wistfully.

"We can."

"You're kidding. What—the strat boards?"

"Yup."

She paused. "There are a lot of places we could put that money, Scott."

Yes, there were, but I elected to put it on the counter of a butcher shop in exchange for four small sirloin steaks. And at the grocer I picked up basmati rice and fresh asparagus spears and real butter. There's no point living if you can't, at least occasionally, *live.*

Kait and David made their home in a converted storage space over Janice and Whit's garage. As awful as that sounds, they had managed to turn a chilly peaked-roof attic into a relatively warm and comfortable nest, furnished with Whit's cast-off sofa and a big wrought-iron bed David had inherited from his parents.

The attic also afforded them a little distance from Whit himself, whose charity they were in no position to refuse. Whit was a dignified Copperhead and disapproved of street fighting; but he took his politics seriously and could be counted on for a little accommodationist lecture whenever the conversation lagged.

I picked up Kait and David and drove them to the small apartment I shared with Ashlee. Kait was quiet in the car, putting on a brave face but obviously worried for her husband. David compensated by chattering about the news (the ousting of the Federal Party, the fighting in San Salvador), but by his voice and gestures he was also nervous. Reasonably so. None of us mentioned China even in passing.

David Courtney hadn't impressed me when Kait first introduced him last year, but I had come to like him very much. He was just twenty years old and displayed that emotional blandness—psychologists call it "lack of affect"—that is the style of this generation raised in the shadow of Kuin. Underneath it, however, David proved to be a warm and thoughtful young man whose affection for Kait was unmistakable.

He was not especially handsome—he had picked up a facial scar in the Lowertown fires of 2028—and he was certainly not rich or well-connected. But he was employed (or had been, until the draft notice arrived) driving a loader at the airport, and he was bright and adaptable, vital qualities in these dark days of a dark century.

Their wedding had been a tiny affair, subsidized by Whit and held in a church in Whit's parish where half the deacons were probably closet Copperheads. Kait had worn Janice's old wedding dress, which revived some awkward memories. But it was a fine event by modern standards and both Janice and Ashlee had been moved to tears by the ceremony.

Kaitlin went on up to the apartment as David and I set the car's alarms and security protocols. I asked him how Kait was dealing with his impending departure.

"She cries sometimes. She doesn't like it. I think she'll be okay, though."

"How about you?"

He brushed his hair away from his eyes, revealing for a moment the scar tissue that marred his forehead. He shrugged.

"All right so far," he said.

I offered to broil the steaks, but Ashlee wouldn't have it. We hadn't seen steak for the better part of a year and she wasn't about to entrust these to my care. I could chop the onions, she suggested, or better, keep Kait and David company and stay the hell out of the kitchen.

Maybe the steaks were a bad idea. They were celebration food, but there was nothing to celebrate tonight. Kait and David exchanged troubled glances and were clearly making an effort to rise above their anxiety, an effort not even briefly successful. By the time Ash served dinner we were all clearly playing a game of mutual denial.

Ashlee and I had rented this fifth-floor apartment shortly after we were married, six years ago in July. Rent was controlled under the Stoppard Act but building maintenance was casual to the point of sloppy. The upstairs neighbor's water pipes had leaked through our kitchen cupboards, until Ash and I went up there with plumbing tools and PVC and patched up the problem ourselves. But our living-room windows looked southwest across low suburbs—shingles, solar cells, treetops—and tonight there was a big moon riding the horizon, almost bright enough to read by.

"Hard to believe," Kait said, also entranced by the moon, "people used to live up there."

A lot of things about the past had become hard to believe. Last year I had watched through this same window when the abandoned Corning-Gentell orbital factory burned its way through the atmosphere, shedding molten metal like a Fourth of July sparkler. A decade ago there had been seventy-five human beings living in Earth orbit or beyond. Today there were none.

I stood up to open the curtains a little wider. That was when I noticed the old GM efficiency vehicle parked in front of the barred door of the Mukerjee Dollar Bargain Store, and the bearded man's face in the automobile window, illuminated, until he looked away, by the glare of a sulfur-dot streetlight.

I couldn't say for sure that this was the same twitch who had been haunting my table at the Nicollet Mall, but I would have been willing to bet on it.

I didn't mention this to the family, just sat back down and made myself smile—all our smiles were fabricated tonight. David talked a little more, over coffee, about what he might be facing with the Uniforces over the term of his conscription. Unless he was lucky enough to land a clerical or tech position, he would probably end up in China with the infantry. But the fighting couldn't go on much longer, he told Kait, so that was okay; and we all pretended to believe this absurd untruth.

David would have been deferred, of course, had Kaitlin been pregnant, but that was not a possibility. The infection she had picked up in Portillo had scarred her uterus and left her infertile. She and

David could still have children but they would have to be conceived in vitro, a process none of us could afford. To my knowledge David had never even raised that subject—the impossibility of a childbirth deferral—with Kait. He loved her, I believe, very genuinely. Deferral marriages were common enough in those days, but it was never an issue for David and Kaitlin.

Ashlee served coffee and made cheerful conversation while I tried not to think about the man outside. I found myself watching Kait as she quietly watched David, and I felt very proud of her. Kait had not led a simple life (none of us had, deep as we were in the Age of the Chronoliths), but she had come to possess an immense personal dignity that at times seemed to shine through her skin like a bright light. It was the miracle of our brief time together that Janice and I had produced, all unaware, this powerfully alive human soul. We had propagated goodness, in spite of ourselves.

Kait and David needed their last few hours together, however. I asked Ashlee to drive them back home. Ash was surprised by the request and gave me a sharp inquisitive look, but agreed.

I shook David's hand warmly and wished him the best. I gave Kait a long hug. And when the three of them were gone I went into the bedroom and fetched my pistol from the top shelf of the linen cupboard and unlocked and removed the trigger guard.

I already mentioned, I think, that I had grown up in the anti-gun revulsion of the early decades of the century. (This century which hovers, as I write these words, on the brink of its last quarter . . . but I don't mean to get ahead of myself.)

Handguns had come back into vogue during the troubles. I did not like owning one—among other things, it made me feel like a hypocrite—but I had become convinced that it was prudent. So I had taken the required courses, filled out all the forms, registered both the weapon and my genome with ATF, and purchased a small-caliber handgun that recognized my fingerprints (and no one else's) when I picked it up. I had owned this device for some three years now and I had never fired it outside of the training range.

I put it in my pocket and walked down four flights of stairs to the lobby of the building and then across the street toward the parked car.

The bearded man in the driver's seat showed no sign of alarm. He smiled at me—smirked, in fact—as I approached. When I was close enough to make myself heard I said, "You need to explain to me what you're doing here."

His grin widened. "You really don't recognize me, do you? You don't have the faintest idea."

Which was not what I had expected. The voice did sound familiar, but I couldn't place it.

He stuck his hand out of the car window. "It's me, Scott—Ray Mosely. I used to be about fifty pounds heavier. The beard is new."

Ray Mosely. Sue Chopra's understudy and hopeless courtier.

I hadn't seen him since before Kait's adventure in Portillo—since I retired from all that business to make a new life with Ashlee.

"Well, damn," was all I managed.

"You look about the same," he said. "That made it easier to find you."

Without the body fat he looked almost gaunt, even with the beard. Almost a ghost of himself. "You didn't have to stalk me, Ray. You could have come up to the table and said hello."

"Well, people change. For all I know you could be a fire-breathing Copperhead by now."

"Fuck you, too."

"Because it's important. We kind of need your help."

"Who's 'we'?"

"Sue, for one. She could use a place to stay for a little while."

I was still trying to cope with that information when the rear window rolled down and Sue herself poked her big ungainly peanut-shaped head out of the darkness.

She grinned. "Hey there, Scotty," she said. "We meet again."

Nineteen

In the past seven years I had told Ashlee a great deal about Sue Chopra and her friends. That didn't mean Ash was pleased to come home and find two of these worthies occupying her living-room sofa.

It had seemed obvious to me, after Portillo, that I would have to choose between my life with Ashlee and my work for Sue. Sue persisted in her belief that the advance of the Chronoliths could be turned back, given the right technology or even the appropriate degree of understanding. Privately, I doubted it. Consider the word itself, "Chronolith"—an ugly portmanteau word coined by some tone-deaf journalist shortly after Chumphon, a word I had never liked but which I had come to appreciate for its aptness. *Chronos*, time, and *lithos*, stone, and wasn't that the heart of the matter? Time made solid as rock. A zone of absolute determinacy, surrounded by a froth of ephemera (human lives, for instance) which deformed to fit its contours.

I did not wish to be deformed. The life I wanted with Ashlee was the life the Chronoliths had stolen from me. We had come back from Tucson, Ash and I, to lick our wounds and to take from each other what strength we were able to give. I could not have given Ashlee much if I had gone on working for Sulamith Chopra, if I had continued to dip into the tau turbulence, if I persisted in making myself an instrument of fate.

Not that we had lost contact entirely. Sue still called on me occasionally for consultation, though there was little I could do professionally without access to her mil-spec code incubators. More often, she called to keep me up to date, share her optimistic or pessimistic moods, gossip. She took, I think, a vicarious pleasure in the life I had made for myself—as if it were somehow exotic; as if there weren't a million families like mine, making do in hard times. Certainly I had not expected her to arrive at my doorstep in this cloak-and-dagger fashion.

Ash had exchanged a few words with Sue on the phone but they had never been formally introduced, and Ray was a stranger to her. I made the introductions with a gusto that was perhaps too obviously insincere. Ashlee nodded and shook hands and retreated to the kitchen "to make coffee," i.e., to work out her concerns about their presence here.

It *was* only a visit, Ray insisted. Sue still maintained her network of connections with the remaining Chronolith researchers, and she had been doing some connecting during this trip west. The vascular ebb and flow of federal funding had turned her way once again, though she still had detractors in Congress. These days, she said, all her work was stealthy, half-hidden, concealed by one agency from another, embedded in bureaucratic rivalries she barely understood. Yes, she was in Minneapolis on business, but basically she just wanted a friendly place to stay for a couple of evenings.

"You could have called ahead."

"I suppose so, Scotty, but you never know who's listening. Between the closet Copperheads in Congress and the crazies on the street . . ." She shrugged. "If it's inconvenient, we'll take a hotel room."

"You'll stay here," I said. "I'm just curious."

Plainly there was more to this than a friendly reunion. But neither she nor Ray would volunteer details, and I guessed that was all right with me, at least for tonight. Sue and all her furor and obsession seemed a long time gone. Many things had changed since Portillo.

Oh, I still watched the news of Kuin's advances, when the bandwidth allowed, and I still occasionally wondered what "tau turbulence" might mean and how it might have affected me. But these were night fears, the kind of thing you think about when you can't sleep and rain taps on the window like an unwelcome visitor. I had given up attempting to understand any of this in Sue's terms—her conversations with Ray always veered too quickly into C-Y geometry and dark quarks and such esoteric matters. And as for the Chronoliths themselves . . . should I be ashamed to admit that I had achieved a private, separate peace with them? That I was resigned to my own inability to influence these vast and mysterious events? Maybe it was a small treason. But it felt like sanity.

It was disturbing, then, to be back in the presence of Sue, whose obsessions still burned very brightly. She was polite when we talked about old times or familiar faces. But her eyes brightened and her voice gained a decibel as soon as talk turned to the recent advent of the Freetown Chronolith or the advance of the Kuinist armies into Nigeria.

I watched her while she talked. That gloriously uncontrollable crown of coiled hair had grayed at the fringes. When she smiled, the skin at the corners of her eyes wrinkled complexly. She was skinny and looked a little careworn whenever the glow of her fervency ebbed.

And Ray Mosely, incredibly, was still in love with her. He did not, of course, say this. I suspect Ray experienced his love for Sulamith Chopra as a private humiliation, forever invisible to outsiders. But it wasn't invisible. And maybe he had made his own bargain with it: better to nurse a futile affection than to concede to lovelessness. Bearded as he was, thin now almost to the point of anorexia, his hair receding like a childhood memory, Ray still gave Sue those deferential glances, still smiled when she smiled, laughed when she laughed, rose to her defense at the first hint of criticism.

And when Sue nodded at Ashlee in the kitchen and said, "I envy you, Scotty. I always wanted to settle down with a good woman," Ray chuckled obediently. And winced, all at once.

Before I went to bed I turned out the sofa-bed and shook out a set of spare blankets. This could only have been torture for Ray, sleeping next to Sue in absolute and unquestioned chastity, listening to the sound of her breath. But it was the only accommodation I had to offer, apart from the floor.

Before I went to bed myself I took Sue aside. "It's good to see you," I told her. "I mean it. But if you want more from me than a couple of nights on a fold-out, I want to know."

"We'll talk about that later," she said calmly. "Night, Scotty."

Ashlee, in bed, was less sanguine. It was great to meet these people who had once meant so much to me, she said—it made all those stories I had told her come to life. But she was afraid of them, too.

"Afraid?"

"The way Kait's afraid of the draft. For the same reason. They want something from you, Scott."

"Don't let it worry you."

"But I have to worry. They're smart people. And they wouldn't be here if they didn't think they could talk you into . . . whatever it is they want you to do."

"I'm not so easy to convince, Ash."

She rolled on her side, sighing.

• • •

In seven years Kuin had still not planted a Chronolith on American soil, at least not north of the Mexican border. We remained part of an archipelago of sanity in a world besieged by madness, along with northern Europe, southern Africa, Brazil, Canada, the Caribbean Islands, and sundry other holdouts. Kuin's impact in the Americas had been broadly economic, not political. Global chaos, especially in Asia, had dried up foreign demand for finished goods. Money drained out of the consumer-goods industries and was funneled into defense. It made for relatively low unemployment (apart from the Louisiana refugees) but lots of spot shortages and some rationing. Copperheads claimed that the economy was being gradually Sovietized, and in this, at least, they may have had a point. There was still no real pro-Kuin sentiment in Congress or the White House. Our Kuinists (and their radical A-K counterparts) were street fighters, not organizers. At least, so far. Respectable Copperheads like Whit Delahunt were another matter—they were everywhere, but they walked very softly.

I had read some of the Copperhead literature, both the academic writers (Daudier, Pressinger, the Paris Group) and the populist hacks (Forrestall's *Clothing the Emperor* when it hit the bestseller list). I had even sampled the works of the musicians and novelists who were the public face of the Kuinist underground. Impressive as some of this was *prima facie*, it nevertheless struck me as wishful at best, at worst as an attempt to ingratiate either the nation or more likely the writer to some inevitable Kuinist autarchy.

And still there was no direct evidence of the existence of Kuin himself. No doubt he *did* exist, perhaps somewhere on the southern Chinese mainland, but most of Asia was closed to media and telecommunications, its infrastructure in a state of radical collapse and millions dead in the famine and unrest. The chaos that helped create Kuin also served to shield him from premature exposure.

And was the technology necessary to create a Chronolith already in Kuin's hands?

Yes, probably, Sue told me.

This was Sunday morning. Ashlee, still nervous, had gone off to visit her cousin Alathea in St. Paul. (Alathea eked out a living selling decorative copper pots door to door. Visiting Alathea on Sundays was an expression of familial piety on Ashlee's part, since Alathea was a disagreeable woman with eccentric religious beliefs and no talent for housekeeping.) I sat with Sue at the kitchen table, picking at breakfast and generally savoring my day off, while Ray went out to hunt for a source of fresh coffee—we had used up the house supply.

There were, Sue told me, only a handful of people in the world who understood contemporary Chronolith theory well enough to envision the means to create one. She happened to be one of them. That was why the federal government had taken such an ambivalent interest in her, alternately helping and hindering her work. But that wasn't the big problem right now. The big problem, she said, was that the increasingly desperate Chinese government had years ago established its own intensive research programs into the practicality of tau-bending technology and had isolated these facilities from the international community.

And why was that a problem?

Because the fragmented Chinese government had finally collapsed under the weight of its own insolvency, and those same research facilities were presumably under the direct control of Kuinist insurgents.

"So it all fits into place," she said. "Somewhere in Asia there's a Kuin, and he has the technology in his hands. We're only a couple of years away from the Chumphon conquest, and that looks like an entirely plausible event. We can't do anything about it, either. All of Southeast Asia is in the hands of various Kuinist insurgent movements—it would take a huge army to occupy the hills above Chumphon, and that would mean recommitting troops and supplies from China, which nobody is willing to do. So it comes together very, very neatly . . . you might say, inevitably."

"These are the shades of things that *must* be."

"Yes."

"And we're helpless to stop it."

"Well, I don't know, Scotty. I think maybe there *is* something I can do." Her smile was both mischievous and sad.

But the whole subject made me uneasy, and I tried to divert her by asking whether she had heard from Hitch Paley lately. (I hadn't: not since Portillo.)

"We're still in contact," she said. "He'll be passing through town in a couple of days."

I suppose it's evidence of Sue's innate (if awkward) charm that by the following evening Ashlee was sitting beside her on the sofa, listening raptly to Sue's interpretation of the Age of Chronoliths.

As I joined them, Ash was saying, "I still don't understand why you think it's so important to *destroy* one."

Sue, pondering her response, looked as intensely thoughtful as a religious zealot.

Which, perhaps, she was, at least on her own terms. In her pop-physics seminar at Cornell she had been fond of comparing the particle zoo (hadrons, fermions, and all the varieties of their constituent quarks) to the deities of the Hindu pantheon—all distinct, yet all aspects of a single encompassing Godhead. Sue was not conventionally religious and she had never even visited her parents' native Madras; she used the metaphor loosely and often comically. But I recalled her description of two-faced Shiva: the destroyer and bringer of life, the ascetic youth and the lingam-wielding impregnator—Sue had detected the presence of Shiva in every duality, every quantum symmetry.

She put the tips of her fingers together. "Ashlee, tell me how you define the word 'monument.' "

"Well," Ash said tentatively, "it's a thing, a structure, like a building. It's, you know, architecture."

"So how is it different from a house or a temple?"

"I guess you don't *use* a monument, the way you use a house or a church. It just sort of stands there announcing itself."

"But it does have a purpose, right? The way a house has a purpose?"

"I don't know if I would say it's *useful* . . . but I guess it serves a purpose. Just not a very practical one."

"Exactly. It's a structure with a purpose, but the purpose isn't practical, it's spiritual . . . or at least symbolic. It announces power and preeminence or it commemorates some communal event. It's a physical structure but all its meaning, all its utility, is invested in it by the human mind."

"Including the Chronoliths?"

"That's the point. As a destructive weapon, a Chronolith is relatively trivial. By itself, it achieves nothing in particular. It's an inert object. All its significance lies in the realm of meaning and interpretation. And that's where the battle is, Ashlee." She tapped her forehead. "All the strangest architecture is right up here. Nothing in the physical world compares to the monuments and the cathedrals we build inside our own skulls. Some of that architecture is simple and true and some of it is baroque and some of it is beautiful and some of it is ugly and perilously unsound. But that architecture matters more than any other kind, because we make the future out of it. History is just a fossil record of what men and women construct out of the contents of their minds. You understand? And the genius of Kuin has nothing to do with the Chronoliths; the Chronoliths are just technology, just people making nature jump through hoops. The genius of Kuin is that he's using them to colonize the world of the mind, to build his own architecture directly into our heads."

"He makes people believe in him."

"In him, in his power, in his glory, in his benevolence. But above all in his *inevitability*. And that's what I want to change. Because *nothing* about Kuin is inevitable, absolutely nothing. We build Kuin every day, we manufacture him out of our hopes and fears. He *belongs* to us. He's a shadow we're all casting."

This in itself was nothing new. The politics of expectation had even been debated in the press. But something about this speech made the hairs on my arms stand erect. The degree of her conviction, her casual eloquence. But I think it was more. I think I understood for the first time that Sue had declared a private and very personal war on Kuin. More: that she believed she was at the very center of the conflict now—anointed by the tau turbulence, promoted directly into the Godhead.

I met Kaitlin for a Sunday dinner out, strictly fast food, this representing the last of the weekend's windfall money.

Kait came down from the apartment over Whit's garage looking brave but inconsolable. She had passed her first couple of nights without David, and it showed. Her eyes were shadowed, her complexion sallow for lack of sleep. The smile she gave me was almost furtive, as if she had no business smiling while David was at war.

We shared beanpaste sandwiches at a once-brightly-colored but lately scabrous People's Kitchen. Kait knew that Sue Chopra and Ray Mosley were in town and we talked a while about that, but Kait was plainly not much interested in what she called "the old days." She had been troubled by nightmares, she said. In her dreams she was back in Portillo, but this time with David, and David was in some mortal danger from which Kait could not rescue him. She was knee-deep in sand, in the dream, the Kuin of Portillo looming over her, nearly alive, gnarled and malevolent.

I listened patiently and let her wind down. The dream wasn't difficult to interpret. Finally I said, "Have you heard from David?"

"A phone call after his bus got into Little Rock. Nothing since then. But I guess boot camp keeps you busy."

I guessed it did. Then I asked how her mother and Whit were dealing with it.

"Mom is a help. As for Whit—" She fluttered her hand. "You know how he is. He doesn't approve of the war and sometimes he acts like David is personally responsible for it—as if he had a choice about the draft notice. With Whit it's all big issues, there's no *people* involved, except as obstacles or bad examples."

"I'm not sure the war is doing any good either, Kait. If David had wanted to duck the draft, I would have helped him dig a hole."

She smiled sadly. "I know. David knew that, too. The odd thing is that Whit wouldn't hear of it. He doesn't like the war but he couldn't sanction breaking the law, putting the family in legal jeopardy and all that crap. The thing is, David figured Whit would probably inform on him if he tried to evade the conscription drive."

"You think that's true?"

She hesitated. "I don't hate Whit . . ."

"I know."

"But yes, I think he might be capable of that."

It was perhaps not surprising that she suffered from nightmares.

I said, "Janice must be around the house more since her job evaporated."

"She is, and it's a help. I know she misses David too. But she doesn't talk about the war, or Kuin, or Whit's opinions. That's strictly forbidden territory."

Janice's loyalty to her second husband was remarkable and probably admirable, though I had a hard time seeing it that way. When does loyalty become martyrdom, and just how dangerous *was* Whitman Delahunt? But I couldn't ask Kait these questions.

Kait couldn't answer them, any more than I could.

By the time I got home Ashlee had already gone to bed. Sue and Ray were awake at the kitchen table, talking in low tones over a map of the western states. Ray clammed up when I passed through, but Sue invited me to sit down and join them. I declined politely, much to Ray's relief, and instead joined Ashlee, who was curled up on her left side with the sheet tangled at her feet and a night breeze raising goosebumps on the slope of her thigh.

Should I feel guilty because in the end I hadn't sought or achieved a private martyrdom—like Janice, bound to Whit by her sense of duty; like David, aimed at China like a bullet and about as disposable; or like my father, for that matter, who had justified his life as a martyrdom? (I was *with* her, Scotty.)

When I rolled into bed Ashlee stirred and mumbled and pressed herself against me, warm in the cool of the night.

I tried to imagine martyrdom running backward like a broken clock. How sweet to abdicate divinity, to climb down from the cross, to travel from transfiguration to simple wisdom and arrive at last at innocence.

Twenty

Hitch came into town missing two fingers from his left hand and walking with a limp. It seemed to me he didn't smile as readily as he used to, either, though he smiled at Sue and gave me an appraising look that was friendly enough. Certainly he did not make Ashlee smile.

Ashlee worked at the city water-treatment plant, writing the status reports required by state and federal regulations and staffing an Accounts Receivable desk for the financial manager. She came home tired and she nearly fainted at the sight of Hitch Paley, even though Hitch was dressed in a respectable suit and had even attempted a necktie. Hitch remained a bad memory for Ashlee—Hitch had been with her when she lost Adam.

She did not, of course, recognize former FBI desk man Morris Torrance, now even balder than Ray Mosely, who had also arrived in the big utility van parked out front. I attempted an introduction, but Ashlee said in a flat tone, "We can't sleep all these people, Scott. Not even for a night."

The catch in her voice reflected a little fear, a lot of resentment.

"No need for that," Hitch said hastily. "I just rented a couple of rooms at the Marriott. Good to see you, Ashlee."

"You too, I guess," she said.

"And thank you for accommodating us in the meantime," Sue Chopra put in. "I know it's been an inconvenience."

Ashlee nodded, mollified perhaps by the sight of Sue with her duffel packed. "The Marriott?"

"Our fortunes," Sue said, "have changed."

I walked out to the van with Hitch while Sue and Ray finished packing. Hitch tucked Sue's duffel into the cargo bin. Then he put his hand on my shoulder. "I could use some help tomorrow, Scotty, if you think you can make the time."

"Help with what?"

"Spending money on heavy machinery. Diesel generators and like that."

"I don't know much about machinery, Hitch."

"Mainly I want your company."

"Tomorrow's a working day."

"Running that flea market table? Take the day off."

"I can't afford to."

"Yeah, you can. We're budgeted for that."

He named an hourly wage for an eight-hour day. A princely sum for the simple act of riding shotgun with him, particularly from a man whose friends had been begging me for sofa space just a few days ago. Hitch had obviously come into town with money, and the offer was tempting. But I was reluctant to accept it.

"Figure it out," he said. "We have a Department of Defense charge account, at least for the time being. The cash is available and I know you can't afford to take time off on short notice. And we really need to discuss a few things."

"Hitch—"

"And what can it hurt?"

That was the pertinent question. "I'm sensing there's more here than meets the eye."

"Well, yeah. There is. We can talk about it tomorrow. I'll call from the hotel, we'll make plans."

I said, "Why me?"

"Because there's an arrow pointed at you, my friend." He hoisted himself into the driver's seat, grimacing as he pulled his lame leg after him. "Or at least that's what Sue thinks."

And so, in the sunny morning light, I drove with Hitch Paley into the shabby industrial parks west of the river. The van's air conditioning was broken. (Which was only to be expected: Spare parts were at premium, most of them going to the military.) The air outside was dry and climbing toward oven heat and Hitch drove with the tinted windows up but the vents wide open. By the time we reached our destination the interior reeked of hot vinyl and motor oil and sweat.

Hitch had made an appointment with the sales manager of a machine and machine-parts distributor called Tyson Brothers. I followed Hitch through reception and sat in the man's office examining his wilted ficus and his generic wall art while Hitch negotiated the outright purchase of two small earthmovers and enough portable generators to power a small town, plus copious spare parts. The sales guy was obviously curious—he asked twice whether we were independent contractors and seemed vexed when Hitch deflected the question. But he was just as obviously delighted to write up the order. For all I know, Hitch may have saved Tyson Brothers from bankruptcy, or at least postponed that inevitable hour.

In any case, he debited more money in a couple of hours than I had earned over the course of the last year. He left a contact number with the distributor and told him someone would be in touch to arrange delivery, waved his good right hand at the receptionist and sauntered back out into the heat. In the van I said, "You're doing what, exactly—digging a hole and lighting it up?"

"We're a little more ambitious than that, Scotty. We're going to bring down one of those Kuin stones."

"With a handful of earthmovers?"

"That's just filling in the shortfall. We've got very nearly a battalion of military engineers and gear ready to roll when Sue says the word."

"You seriously mean to demolish a Chronolith?"

"Sue says we can. She thinks."

"Which one were you planning to take down?"

"The one in Wyoming."

"There is no Chronolith in Wyoming."

"Not yet there isn't."

Hitch explained all this as he understood it. Sue filled in the details later.

It had been a busy few years for Sulamith Chopra.

"You dropped out of it," Hitch said, "made a little life for yourself with Ashlee, and more power to you, Scotty, but the rest of us didn't exactly stand still just because you stopped breeding our code."

I did not then and do not now understand the physics of the Chronoliths, except in the pop-science sense. I know the technology involves the manipulation of Calabi-Yau spaces, which are the smallest constituent parts of both matter and energy, and that it uses a technique called slow fermionic decohesion to do this at practical energy levels. As to what *really* happens down there in the tangled origami of spacetime, I remain as ignorant as a newborn infant. They say nine-dimensional geometry is a language unto itself. I don't happen to speak it.

But Sue did, and I think the depth of her understanding was

unappreciated. The federal government had both cultivated her as an ally and pursued her as a liability, but they had also consistently underestimated her. She was so completely at ease with Calabi-Yau geometry that I came to believe a part of her lived in that world—she had inhabited these abstractions the way an astronaut might inhabit a strange and distant planet. There is no such thing as a paradox, Sue once said to me. A paradox, she said, is just the illusion created when you look at an *n*-dimensional problem through a three-dimensional window. "All the parts connect, Scotty, even if we can't see the loops and knots. Past and future, good and evil, here and there. It's all one thing."

In more particular terms, Sue's collaborators had already succeeded in producing tau-turbulent events on a small scale. Grains of sand to Kuin's Chronoliths, of course, but in principle the same. Now Sue believed she could disrupt the arrival of a Chronolith by performing this same manipulation in the physical space where the Chronolith was about to manifest.

She had been urging this action for most of a year, but the global systems that monitored and predicted arrivals were either highly classified or in disarray, or both, and it had taken time for the military bureaucracy to examine her proposals and approve them. Wyoming was the first real opportunity, Hitch said—and maybe the last. And even Wyoming wasn't without its dangers; it had become a mecca for Copperhead militias of various (often incompatible) political stripes. The good news was a generous three-week arrival-warning window, plus full military support. The effort was not being publicized, for fear of attracting yet more Kuinists; it would be stealthy, but it would not be halfhearted.

That was all well and good, I told Hitch, but it didn't explain why I was sitting in his truck listening to what sounded increasingly like a sales pitch.

Hitch became solemn. "Scotty," he said, "this isn't anything like a pitch. At least not from me. I like you as a person but I'm not convinced you'd be an asset to this particular expedition. I respect all that you achieved here, and God knows it's hard enough keeping a family together in this day and age, but what we need are technicians and engineers and guys who can handle heavy equipment, not somebody who sells secondhand crap at a flea market."

"Gee, thanks."

"No offense. I mean, am I wrong?"

"No, you're not wrong."

"It's Sue who wants you with us, for reasons she just sort of hints at."

"You mentioned an arrow."

"Well, it's more like a game of connect-the-dots. Can I tell you a story?"

"If you keep your eyes on the road." Half the streets in Minneapolis had reverted to their unmonitored status, nothing to prevent a collision but a vehicle's own built-ins. Hitch had come close enough to a peddler's cart to set the proximity alarms shrilling.

"I hate traffic," he said.

He had been in El Paso six months ago, doing his thing on Sue's behalf, tracking down death threats she had been receiving at her home terminal, an address no one but a few close associates should have had.

Morris Torrance was theoretically in charge of Sue's security, but it was always Hitch who did the leg work. He was well-connected in Kuinist circles and he possessed enough street credibility to impress any number of thugs. He was good in a fight and no doubt handy with weapons of all kinds, though I didn't ask.

Morris had traced the threats to one of the big Kuinist cells operating out of Texas, and Hitch went to El Paso to ingratiate himself with the local street armies. "But I made the obvious mistake," he told me. "I asked too many questions too soon. You can get away with that if the mood is right. But those Texans are fucking paranoid. Somewhere down the road, somebody decided I was a bad risk."

In the end, five Kuinist shock troops had dragged him into the back lot of an auto-repair shop and questioned him with the aid of a saw-toothed machete.

Hitch held up his left hand and showed me the stumps of his first and second fingers. Both had been severed below the knuckle. Both had been carefully sutured, but the cut had obviously been rough. I thought about that. I thought about the pain.

"Don't flinch," he said. "It could have been worse. I managed to get away."

"You acquired that limp at the same time?"

"A small-caliber bullet in the muscle tissue. As I was leaving the scene. They had this ancient pistol, some twentieth-century junk piece with the stock half rusted off. But the thing is, Scotty, I recognized the one who shot me."

"You recognized him?"

"And I think he knew me, too, or at least knew I seemed familiar. If he hadn't been a little shook up he might have been a better shot. It was Adam Mills."

I scooted away from him almost instinctively, pushed myself up against the passenger door, feeling cold despite the summer heat.

"Can't be," I said.

"Fuck me if it wasn't. He didn't die in Portillo—he must have got out with the refugees."

"And you ran into him in El Paso? Just like that?"

"It's not a coincidence, Sue says. It's tau turbulence. It's a meaningful synchronicity. And we connect to Adam right through *you*, Scotty. Adam Mills is the arrow, and he's pointed straight at you."

"I don't accept that."

"You don't have to, far as I'm concerned. I didn't want to accept that bullet in my leg, either. If it matters, I had to kill a couple of people to get this information to Sue. What she makes of it, what you make of it, that's not my business."

"You killed a couple of people?"

"What exactly do you think I do, Scotty? Travel around the country using moral suasion? I've killed people, yeah." He shook his head. "This is exactly what makes me nervous. You look at me and you see this big colorful friend you used to hang out with in Chumphon. But I had killed a man before I ever met you, Scotty. Sue knows that. I was dealing drugs back there, you know, not retailing swimwear. You get in situations sometimes. Then and since. I don't have your kind of conscience. I know you think you're some kind of moral leper because you fucked up with Janice and Kait, but deep down, Scotty, you're a family man. That's all."

"So what does Sue want with me?"

"I wish I knew."

Twenty-one

The Marriott didn't attract many guests in these diminished days. Sue was alone in the pool and sauna room, though Morris Torrance stood watch outside the entrance.

She looked up at me from the roiling waters of the whirlpool bath. She wore a fire-engine-red single-piece bathing suit and a yellow elastic hair cap, neither item flattering to her, but Sue had always been indifferent to fashion. Even in the whirlpool she wore her huge archaic eyeglasses, framed in what looked like scuffed black Bakelite. She said, "You should try this, Scotty, it's very relaxing."

"I'm not in the mood."

"Hitch has been talking to you, I gather?"

"Yes."

She sighed. "Well, give me a minute."

She lifted her pear-shaped body out

of the Jacuzzi and peeled off the headgear, her hair springing out like a caged animal. "I like the deck chairs by the window," she said, "if you're not too warm in those clothes."

"I'm all right," I said, though the air was tropical and reeked of chlorine. The discomfort seemed somehow appropriate.

She stretched out a bath towel and seated herself regally. "Hitch told you about Adam Mills?"

"Yes, he did. I haven't told Ashlee yet."

"Don't, Scotty."

"Don't tell Ashlee? Why, are you planning to tell her yourself?"

"Certainly not, and I hope you won't, either."

"She thinks he may be dead. She has a right to know if that's not true."

"Adam is alive, no doubt about it. But you have to ask yourself: What purpose would it serve to tell Ashlee? Is it really better for Ash to know that Adam is alive and that he's a murderer?"

"A murderer? *Is* he?"

"Yes. We established that fact beyond any doubt. Adam Mills is a devoted hard-core Kuinist and a multiple murderer, a hatchetman for one of the most vicious P-K gangs in the country. Do you think Ashlee needs to know that? Do you want to tell her her son is leading the kind of life that will likely get him killed or imprisoned in the very near future? And if that happens, do you want to watch her grieve all over again?"

I hesitated. I had been putting myself in Ashlee's position: If I had been wondering for seven years whether Kait had survived Portillo, any information would have been welcome.

But Adam was not Kaitlin.

"Look at what she's gained since Portillo. A job, a family, a real life—*equilibrium*, Scotty, in a world where that's a rare commodity. Obviously you know her better than I do. But think about it before you take all that away from her again."

I decided to shelve the question. It wasn't what had brought me here, not primarily. "I'd be taking all that away from her just as surely if I went out west with you—which is what Hitch claims you want."

"Yes, but only for a little while. Scotty, will you please sit down? I hate talking *up*. It makes me nervous."

I pulled a second deck chair in front of hers. Beyond the steam-hazed window, the city baked in afternoon sunlight. Sunlight glittered off windows, rooftop arrays, mica-studded sidewalks.

"Now listen to me," she said. "This is important, and I want you to keep an open mind, hard as that may be under the circumstances. I know there are a lot of things we've kept from you, but please understand, we had to be careful. We had to make sure you hadn't changed your mind about Kuin—no, don't act insulted, stranger things have happened—or that you weren't caught up in Copperhead circles like Janice's husband, whatsisname, Whitman. Morris keeps insisting we can't trust *anyone*, though I told him you'd be all right. Because I know you, Scotty. You've been in the tau turbulence almost from the beginning. Both of us have."

"We have a sacred kinship. Bullshit, Sue."

"It's *not* bullshit. It's not just conjectural, either. Admittedly, I'm interpreting, but the math suggests—"

"I really don't care what the math suggests."

"Then just listen to me, and I'll tell you what I think is the truth."

She looked away, her eyes distantly focused. I didn't like the expression on her face. It was earnest and aloof, almost inhuman.

"Scotty," she said, "I don't believe in destiny. It's an archaic concept. People's lives are an incredibly complex phenomenon, far less predictable than the lives of stars. But I also know that tau turbulence splashes causality up and down the timeline. Is it really a coincidence that you and Hitch both ended up working for me, or that Adam Mills shared the turbulence with us in Portillo? In either case you can construct a logical sequence of events that's almost but not quite satisfying as an explanation. I connected with Hitch Paley through the events at Chumphon, not quite at random;

you met Ashlee because both of you had children caught up in the same haj, fine. But, Scotty, step back and take a longer look. It knits together way too neatly. The antecedent causes are insufficient. There has to be a *postcedent* cause."

Hitch tangling with Adam, for that matter. More than coincidence. But also uninterpretable. "That's an item of faith," I said softly.

"Then look at *me*, Scotty! Look at the power I hold in these two hands!" She turned her pale palms up. "The power to bring down a fucking Chronolith! That makes me *important*. It makes me a player in the resolution of these events. Scotty, I *am* a postcedent cause!"

"There is such a thing," I said, "as megalomania."

"Except I didn't make this up, any of this! It's not a fantasy that I happen to understand Chronolith physics as well as anyone on the planet—and I'm not being vain, either. It's not a fantasy that you and Hitch were at Chumphon and Portillo or that you and I were at Jerusalem. Those are *facts*, Scotty, and they demand an interpretation that goes beyond happenstance and blind chance."

"Why do you want me in Wyoming?"

She blinked. "But I don't. I don't *want* you there. You're probably safer here. But I can't ignore the facts, either. I believe—and yes, this *is* intuition, probably unscientific, but I don't care—I believe you have a role to play in the endgame of the Chronoliths. For good or ill, I don't really know, though I'm sure you wouldn't do anything to hurt me or to further the interests of Kuin. I think it would be better if you came with us because you carry something special with you. The fact of Adam Mills is like a billboard. Chumphon, Jerusalem, Portillo, Wyoming. *You.* You may not like it, Scotty, but you *matter*." She shrugged. "That's what I believe, and I believe it very fervently. But if I can't convince you to come, you won't come, and maybe that's what our destiny is, maybe that's how we're tied together, by your refusal."

"You can't put that weight on me."

"No, Scotty, I can't." She blinked sadly. "But I can't take it away, either."

None of this sounded quite sane to me. No doubt because of my mother, I had developed a sensitive ear for the irrational. Even as a child I had known at once when my mother began to veer into madness. I recognized the grandiose assertions, the inflated self-importance, the hints of imminent threat. And it always provoked the same reaction in me, a withdrawal verging on disgust, a rapid emotional deep-freeze.

"Do you remember Jerusalem?" Sue asked. "Remember those young people, the ones who were killed? I think of them often, Scotty. I think of that young girl who came to me just when the Chronolith was arriving, when the tau turbulence was peaking. Her name was Cassie. Do you remember what Cassie said?"

"She thanked you."

"She thanked me for something I hadn't done, and then she died. I think it's possible she was as deep in the tau turbulence as anyone can be, that the fact of her death had spilled over into the last minutes of her life. I don't know exactly *why* she thanked me, Scotty, and I'm not sure she knew, either. But she must have sensed something . . . momentous."

Sue turned her eyes away from me almost sheepishly, an expression that returned us to the scale of the merely human. "I need to live up to that," she said. "At least, I need to try."

Every two people who have ever fallen in love have a special place. A beach, a back yard, a park bench by a library. For Ashlee and me it was a landscaped park a few blocks east of our apartment, an ordinary suburban park with a concrete-rimmed duck pond and a playground and a cut-grass softball field. We had come here often in the days after Portillo, when Ash was recovering from the loss of Adam and after I had severed my contacts with Sue and company.

I had proposed marriage to her here. We had brought food for a picnic, but storm clouds came careening over the horizon and rain began to fall suddenly and copiously. We ran as far as the softball field and sheltered on the roofed bleachers. The air grew colder and the wet wind prompted Ashlee to curl against my shoulder. The park's huge elms reared back from the storm, branches laced like fingers together, and I chose that moment to ask Ashlee whether she would consent to be my wife, and she kissed me and said yes. It was as simple and as perfect as that.

I took her there again.

The city had created perhaps too many of these parks in the urban-upgrade mania of the early century. Several had been rezoned for poverty housing or had deteriorated beyond all utility. This one was an exception, still stubbornly claimed by local families, defended by a host of local ordinances, patrolled after dark by community volunteers. We arrived in the late afternoon of a day cooler than the scorching day before, the kind of summer day so fine you want to fold it up and put it in your pocket. There were picnickers by the pond, toddlers swarming over the recently repainted swing sets and climbing gear.

We sat down on the untenanted softball bleachers. We had bought takeout food on the way to the park, stringy little chicken pieces fried in batter. Ashlee picked at hers listlessly. Her unease was obvious in every gesture. I suppose mine was, too.

I had originally planned (at least, perhaps) to tell her about Adam today. Lately I had understood that I wouldn't. It was a decision by default, arguably a failure of courage. I still believed Ash deserved to know Adam was alive. But Sue was right, too. The news would hurt more than it would heal.

I couldn't bring myself to hurt Ash that badly, much as my conscience protested.

It's out of decisions like this, I suppose, that fate is constructed, board and nails, like a gallows.

"You remember the boy?" Ashlee asked, dabbing her lips with a napkin. "The little boy in the ball game?"

We had come here one Saturday not long after our wedding. There had been a Little League practice game in progress, two coaches and a few parents sharing the bleachers with us. The batter was a kid who looked like he'd been raised on steak and steroids, the kind of eleven-year-old who has to shave before school. The pitcher, contrarily, was a fair-haired waif with a talent for sinker balls. Unfortunately he left one up and over the plate. The ball came off the bat and back to the mound before the elfin pitcher had time to get a glove up—something off toward first base had distracted him—and as he turned his head he was struck squarely in the temple.

Silence, then gasps and a couple of screams. The pitcher blinked at the ground and fell, fell loose-limbed and suddenly, and lay motionless on the bare dirt patch that served as a mound.

Here's the odd part. We weren't parents or participants, just casual observers on a lazy day off, but I was on the phone to Emergency Services before anyone else in the bleachers had thought to reach into his pocket; and Ashlee, who had some RN training, reached the mound before the coach.

The injury wasn't serious. Ash kept the boy still and calmed the terrified mother until the paramedics arrived. Nothing unusual about the incident except that Ash and I had both been so quick off the mark.

"I remember," I told her.

"I learned something that day," Ashlee said. "I learned we're both ready for the worst. Always. Maybe, on some level, *expecting* it. Me, I guess it's because of my dad." Ashlee's father had been an alcoholic, which often enough forces a child into premature adulthood, and he had died of liver cancer when Ashlee was just fifteen. "You because of your mom." Expecting the worst: Well, yes, of course. (And her voice rang briefly in my head: *Scotty, stop looking at me like that!*)

"What that tells me," Ashlee said, choosing her words carefully, not meeting my eyes, "is that we're pretty strong people. We've faced up to some difficult things."

Difficult as a murderous child, resurrected from the dead?

"So it's all right," Ashlee said. "I trust you, Scott. To do what you think is right. You don't have to break it to me gently. You're going away with them, aren't you?"

"Just for a little while," I said.

Twenty-two

We crossed the state border into Wyoming on the day the governor abdicated.

One of the so-called Omega militias had occupied the legislature for most of a week, holding Governor Atherton among the sixty hostages. The National Guard finally cleared the building but Atherton resigned as soon as he was released, citing health reasons. (Good ones: He had been shot through the groin and the wound had been allowed to grow septic.)

Emotions ran high, in other words, out here in big sky country, but all that political ferment was invisible from the road. Where we crossed into the state, the highway was potholed and the vast ranchlands on either side had gone feral and dry in the wake of the retreating Oglalla Aquifer. Flocks of starlings populated the rusted ribs of irrigation piping.

"Part of the problem," Sue was saying, "is that people see the Chronoliths as a kind of magic—but they're not, they're technology, and they *act* like technology."

She had been talking about the Chronoliths for at least five hours, though not exclusively to me. Sue insisted on driving the last van in the convoy, which contained our personal effects and her notes and plans. We—Hitch or Ray or I—tended to rotate through the passenger seat. Sue had added a kind of nervous loquaciousness to her customary obsessive behavior. She had to be reminded to eat.

"Magic is unlimited," she said, "or limited only by, allegedly, the skill of the practitioner or the whims of the supernatural world. But the limits on the Chronoliths are imposed by nature, and they're very strict and perfectly calculable. Kuin broadcasts his monuments roughly twenty years into the past because that's the point at which the practical barriers become insurmountable—any farther back and the energy requirements go logarithmic, shoot up toward infinity for even a very tiny mass."

Our convoy consisted of eight large enclosed military cargo trucks and twice that number of vans and personnel carriers. Sue had put together, over the years, a small army of like-minded individuals—in particular the academics and grad students who had assembled the tau-intervention gear—and they were bookended, in this expedition, by the military posse. All these vehicles had been painted Uniforces blue so that we would resemble any number of other military convoys, a common-enough sight even on these underpopulated western highways.

Some miles past the border we pulled over to the margin of the road on a cue from the lead truck, lining up for gas at a lonely little Sunshine Volatiles station. Sue switched off the forced-air cooler and I rolled down a side window. The sky was boundless blue, marked here and there with wisps of high cloud. The sun was near zenith. Across a brown meadow, more sparrows swirled over an ancient rust-brown oil derrick. The air smelled of heat and dust.

"There are all kinds of limits on the Chronoliths," Sue went on, her voice a sleepy drone. "Mass, for instance, or more precisely mass-*equivalency*, given that the stuff they're made of isn't conventional matter. You know there's never been a Chronolith with a mass-equivalency greater than roughly two hundred metric tonnes? Not for lack of ambition on Kuin's part, I'm sure. He'd build them to the moon if he thought he could. But again, past a certain point, the energy bill shoots up exponentially. Stability suffers, too. Secondary effects become more prominent. Do you know what would happen to a Chronolith, Scotty, if it was even a fraction over the theoretical mass limit?"

I said I did not.

"It would become unstable and destroy itself. Probably in a spectacular fashion. Its Calabi-Yau geometry would just sort of *unfold*. In practical terms, that would be catastrophic."

But Kuin had not been so unwise as to allow that to happen. Kuin, I reflected, had been pretty savvy all along. And this did not bode well for our quixotic little voyage into the sun-ridden western lands.

"I could use a Coke," Sue said abruptly. "I'm dry as a bone. Would you fetch me a Coke from the gas station, if they have any to sell?"

I nodded and climbed out of the van onto the pebbly margin of the road and walked up past the row of idling trucks toward the Sunshine depot. The fuel station was a lonely outpost, an old geodesic half dome shading a convenience store and a row of rust-spackled holding tanks. The tarmac was lined with miniature windrows of loose dirt. An old man stood in the doorway, shading his eyes with his hand and looking down the long row of vehicles. This was probably more custom than he had seen in the last two weeks. But he didn't look particularly happy about it.

Automated service modules groped under the carriage of the lead truck, refueling and cleaning it. Charges were displayed on a big overhead panel, its lens gone opaque in the wash of sun and grit.

"Hey," I said. "Looks like it hasn't rained around here for a while."

The gas-station attendant lowered his hand from his eyes and gazed at me obliquely. "Not since May," he said.

"You got any cold drinks in there?"

He shrugged. "Soda pop. Some."

"Can I have a look?"

He moved out of the doorway. "It's your money."

The interior shade seemed almost frigid after the raw heat of the day. There wasn't much stock on the store's shelves. The cooler held a few Cokes, root beers, orange pop. I selected three cans at random.

The attendant rang up the sale, peering at my forehead so intently that I began to feel branded. "Something wrong?" I asked him.

"Just checking for the Number."

"Number?"

"Of the Beast," he said, and pointed to a bumper sticker he had attached to the front of the checkout desk: I'M READY FOR THE RAPTURE! HOW ABOUT YOU?

"I guess all I'm ready for," I said, "is a cold drink."

"What I figured."

He followed me out of the store and squinted down the line of trucks. "Looks like the circus came to town." He spat absentmindedly into the dust.

"Is there a key to the toilet?"

"On the hook around the side" He hooked a thumb to the left. "Show some mercy and flush when you're done."

The location of the arrival—identified by satellite surveillance and refined by on-the-spot measurement of ambient radiation—was as enigmatic and as unenlightening as so many other Chronolith sites.

Rural, small-town, or otherwise relatively undestructive Chronoliths were generally labeled "strategic," whereas city-busters like the Bangkok or Jerusalem stones were "tactical." Whether this was a meaningful distinction or just happenstance was subject to debate.

The Wyoming stone, however, clearly fell into the "strategic" category. Wyoming is essentially a high, barren mesa interrupted by mountains—"the land of high altitudes and low multitudes," a twentieth-century governor had called it. Its oil reserves and its cattle business were hardly vulnerable to a Kuin stone, and in any case the projected arrival site featured neither of those resources—featured nothing at all, in fact, apart from a few crumbling farm structures and prairie-dog nests. The nearest town was a post-office village called Modesty Creek, fifteen miles up a two-lane tarmac road that ran through brown meadowland and basalt outcroppings and sparse stands of cottonwood. We traversed this secondary road at a cautious speed, and Sue took time off from her monologue to admire the waves of sage and wild nettles as we approached our destination.

What purpose, I asked her, could a Chronolith serve in a place like this?

"I don't know," she said, "but it's a good and reasonable question to ask. It must mean *something*. It's like playing a game of chess and suddenly your opponent moves his bishop off to the rim for no apparent reason. Either it's an implausibly stupid mistake, or it's a gambit."

A gambit, then: a distraction, false threat, provocation, lure. But it didn't matter, Sue insisted. Whatever purpose the Chronolith was meant to serve, we would nevertheless prevent its arrival. "But the causality is extremely tangled," she admitted. "Very densely knotted and recomplicated. Kuin has the advantage of hindsight. He can work against us in ways we can't anticipate. We know very little about him, but he might know a great deal about us."

By nightfall we had pulled all our vehicles off the road. An advance party had already scouted the site and marked its rough perimeter with survey stakes and yellow tape. There was enough light left in the sky for Sue to lead some of us up a rise, and from there we looked out across a meadow as prosaic as the surveyed ground of a shopping-mall project.

This was wild country, originally part of a privately-owned land parcel, never cultivated and seldom visited. At dusk it was a solemn place, rolling prairie edged on its eastern extremity by a steep bluff. The soil was stony, the sagebrush gray at the end of a dry summer. It would have been utterly quiet if not for the sound of the engineering crew pumping compressed air into the frames of a dozen inflatable quonsets.

Atop the bluff, an antelope stood in silhouette against the fading blue of the sky. It raised its head, scented us, trotted out of view.

Ray Mosely stepped up behind Sue and took her arm. "You can sort of feel it," he said, "can't you?"

The tau turbulence, he meant. If so, I was immune to it. There might have been a faint scent of ozone in the air, but all I could feel for certain was the cooling wind at my back.

"It's a pretty place," Sue said. "But stark."

In the morning we filled it with earthmovers and graders and razored all its prettiness away.

The civilian telecom network, like so many other public works, had lately fallen into disrepair. Satellites dropped out of their orbits and were not replaced; lightpipes aged and cracked; the old copper wires were vulnerable to weather. Despite all that I was lucky enough, the following night, to get a voice line through to Ashlee.

Our first day at the dig had been enormously busy but surprisingly productive. Sue's technical people had triangulated the center of the arrival site, where the military engineers graded a level space and poured a concrete slab to serve as a foundation for the tau-variable device, called "the core" for short. It wasn't, of course, a nuclear core in the conventional sense, but the fragment of exotic matter it was designed to produce required similar shielding, both thermal and magnetic.

Smaller foundations were poured for the several redundant diesel generators that would power it and for the smaller generators that ran our string of lights and our electronics. By the second sunset we had turned our isolated highland into an industrial barrens of almost Victorian bleakness and had frightened away an astonishing number of jackrabbits, prairie dogs and snakes. Our lamps glowed in the darkness like the ancient sentinel fires of the Crow or the Blackfoot, the Sioux or the Cheyenne; the air stank of volatiles and plastic.

Sue had assigned me lookout duty, but that was so obviously a piece of make-work that I had traded it for the less glamorous but infinitely more useful work of digging pit latrines and hauling lime. Just before sunset, numb with exhaustion, I carried my pocket terminal to the rising ground below the bluff and established the link with Ashlee. There was bandwidth enough for voice, not images, but that was all right. It was her voice I needed to hear.

Everything was fine, she said. The money Hitch had advanced us was paying some bills we had long needed to pay, and she had even taken Kaitlin out to a couple of movies. She didn't understand, she said, why it had been necessary to leave Morris Torrance there to keep an eye on her—he was sitting in his car on the street outside the apartment. He wasn't a nuisance, she said, but he made her feel like she was under surveillance.

Which she was. Sue had been worried that Kuinist elements might have traced her to Minneapolis, and I had insisted on protection for Ash—which took the form of the venerable but well-trained Morris Torrance doing reluctant guard duty. I had refused to leave Ashlee without protection if there was even a vague threat to her safety; Sue had chosen Morris.

"He's a nice enough guy," Ash said, "but it's a little unnerving, being shadowed by him."

"Just until I get back," I told her.

"Too long."

"Think of it as a way to preserve my peace of mind."

"Think of it as a reason to come back soon."

"Soon as I can, Ash."

"So what's it like . . . Wyoming?"

I lost a syllable or two of that to dropout but took the gist. "Wish you could see it. The sun's just gone down. The air smells like sagebrush." The air smelled like creosote and lime and hot metal, but I preferred the lie. "The sky's almost as pretty as you are."

". . . Bullshit."

"I spent the day digging a latrine."

"That's more like it."

"I miss you, Ash."

"You too." She paused, and there was a sound that might have been the security bell back home; then she said, "I think there's somebody at the door."

"I'll call tomorrow."

". . . Tomorrow," she echoed, and then the line shut down completely.

But I couldn't reach her the next day. We couldn't get a line through anywhere east of the Dakotas, despite all the multiple redundancies still embedded in the networks. A bunch of nodal servers must have gone down, Ray Mosely told me, possibly due to yet another act of Kuinist sabotage.

It was because of the communications problem that the DOD media guru decided to alert the press a day earlier than we had planned. There were lots of network video stringers still covering the unrest in Cheyenne, but it would take them at least another twenty-four hours to get to Modesty Creek—where they were needed.

That next night the engineers erected a circle of achingly bright sulfur-dot lamps. We worked while the air was cool and the moon was up, carving a blockhouse out of the dry earth a mile from the touchdown site, burying cables and unrolling enormous lengths of link fence. The fencing would keep out both sightseers and Kuinists, should any of them get wind of the effort. Hitch opined that it would keep out antelopes but not any number of larger mammals, not without an armed guard. But we had that, too.

I crawled into my cot at sunrise bleeding from both my hands. The siege was about to begin.

Twenty-three

Until now we'd had the site to ourselves. Shortly, the world would be with us.

And everything that implied. Not just press people, but Kuinists of all stripes . . . though we hoped the isolated location and short notice would preclude a massive haj. ("This is *our* haj," Sue had said more than once. "This one belongs to *us*.")

So our Uniforces troops arrayed themselves around our fenced perimeter and up along the bluff, and we notified the Highway Patrol and state officials, who were deeply unhappy with us for making our work public but lacked the authority to shut us down. Ray Mosely figured we had at most twelve hours before the first outsiders began to arrive. We had already managed to erect a cranelike superstructure above the poured foundation that would support the tau core, and to rig and test all our ancillary equipment. But we weren't finished.

Sue hovered around the large flatbed truck which contained the core itself, second-guessing the engineers, until Ray and I distracted her with lunch. We choked down mil-surplus meals under a canvas tent while Ray walked us through a checklist. The work was ahead of schedule, which served to calm some of Sue's fears.

At least briefly. Sue was what the doctors call "agitated." In fact she gave every indication that she was on the brink of nervous collapse. She moved restlessly and aimlessly, drummed her fingers, blinked, confessed she hadn't been able to sleep. Even when she was engaged in conversation, her eyes tended to stray toward the concrete core emplacement and the glittering steel tubing of the support structure.

She continued to talk relentlessly about the project. Her immediate fear was that the press might be delayed or the Chronolith arrive prematurely. "It's not so much what we do here," she said, "as what we're *seen* to do here. We don't succeed unless the world *sees* us succeed."

(And I considered what a slender reed that really was. We had only Sue's assurance that destroying a Chronolith at the moment of its arrival might tip the balance of this shadow war—might destabilize the feedback loop on which Kuin allegedly depended. But how much of that was calculation, how much wishful thinking? By virtue of her position and her fervent advocacy Sue had been able to carry us all along with her, invested as she was with the authority of her mathematics and her profound understanding of tau turbulence. But that didn't mean she was necessarily right. Or even, necessarily, sane.)

After lunch we watched as a crew of stevedores and a crane operator lifted the tau core from its crate and hauled it as delicately as if it were compressed dynamite to its resting place. The core was a sphere three meters in diameter, anodized black and studded with electronic ports and cable bays. I gathered from what Sue had told me that it was essentially a magnetic bottle in which some exotic form of cold plasma was already contained. When the core was activated, an array of internal high-energy devices would initiate fermionic decohesion and a few nearly massless particles of tau-indeterminate matter would be created.

This material, Sue claimed, would be sufficient to destabilize the arriving Chronolith attempting to occupy its space. What *that* meant was still unclear, at least to me. Sue said the interaction of the competing tau spaces would be violent but not "unduly energetic," i.e., it would probably not wipe out all of Modesty County and us along with it. Probably.

By sunset the core was fixed in place and linked to our electronics through a bundle of lightpipes and conductors jacketed in liquid nitrogen. We still had much to do, but the heavy lifting and digging was essentially finished. The civilians celebrated with grilled flank steaks and generous rations of bottled beer. A bunch of the older engineers gathered by the roadside after dinner, talked about better days and sang old Lux Ebone songs (much to the chagrin of the young Uniforces troops). I joined in on the choruses.

We suffered our first casualty that night.

Isolated we might have been, but there was still occasional traffic on the two-lane county road that had brought us here. We had men north and south along the roadside, soldiers wearing the orange brassards of a highway work crew. They carried glow torches and waved on anyone who seemed more than casually curious about our trucks and gear. The strategy had worked reasonably well so far.

Not long after moonrise, however, a man in a verdigris-green landau cut his motor and lights at the top of the northern rise and rolled silently into the breakdown lane not fifty feet from our lead truck, in the shadows where the glow of the camp lights began to fade.

He stepped out onto the gravel berm with his back to two approaching security personnel, and when he turned he revealed a heavy indeterminate shape that proved to be a pump-action shotgun of ancient provenance. He turned and fired it at the Uniforces men, killing one and permanently blinding the other.

Fortunately the chief of security that night was a bright and well-trained woman named Marybeth Pearlstein, who witnessed the act from a watch station fifty feet up the road. A scant few seconds later she came around the bumper of the nearest truck with her rifle at ready and took down the assailant with one well-placed shot.

The assailant turned out to be a Copperhead crank well known to local police. A County Coroner's truck pulled up two hours later and took the bodies away; an ambulance carried the survivor into the Modesty County medical center. There might have been an inquest, I suppose, if events had turned out differently.

What I didn't know—

That is, what I learned later—

Pardon me, but fuck these stupid and impotent words.

Can you hear it, grinding away under the printed page, this outrage disinterred from the soil of too many years?

What I didn't know was that several of the Texas PK militia—the people Hitch had told me about, the people who had taken two of his fingers—had already followed a trail of clandestine connections as far as the home of Whitman Delahunt.

Whit, it seemed, had kept his colleagues informed of my comings and goings ever since I had traveled to Portillo in search of Kaitlin. Even then, the PK and Copperhead elites had taken an interest in Sue Chopra: as a potent enemy, or worse, a commodity, a potential resource.

I don't imagine Whit could have foreseen the consequences of his actions. He was, after all, only sharing some interesting information with his Copperhead buddies (who shared it with their friends, and so on down the line from Whit's suburban universe all the way to the underground militant cadres). In Whit's world consequences were always remote; rewards were immediate, else they were not rewards. There was nothing genuinely political about Whit Delahunt's Copperhead leanings. For Whit the movement was a kind of Rotary or Kiwanis, dues paid in the coin of information. I doubt he ever really believed in a physical, substantial Kuin. Had Kuin appeared before him, Whit would have been as dumbfounded as a Sunday Christian confronted by the Carpenter of Galilee.

Which is not, I hasten to add, an *excuse.*

But I'm sure Whit never envisioned these Texas militiamen knocking at his door well after midnight, entering his home as if it were their own (because *he* was one of their own) and extracting from him at gunpoint the address of the apartment where Ashlee and I lived.

Janice was present when this invasion took place. She tried to persuade Whit not to answer the invaders' questions, and when he ignored her she tried to phone the police. For this unsuccessful effort she received a pistol-whipping that broke her jaw and fractured her collarbone. They both would have been killed, I'm sure, if not for Whit's promise to keep Janice under control—he had nothing to gain by reporting any of this and I'm sure he told himself he was helpless to stop it—and his potential further utility to the movement.

What neither Whit nor Janice could have known was that one of the militiamen had taken a longtime personal interest in the activities of Sue Chopra and Hitch Paley—this was, of course, Adam Mills. Adam had returned to his hometown in a frenzy of antinostalgia, delighted that the threads of his life had knotted back on themselves in such a strange and satisfying fashion. It gave him a sense of destiny, I suppose; a feeling of profound personal significance.

Had he known the phrase, he might have considered himself "deep in the tau turbulence." Adam had lost two fingertips to frostbite in the aftermath of Portillo—not coincidentally, the same fingertips he later subtracted by machete from Hitch—and this had left him with a feeling of entitlement, as if he had been anointed by Kuin himself.

Kait, thank God, was asleep in the apartment over the garage during these events. There was noise, but not enough to wake her. She wasn't involved.

At least, not yet.

Sleepless in the aftermath of the roadside shooting, I walked a little while with Ray Mosely on the cluttered ground between the core tower and the quonsets.

Much of the camp had finally settled down, and apart from the muted hum of the generators there was not much noise. In effect, it was possible at last to hear the silence—to appreciate that there *was* a silence, deep and potent, out there beyond the pretension of the light.

I had never been close to Ray, but we had grown a little closer over the duration of this trip. When I first met him he was the kind of book-smart, underconfident overachiever who fears nothing so much as his own vulnerability. It had made him defensive and brittle. He was still that person. But he was also the end result of years of compulsive denial, middle-aged now and a little more cognizant of his own shortcomings.

"You're worried about Sue," he said.

I wondered whether I ought to talk about this. But we were alone, out of earshot. Nobody here but me and Ray and the jackrabbits.

I said, "She's obviously under stress. And she's not dealing with it particularly well."

"Would you? In her position?"

"Probably not. But it's the way she talks. You know what I mean. It starts to sound a little relentless. And you begin to wonder—"

"Whether she's sane?"

"Whether the logic that brought us here is as airtight as she thinks it is."

Ray seemed to consider this. He put his hands in his pockets and gave me a rueful smile. "You can trust the math."

"I'm not worried about the math. We're not here for the *math*, Ray. We're ten or fifteen leaps of faith beyond that."

"You're saying you don't trust her."

"What does that mean? Do I think she's honest? Yes. Do I think she means well? Of course she means well. But do I trust her judgment? At this point, I'm not sure."

"You agreed to come here with us."

"She can be convincing."

Ray paused and looked out into the darkness, out past the tau core in its steel framework, to the scrub and the moonlit wildgrass and the stars. "Think about what she's given up, Scott. Think about the life she could have had. She could have been loved." He smiled wanly. "I know it's obvious how I feel about her. And I know how ridiculous that is. How fucking clownlike. How stupid. She's not even heterosexual. But if not me, it could have been someone else. One of those women she's always dating and ignoring, splicing in and out of her life like a spare reel of film. But she pushed those people away because her work was important, and the harder she worked the more important her work became, and now she's given herself to it altogether, she *belongs* to it. Every step she ever took was a step toward this place. Right now I think even Sue must be wondering whether she's delusional."

"So we owe her the benefit of the doubt?"

"No," Ray said. "We owe her more than that. We owe her our loyalty."

Fond as ever of having the last word, he chose that moment to turn and head back for camp.

I stayed behind, standing mute between the moon and the floodlights. From this distance the tau core seemed a small thing. A very small thing with which to lever such a long result.

• • •

When I did sleep I slept soundly and long. I woke at noon under the translucent roof of the inflated quonset, alone but for a few off-shift security staff and exhausted night crew.

No one had thought to wake me. Everyone had been too busy.

I stepped out of the shade of the quonset into blistering sunlight. The sky was viciously bright, a thin blue veneer between the prairie and the sun. But it was the noise that struck me more immediately. If you've ever been near a sports stadium on the day of a game you know that sound, the rumble of massed human voices.

I found Hitch Paley by the food tent.

"More press than we bargained for, Scotty," he said. "There's a whole mob of them blocking the road. We got Highway Patrol trying to clear them off the tarmac. You know we've already been denounced in Congress? People covering their asses in case we don't bring this off."

"You think we have a chance?"

"Maybe. If they give us time."

But no one wanted to give us time. The Kuinist militias were arriving by the truckload, and by the following morning the shooting had begun in earnest.

Twenty-four

I know what the future smells like.

The future, that is, imposed on the past; past and future mingled like two innocuous substances which when combined produce a toxin. The future smells like alkaline dust and ionized air, like hot metal and glacier ice. And not a little like cordite.

The night had been relatively quiet. Today, the day of the arrival, I woke from a round of exhausted sleep to the sound of sporadic gunfire—not close enough to inspire immediate panic; close enough that I dressed in a hurry.

Hitch was back at the food tent, complacently eating cold baked beans from a paper bowl. "Sit down," he said. "It's under control."

"Doesn't sound like it."

He stretched and yawned. "What you hear is a bunch of Kuinists south along the road having words with security. Some of them are armed but all they want to do is shoot into the air and shake their fists. Basically, they're spectators. What we also have is an equal number of journalists trying to get closer than the perimeter fences. The Uniforces are sorting them out. Sue wants them close to the arrival but not, you know, *too* close."

"So how close is too close?"

"That's an interesting question, isn't it? The wonks and the engineers are all clustered down by the bunker. The press people are setting up a little farther east."

The bunker, so-called, was a trench emplacement with a wooden roof, located a mile from the core, where Sue had set up gear to monitor and initiate the tau event. The trench was equipped with heaters to provide at least a little protection against the cold shock, and in a worst-case scenario the bunker was defensible against small-arms fire.

The core itself remained almost preposterously vulnerable, but the Uniforces people had pledged to protect it as long as they could keep our perimeters intact. The good news was that this ragtag crew of Kuinists down the road did not (Hitch said) constitute anything like a superior force.

"We may just pull this off, Scotty," he said. "Given a little luck."

"How's Sue?"

"I haven't seen her since sunrise, but—how is she? Wound up, is how she is. It wouldn't surprise me if she blew an artery." He looked at me oddly. "Tell me something. How well do you know her?"

"I've known her since I was a student."

"Yeah, but how well? I've worked for her a long time too, but I can't honestly say I *know* her. She talks about her work—and that's all she talks about, at least to me. Is she ever lonely, afraid, angry?"

This was an incongruous conversation to be having, it seemed to me, with the sound of rifle fire still popping down the road. "What's your point?"

"We don't know anything about her, but here we are, doing what she tells us. Which strikes me as peculiar, when I think about it."

It struck me as peculiar, too, at least at that moment. What *was* I doing here? Nothing but risking my life, certainly nothing useful. But that wasn't what Sue would say. You're waiting for your time, she would say. Waiting for the turbulence.

I thought of what Hitch had told me in Minneapolis, his flat declaration that he had killed people. "How well do any of us know each other?"

"It's cooler this morning," Hitch said. "Even in the sun. You notice that?"

It was some days before this that Adam Mills had arrived at his mother's door along with five thuggish friends and an assortment of concealed weapons.

I won't dwell on this.

Adam, of course, was psychotic. Clinically psychotic, I mean. All the markers were there. He was antisocial, a bully and, in a certain perverse way, a natural leader. His mental universe was a cluttered attic of secondhand ideology and blatant fantasy, all centered on Kuin or whatever it was he imagined Kuin to be. He had never formed the natural human attachment to family or friends. He was by all evidence absent a conscience.

Ashlee, in her darker moods, would blame herself for what Adam had become; but Adam was a product of his brain chemistry, not his upbringing. A genome profile and some simple blood tests would have flagged his problem at an early age. He might even have been treatable, to some limited extent. But Ash had never had the money for that kind of up-market medical intervention.

I cannot imagine, and I do not wish to imagine, what Ashlee endured in her few hours with Adam. At the end of it she had revealed the location of the arrival site in Wyoming and the fact that I was there along with Hitch Paley and Sue Chopra—and the key fact, which was that we expected to disable a Chronolith.

She is not to be blamed for this.

The result was that Adam had reliable information about the Kuin stone and our efforts to destroy it a good forty-eight hours before the news reached the press.

Adam promptly headed west, but he left two of his followers behind to prevent Ashlee from making any inconvenient calls. He could have simply killed her, but he elected instead to keep her in reserve, possibly as a hostage.

Bad as this was, it was not the worst of it.

The worst of it was that Kaitlin came to the apartment not long after Adam left, still ignorant of what had happened to Janice and expecting to join Ashlee for a leisurely lunch and maybe a movie in the evening.

The statistical measurement of low-level ambient radiation had been refined since Jerusalem and Portillo. Sue's people were able to establish a much more accurate countdown for this arrival. But we didn't need a countdown to feel it in the air.

Here's how it stood when I climbed out of the bunker for a last breath of fresh air, some twenty minutes before the core was due to be activated.

There had been more gunfire south along the highway and sporadically at various points along the perimeter fence. So far, local and state police had managed to contain the Kuinists—there was a lot of anti-Kuinist sentiment in Wyoming since the storming of the State House, not least among civil servants and police. One Uniforces soldier had been injured by an Omega militiaman attempting to run the fence in an ATV, and four armed Kuinists of unknown affiliation had been shot to death in an effort to storm the northern checkpoint earlier this afternoon. Since then there had been only gestures and scattered arrests . . . although the crowd was still growing.

Sue had allowed a body of journalists to set up recording equipment well behind the bunker, and I was able to see them from where I stood, a line of trucks and tripods about a football field's length to the east. There were dozens of these people, most diverted here from Cheyenne, and they represented all the major news providers and not a few of the more respectable independents. As many of them as there were, they seemed lost in the brown vastness of the land. A second contingent of independent journalists had set up their gear on the bluff above the site, a little closer than Sue would have liked, but our media liaison called these folks "very dedicated and insistent"—that is, stubborn and stupid. I could see their cameras, too, bristling above the rim rock.

Many of our machine operators and manual laborers had already left the site. The remaining civilian engineers and scientific crew were either crowded into the bunker now or watching from behind the line of journalists.

The tau core was suspended in its steel frame over the concrete pad like a fat black egg. A plume of dust in the near distance was Hitch Paley, bringing the last van of our original convoy up the graded access road from the highway to park it near the bunker. All these vehicles had been cold-proofed against the arrival.

Also obvious was the tau chill, the premonitory coolness of the air—and not just of the air but of everything, earth and flesh, blood and bone. We had lost only a fraction of a centigrade degree at this stage. The cold shock was just beginning to ramp up, but it was already perceptible, a delicate prickling of the skin.

I took out my phone and made yet another attempt to reach Ashlee. The call failed to go through, just as all my calls had failed to go through for most of a week now. Sometimes there was a general failure message from the system, sometimes (as now) only a blank screen and a whisper of distorted audio. I put the phone away.

I was surprised when Sue Chopra opened the steel bunker door and stepped out behind me. Her face was wan and she was visibly trembling. She shaded her eyes against the sun.

I said, "Shouldn't you be down below?"

"It's all clockwork now," she said. "It runs itself."

She stumbled over a mesquite root and I took her arm. Her arm was cold.

"Scotty," she said, as if recognizing me for the first time.

"Take a deep breath," I said. "Are you all right?"

"Just tired. And I didn't eat." She shook her head quizzically. "The question that keeps coming to mind . . . did something *bring* me here? Or did I bring *myself*? That's the strange thing about tau turbulence. It gives us a destiny. But it's a destiny without a god. Destiny with no one in charge."

"Unless it's Kuin."

She frowned. "Oh, no, Scotty. Don't say *that.*"

"Not long now. How's it look downstairs?"

"Like I said. Clockwork. Good, solid numbers. You're right, I need to go back . . . but will you come with me?"

"Why?"

"Because there's actually a fairly high level of ionizing radiation out here. You're getting a chest X-ray every twenty minutes." And then she smiled. "But mainly because I find your presence reassuring."

It was a good enough reason, and I would have gone with her, but that was when we felt the crump of a distant explosion. The sound of gunfire erupted again, much closer than it should have been.

Sue instinctively dropped to her knees. Idiotically, I remained standing. The firing began as a pop-pop staccato but immediately increased to a nearly continuous volley. The fence (and a big gate) was yards behind us. I looked that way and saw Uniforces personnel taking cover and raising their weapons, but the source of the fire wasn't immediately obvious.

Sue had fixed her eyes on the bluff. I followed her gaze.

Wispy smoke issued from the Uniforces observation point there.

"The *journalists*," she whispered.

But of course they weren't journalists. They were Kuinists—a group of militiamen bright enough to have highjacked a network truck outside of Modesty Creek and savvy enough to have passed themselves off plausibly to our media-handlers at the gate. (Five genuine net newspeople were later found beaten and strangled in the rabbitbrush twenty miles down the road.) A dozen less presentable Kuinists in unmarked cars were smuggled in as technicians; weapons were effectively hidden amidst a cargo of lenses, broadcast apparatus, and imaging gear.

These people installed themselves on the bluff overlooking the tau core, near the Uniforces observation point. When they saw Hitch bring the last truck up to the bunker, they understood that to mean that the arrival was imminent. They destroyed the Uniforces outpost with an explosive device, picked off any survivors, then focused their efforts on the tau core.

I saw the puffs of smoke from their rifles, faint against the blue sky. They were too far from the core for accurate marksmanship, but sparks flew where their bullets struck the steel frame. Behind us, Uniforces gatekeepers began to return fire and radioed for support. Unfortunately the bulk of the forces were concentrated at the south gate, where the Kuinist mob had begun to fire on them in earnest.

Belatedly, I squatted in the dirt next to Sue. "The core is pretty heavily shielded—"

"The core is, I guess, but the cables and connectors are vulnerable—the *instrumentation*, Scotty!"

She rose and ran for the bunker. I had no choice but to follow, but first I waved in Hitch, who had just arrived and must have confused the gunfire from the bluff with the skirmish to the south of us. But when he saw Sue's awkward headlong dash he understood the urgency.

The air was suddenly much colder, and a wind came gusting from the dry prairie, dust-devils marching like pilgrims into the heart of the tau event.

Even the heated concrete-lined bunker was colder than Sue had predicted as the thermal shock began to ramp up. It numbed the extremities, cooled the blood, imposed a strange languid slowness on a sequence of terrifying events. We all struggled into thermally-adaptive jackets and headgear as Hitch sealed the door behind him.

Like clockwork, the tau-core initiation process proceeded; like clockwork, it was immune at this point to human intervention. Technicians sat by their monitors with clenched fists, nothing to do but hope a stray bullet didn't interrupt the flow of data.

I had seen the core's connectors and cables, Teflon-insulated and Kevlar-sheathed and thick as firehoses. I didn't think conventional bullets fired from a great range posed much danger, despite Sue's fears.

But the militiamen had brought more than rifles.

The countdown clock passed the five-minute point when there was the rumble of a distant detonation. Dust shook down from the plank ceiling and the lights in the bunker winked off.

"Hit a generator," I heard Hitch say, and someone else howled, "We're fucking screwed!"

I couldn't see Sue—I couldn't see anything at all. The darkness was absolute. There were nearly forty of us crowded into the bunker behind its elaborate earthworks.

Our backup generator had obviously failed. Auxiliary batteries restored the pilot lights on the electronic gear but cast no useful light. Forty people in a dark, enclosed space. I pictured in my mind the entrance, a steel door set at the top of a concrete stepway maybe a yard from where I stood, fixing the direction in my mind.

And then—the arrival.

The Chronolith reached deep into the bedrock.

A Chronolith absorbs matter and does not displace it; but the cold shock fractured hidden veins of moisture, creating a shockwave that traveled through the earth. The floor seemed to rise and fall. Those of us who hadn't grabbed a handhold fell to the ground. I think everyone screamed. It was a terrible sound, far worse than any physical damage done.

The cold got colder. I felt sensation drain from my fingertips.

It was one of our engineers who panicked and pushed his way to the exit hatch. I supect all he wanted was daylight—wanted it so badly that the need had overcome his reason. I was close enough to see him in the dim light from the console arrays. He found the steps, lunged upward on all fours, touched the door handle. The lever must have been shockingly cold—he screamed even as he put his weight against it. The handle chunked down convulsively and the door sprang outward.

The blue sky was gone, replaced by curtains of screaming dust.

The engineer lurched out. Wind and sand and granules of ice swept in. Had Sue anticipated an arrival as violent as this? Perhaps not—the journalists lined up east of us must have been sprawled in the dirt by now. And I doubted anyone was shooting from the bluff, not anymore.

The thermal shock had peaked but our body temperatures were still dropping. It's an odd sensation. Cold, yes, indescribably cold, but *lazy*, deceptive, narcotic. I felt myself shivering inside my overworked protective clothing. The shivering felt like an invitation to sleep.

"Stay in the bunker!" Sue shouted from somewhere deep in the trench behind me. "You'll all be safer in the bunker! Scotty, *close that door*!"

But few of the engineers and technicians heeded her advice. They spilled out past me into the screeching wind, running—insofar as the cold allowed them to run; more like a stumbling waltz—toward the line of parked vehicles.

Some few even managed to climb inside and start their engines. These vehicles had been proofed against the cold shock, but they roared like wounded animals, pistons grinding against cylinders. Arrival winds had battered down the perimeter fence and the civilian faction of our convoy began to vanish into the teeth of the storm.

West of us, where the Chronolith must have been, I could see nothing but a wall of fog and dust.

I pushed my way up the steps and pulled the hatch shut. The engineer had left some skin on the frigid lever. I left some of my own.

Sue secured some battery lamps and began to switch them on. Maybe a dozen of us remained in the bunker.

As soon we had some light Sue slumped down against one of the inert telemetry devices. I reeled across the room and joined her. Almost fell against her. Our arms touched, and her skin was shockingly cold (as I suppose was my own). Ray was nearby but had closed his eyes and seemed only intermittently conscious. Hitch squatted by the door, stubbornly alert.

Sue put her head on my shoulder.

"It didn't work, Scotty," she whispered.

"We'll think about that later."

"But it didn't *work*. And if it didn't *work*—"

"Hush."

The Chronolith had touched down. The first Chronolith on American soil . . . and not a small one, judging by the secondary effects. Sue was right. We had failed.

"But Scotty," she said, her voice infinitely weary and bewildered, "if it didn't work . . . what am I doing here? What am I *for*?"

I thought it was a rhetorical question. But she had never been more serious.

Twenty-five

I suppose, when history allows a degree of objectivity, someone will write an aesthetic appreciation of the Chronoliths.

Obscene as this idea may seem, the monuments are arguably specimens of art, each one individual, no two quite alike.

Some are crude, like the Kuin of Chumphon: relatively small, lacking detail, like sand-cast jewelry; the work of a novice. Others are more finely sculpted (though they remain as bleakly generic as works of Soviet Realism) and more carefully considered. For instance, the Kuins of Islamabad or Capetown: Kuin as gentle giant, benevolently masculine.

But the most recognizable Chronoliths are the monsters, the city-wreckers. The Kuin of Bangkok, straddling the rude brown water of the Chao Phrya; the Robed Kuin of Bombay; the stern and patriarchal Kuin of Jerusalem, seeming to embrace the world's faiths even as religious relics lie scattered at his feet.

The Kuin of Wyoming surpassed all these. Sue had been right about the significance of this monument. It was the first American Chronolith, a proclamation of victory in the heartland of a major Western power, and if its manifestation in this rural wasteland was an act of deference toward the great American cities, the symbolism remained both brazen and unmistakable.

The cold shock eased at last. We stirred out of our torpor and woke to a dawning awareness of what had happened here and what we had failed to achieve.

Hitch, characteristically, gave first thought to the practical business of staying alive. "Rouse up," he said hoarsely. "We need to be away from here before the Kuinists come looking for us, which probably won't be long. We need to avoid the main road, too."

Sue hesitated, regarding the battery-powered gear lining the wall of the bunker. The instrumentation blinked incoherently, starved for input.

"You too," Hitch said.

"This could be important," she said. "Some of these numbers pegged awfully high."

"Fuck the numbers." He ushered us stumbling to the door.

Sue wailed at the sight of the Chronolith dominating the sky.

Ray came up behind her; I followed Hitch. One of our few remaining engineers, a gray-haired man named MacGruder, stepped out and promptly fell to his knees in an act of pure if involuntary worship.

The Kuin was—well, it beggars description.

It was immense and it was frankly beautiful. It towered above the nearest large landmark, the stony bluff where the saboteurs had parked themselves. Of the tau core and its attendant structures there was, of course, no sign. The skin of ice on the Chronolith was already dropping away—there had not been much moisture in the ambient air—and the monument's details were unobscured save by the mists that sublimated from its surface. Wreathed in its own cloud, it was majestic, immense, tall as a mountain. From this angle the expression on the Kuin's face was oblique, but it suggested a smug complacency, the untroubled confidence of an assured conqueror.

Ice crystals melted and fell around us as a fine cold mist. The wind shifted erratically, now warm, now cool.

The main body of Kuinists had gathered to the south of the site. Many of them must have been disabled by the thermal shock, but the perimeter fence there veered a good couple of miles from the touchdown site, and judging by the renewed crackle of gunfire they were still lively enough to keep the Uniforces engaged. Soldiers closer to us had survived in their thermal gear but seemed disoriented and uncertain—their communications equipment had shut down and they were rallying to the flattened ruins of the east gate.

Of the militiamen who had disabled the tau core there was no sign.

Ray told the remaining engineers and technicians who shuffled out of the bunker to stick with the Uniforces. The journalists in the lee of the bunker must have had a different thought: They barreled past the fallen fence in their bulletproof vans. They had acquired and were no doubt already broadcasting this stunning image, the vast new Kuin of Wyoming. Our failure was an established fact.

Ray said, "Help me get Sue to the van."

Sue had stopped weeping but was staring fixedly at the Chronolith. Ray stood next to her, supporting her. She whispered, "This isn't right. . . ."

"Of course it isn't right. Come on, Sue. We need to get away."

She shook off Ray's hand. "No, I mean it's not *right*. The numbers pegged high. I need a sextant. And a map. There's a topographical map in the van, but—*Hitch*!"

Hitch turned back.

"I need a sextant! Ask one of the engineers!"

"The fuck?" Hitch said.

"A *sextant*!"

Hitch told Ray to get the van started while he hurried back with a digital sextant and a tripod from the survey vehicle. Sue set up the instrument despite the gusting wind and scribbled numbers into her notebook. Ray said, gently but firmly, "I don't think it matters anymore."

"What?"

"Taking measurements."

"I'm not doing this," she said briskly, "for *fun*," but when she tried to fold up the tripod she fainted into Ray's arms, and we carried her to the van.

I picked her notebook out of the icy mud.

Hitch drove while Ray and I got a cushion under Sue's head and a blanket over her body. The Uniforces people tried to flag us down. A guard with a rifle and a nervous expression leaned in the window and glared at Hitch. "Sir, I can't guarantee your safety—"

"Yeah," he said, "I know," and gunned the engine.

We would be safer—Sue would be safer—well away from here. Hitch cut across the flatlands on one of the local roads. These were dirt trails that dead-ended, most of them, at failed ranches or dry cattle tanks. Not an especially promising escape route. But Hitch had always preferred back roads.

Despite the elaborate coldproofing, our engine had sustained damage in the thermal shock. The van was kicking and dying by nightfall, when we came within sight of a cinderblock shed with a crude tin roof. We stopped here, not because the building was in any way inviting—many seasons of rain had come through the empty windows; generations of field mice had built and abandoned nests inside—but because it would serve to disguise our presence and would shelter the van from easy view. We had at least put a few miles behind us.

And with nothing left to do, the sun setting beyond the now-distant but still dominating figure of Kuin and a brisk wind combing the wild grass, we huddled in the vehicle and tried to sleep. We didn't have to try very hard. We were all exhausted. Even Sue slept, though she had revived quickly from her faint and had been alert enough on the drive east.

She slept through the night and was up at dawn.

Come morning, Hitch opened the van's engine compartment and ran the resident diagnostics. Ray Mosely blinked at the noise but then rolled back to sleep.

I woke hungry, remained hungry (we had only emergency rations), and walked past the paint-scabbed wall of the shed to the place on the grassland where Sue had once again unfolded our tripod and sextant.

The surveyor's tool was aimed at the distant Chronolith. Sue had opened a top map and laid it at her feet, the corners weighted with rocks. A brisk wind tousled her coiled hair. Her clothes were dirty and her enormous eyeglasses smudged; but, incredibly, she managed to smile when she noticed me.

"Morning, Scotty," she said.

The Chronolith was an icy pillar silhouetted against the haze-blue horizon. It drew the eye the way any incongruous or shocking thing does. The Kuin of Wyoming gazed eastward from his pedestal, almost directly at us.

Aimed at us, I thought, like an arrow.

I said, trying to restrain the irony, "Are you learning anything?"

"A lot." She faced me. Her smile was peculiar. Happy-sad. Her eyes were wide and wet. "Too much. *Way* too much."

"Sue—"

"No, don't say anything practical. May I ask you a question?"

I shrugged.

"If you were packing for a trip to the future, Scotty, what would you take?"

"What would I *take*? I don't know. What would *you* take?"

"I would take . . . a secret. Can you keep a secret?"

It was an unsettling question. It was something my mother used to ask me when she began to bend into insanity. She would hover over me like a malign shadow and say, "Can you keep a secret, Scotty?"

The secret was inevitably some paranoid assertion: that cats could read her mind; that my father was an impostor; that the government was trying to poison her.

"Come on, Scotty," Sue said, "don't look at me like that."

"If you tell me," I said, "it's not a secret anymore."

"Well, that's true. But I have to tell someone. I can't tell Ray, because Ray is in love with me. And I can't tell Hitch because Hitch doesn't love anyone at all."

"That's cryptic."

"Yes. I can't help it." She glanced at the far blue pillar of the Kuin. "We may not have much time."

"Time for what?"

"I mean, it won't last. The Chronolith. It isn't stable. It's too massive. Look at it, Scotty. See the way it's sort of quivering?"

"That's heat coming off the prairie. It's an optical illusion."

"In part. Not entirely. I've run the numbers over and over. The numbers that pegged back at the bunker. *These* numbers." Her notebook. "I triangulated its height and its radius, at least roughly. And no matter how stingy I am with the estimates, it comes up past the limit."

"The limit?"

"Remember? If a Chronolith is too massive, it's unstable—if I could have published the work they might have called it the Chopra Limit." Her peculiar smile faded and she looked away. "I may be too vain for the work I have to do. I can't let that happen. I have to be humble, Scotty. Because I will, God knows, be *humbled*."

"You're saying you think the Chronolith will destroy itself."

"Yes. Within the day."

"That would hardly be a secret."

"No, of course, but the *cause* of it will be. The Chopra Limit is *my* work. I haven't shared it with anyone, and I doubt anyone else is doing triangulation. The Kuin won't last long enough for accurate measurement."

This was making me nervous. "Sue, even if this is all true, people will know—"

"Know *what*? All anyone will know is that the Chronolith was destroyed and that we were here trying to destroy it. They'll draw the obvious conclusion. That we succeeded, if a little belatedly. The truth will be our secret."

"Why a secret?"

"Because I *mustn't* tell, Scotty, and neither must you. We have to carry this secret at least twenty years and three months into the future or else it won't work."

"Dammit, Sue—*what* won't work?"

She blinked. "Poor Scotty. You're confused. Let me explain."

I couldn't follow every detail of her explanation, but this is what I came away with.

We had not been defeated.

Plenty of press folks were doubtless still reporting the arrival, and they would also witness—in a matter of hours if not minutes—the spectacular collapse of the Chronolith. That broadcast image would (Sue claimed) interrupt the feedback loop and shatter Kuin's aura of invincibility. Win or lose, Kuin would no longer be destiny. He would be reduced to the status of an enemy.

And the world *must* think we had succeeded; the Chopra Limit *must* remain a closely-held secret. . . .

Because, Sue believed, it was not a coincidence that this Chronolith had surpassed the physical limit of stability.

It was, she declared, quite obviously an act of sabotage.

Contemplate that: the sabotage of a Chronolith, by design. Who would commit such an act? Clearly, an insider. Clearly, someone who understood not only the crude physics of the Chronoliths but their finest nuances. Someone who understood the physical limits and knew how to push them.

"That arrow," Sue said almost sheepishly, shocked at the temerity of her words and not a little frightened: "That arrow is pointing at *me*."

Of course it was madness.

It was megalomania, self-aggrandizing and self-abnegating, both at once. Sue had elevated herself to the rank of Shiva. Creator, destroyer.

But a part of me wanted it to be true.

I think I wanted an end to the long and disruptive drama of the Chronoliths—not just for my sake but for Ashlee's, for Kaitlin's.

And I wanted to trust Sue. After a lifetime of doubt, I think I *needed* to trust her.

I needed her madness to be, miraculously, divine.

Hitch was still working on the van when the twelve motorcycles came down the access road in a billow of gray dust. They came from the direction of the Chronolith.

Sue and I scurried back to the shed as soon as we spotted them. By that time Ray had alerted Hitch. Hitch had come out from under the engine block and was loading and passing out our four handguns.

I took one of these gratefully, but just as quickly disliked the way it felt in my hand—cold and faintly greasy. More than the sight of the approaching strangers, who were almost certainly Kuinists but could have been anyone, it was the pistol that made me feel afraid. A weapon is supposed to boost your confidence, but in my case it only served to emphasize how vulnerable we were, how desperately alone.

Ray Mosely tucked his gun under his belt and began frantically thumbing his pocket phone. But we hadn't been able to get a call out for days and he wasn't having any better luck now. The attempt seemed almost reflexive and somehow pitiable.

Hitch held out a gun for Sue, but she pressed her hands to her sides. "No, thank you," she said.

"Don't be stupid."

I was able to hear the motorcycle engines now, the sound of locusts, a plague descending.

"Keep it," she said. "I wouldn't know what to do with it. I'd probably shoot the wrong person."

She looked at me when she said this, and I was inexplicably reminded of the young girl in Jerusalem who had thanked Sue just before she died. Her eyes, her voice, had conveyed this same cryptic urgency.

"We don't have time to argue."

Hitch had taken charge. He was alert and focused, frowning like a chess player facing a skilled opponent. The concrete-block shed possessed a single door and three narrow windows—an easy space to defend but a potential death trap if we were overwhelmed. But the van wouldn't have been any safer.

"Maybe they don't know we're here," Ray volunteered. "Maybe they'll ride on past."

"Maybe," Hitch said, "but I wouldn't count on it."

Ray put a hand on the butt of his pistol. He looked at the door, at Hitch, at the door, as if trying to work out some perplexing mathematical question.

"Scotty," Sue said, "I'm depending on you."

But I didn't know what she meant.

"They're slowing down," Hitch said.

"Maybe they're not Kuinists," Ray said.

"Maybe they're nuns on a day trip. But don't count on it."

• • •

Their disadvantage was, they had no cover.

The land here was flat and grown over with sagegrass. Clearly aware of their vulnerability, the bikers came to an idling stop a distance from the shed, out of easy range.

Watching through the gap in the cinderblocks that passed as a west-facing window, what struck me was the incongruity of all this. The day was fine and cool, the sky as cloudless as crystal. Even the perhaps unstable Chronolith seemed fixed and placid on the horizon. The small sound of sparrows and crickets hung in the air. And yet here were a dozen armed men straddling the road and no help for many miles.

One of the bikers put his helmet in his hand, shook out a flourish of dirty blond hair, and began walking almost lazily down the dirt track toward us.

And:

"I'll be fucked," Hitch said, "if that isn't Adam Mills."

We were deep in the tau turbulence, I guess Sue might have said; in that place where the arrow of time turns on itself and turns again, that place where there are no coincidences.

"We just want the lady," Adam Mills called from a short distance down the road.

His voice was harsh and high-pitched. It was in some ways almost a parody of Ashlee's voice. Bereft, that is, of all warmth and subtlety.

("We have some strange history behind us," Ash had once said. "Your crazy mother. My crazy son.")

"What lady would that be?" Hitch called back.

"Sulamith Chopra."

"I'm the only one here."

"I believe I recognize that voice. Mr. Paley, isn't it? Yes, I've heard that voice. Last time, I think you were screaming."

Hitch declined to answer, but I saw him clench the fingers—what remained of them—of his left hand.

"Just send her out and we'll be away from here. Can you hear me, Ms. Chopra? We don't mean to harm you."

"Shoot him," Ray whispered, "just *shoot* the fucker."

"Ray, if I shoot him, they'll just put a rocket in this window. Of course, they might do that anyhow."

"It's all right," Sue said suddenly and calmly. "None of this is necessary. I'll go."

Which surprised Hitch and Ray, if not me. Some sense of her intention had begun to dawn.

Hitch said, "Now that's just fucking ridiculous. You have no idea—these people are *mercenaries.* Worse, they have a pipeline straight to Asia. They'd be happy to sell you into the hands of some would-be Kuin. You're merchandise, as far as they're concerned."

"I know that, Hitch."

"High-priced merchandise, and for a good reason. You really want to hand over everything you know to some Chinese warlord? I'd shoot you myself if I thought you'd do that."

Sue was as placid now, at least superficially, as a martyr in a medieval painting. "But that's exactly what I have to do."

Hitch looked away. His head was silhouetted in the window. Had it occurred to him to do so, Adam Mills could have taken him out with a well-placed head shot.

Ray, horrified, said, "Sue, *no*," and the tableau was sustained for a fragile moment: Hitch gap-jawed, Ray on the brink of panic. Sue gave me a very quick and meaningful look.

Our secret, Scotty. Keep our secret.

Hitch said, "You mean that."

"Yes, I do."

He turned his weapon away from the window.

The building in which we were trapped had probably been erected during one or another of the state's cyclical oil booms, perhaps to keep prospecting gear out of the rain—not that it seemed to rain much here. The concrete floor was adrift with everything that had blown through the open door frame in fifty or seventy-five years: dust, sand, vegetable matter, the desiccated remains of snakes and birds.

Hitch stood at the west wall where the cinderblocks were water-stained and eroded. Sue and Ray were together in the northwest corner, and I stood across from Hitch at the eastern wall.

The light was dim, despite the brightness of the day, and the air a little cooler than the dry air of the prairie, though that would change as sun began to bake the tin roof. Cross drafts stirred up dust and the scent of ancient decay.

I remember all this vividly. And the sagging wooden roof beams, and the angled sunlight through the empty window, and the dry sagebrush clustered just beyond the doorway, and the glint of sweat on Hitch Paley's forehead as he aimed his pistol—but only tentatively—at Sue.

Sue was pale. A vein pulsed in her throat, but she remained quiet.

"Point that fucking gun away," Ray said.

Ray, in his tangled beard and sweat-stained T-shirt, looked like a middle-aged academic gone feral. His eyes were just that wild. But there was something admirable in this strained declaration of defiance, a fierce if fragile courage.

"I'm serious," Hitch said. "She does not go out that door."

"I have to go," Sue said. "I'm sorry, Ray, but—"

She had taken a single step when Ray slammed her back into the corner, restraining her with his body. "Nobody's going *anywhere*!"

"You going to sit on her till doomsday?" Hitch asked.

"Put your gun down!"

"I can't do that. Ray, you know I can't do that."

And now Ray lifted his own weapon. "Stop threatening her or I'll—"

But this was beyond the bounds of Hitch Paley's patience.

Let me say, in defense of Hitch, that he knew Adam Mills. He knew what was waiting for us out there in the relentless sunlight. He was not about to surrender Sue and I think he would have died rather than surrender himself.

He shot Ray in the right shoulder—at this proximity, a killing wound.

I believe I heard the bullet pass through Ray and strike the stone wall behind him, a sound like a hammerblow on granite. Or it might have been the echo of the gunshot itself, deafening in this enclosed space. Dust rose up around us. I was frozen in my own incredulity.

There was a cough of answering shots from outside and a bullet chinked the cinderblocks near the western window. Sue, suddenly pinned behind the weight of Ray's body, gasped and pushed him aside. She whispered, "Oh, Ray! I'm sorry! I'm so sorry!"

Tears stood in her eyes. There was blood on her tattered yellow blouse and blood on the wall behind her.

Ray wasn't breathing. The wound or the shock had stopped his heart. A blood-bubble formed on his lips and sat there, inert.

He had loved Sue hopelessly and selflessly for many years. But once she had stepped across his motionless legs Sue didn't look back.

She walked toward the door—staggered, but didn't fall.

The air stank of blood and cordite. Outside, Adam Mills was shouting something, but I couldn't make out the words over the ringing in my ears.

The Kuin of Wyoming watched all this from the western horizon. I could see the monument framed in the window behind Hitch, blue on blue, drowsy in the rising heat.

"Stop," Hitch said bluntly.

Sue shuddered at the sound of his voice but took another step.

"I won't warn you again. You know I won't."

And I heard myself say, "No, Hitch, let her go."

• • •

Our secret, Sue had said.

And: *It isn't a secret if you tell someone.*

So why had she shared it with me?

At that moment, I thought I knew.

The understanding was bitter and awful.

Sue took yet another step toward the door.

In the sunlight beyond her a swallow rose out of the dry grass, suspended in the air like a piano note.

"Keep out of it," Hitch told me.

But I was more familiar with handguns now than I had been at Portillo.

When Hitch saw my pistol aimed at him, he said, "This is fucking insane."

"She needs to do this."

Hitch kept his own gun trained on Sue. Sue nodded and approached the door as if each step drew down a failing reserve of strength and courage. "Thank you, Scotty," she whispered.

"I will shoot you," Hitch said, "if you do not stop where you are."

"No," I said, "you won't."

He growled—it was precisely that sound, like a cornered animal. "Scotty, you cowardly fuck, I'll shoot you too, if I have to. Put your weapon down and you, Sue, I said stop *right there.*"

Sue hunched her shoulders as if against the impact of a bullet, but she was already in the frame of the door. She took another step.

For a moment Hitch's weapon wavered—toward me, toward Sue. Then, suddenly resolute, he took aim at her back, the arch of her spine, her big bowed head.

He began—and I know how absurd it seems, to claim to have witnessed this, but in the overweening stillness of the moment, in the shadow of this bright benevolent afternoon and all of us balanced on the fulcrum of time, I swear I saw his meaty, dark finger begin to close on the trigger of the gun.

But I was faster.

The recoil threw back my hand.

Did I kill Hitch Paley?

I'm not an objective witness. I'm testifying in my own defense. But I am, finally, here at the end of my life, honest. I have no more secrets to keep.

The gun recoiled. The bullet was in the air, at least, and then—

And then *everything* was in the air.

Brick, mortar, wood, tin, the dust of ages. My own body, a projectile. Hitch, and the corpse of Ray Mosely. Ray, who had loved Sue far too much to allow her to do what she had to do; and Hitch, who did not love anyone at all.

Did I see (people have asked me) the destruction of the Chronolith? Was I a witness to the fiery collapse of the Kuin of Wyoming? Did I see the bright light and did I feel the heat?

No. But when I opened my eyes again pieces of the Chronolith were falling from the sky, falling all around me. Pieces the size of pebbles, rendered now as conventional matter and fused by the heat of their extinction into glassy blue teardrops.

Twenty-six

In the great release of energy as the Chronolith collapsed, a shockwave swept outward from its perimeter—more wind than heat, but a great deal of heat; more heat than light, but it had been bright enough to blind.

The cinderblock shelter lost its roof and its northern and western walls. I was blown free of it and woke a few yards from the standing fragments.

For some period of time I was not quite coherent or fully conscious. My first thought was for Sue, but Sue was nowhere visible. Gone as well was Adam Mills, and so were his men and their motorcycles, though I did find (later) one overturned Daimler motorbike abandoned in the scrub, its fuel tank cracked, and a single helmet, and a tattered copy of *The Fifth Horseman*.

Do I believe Sue gave herself up to

the Kuinists in the aftermath of the explosion? Yes, I do. The shockwave would likely not have been deadly to anyone in the open. It was the collapse of the stone shed that had caused my concussion and dislocated my shoulder, not the shockwave itself. Sue had been in the doorway, which was still standing.

I found Hitch and Ray partially buried in the rubble, plainly dead.

I spent a few hours trying to dig them out, working with my good hand, until it became obvious that the effort was futile as well as exhausting. Then I rescued some dried rations from the overturned van and ate a little, choking over the food but keeping at least some of it down.

When I tried my phone there was only a clatter of noise, a distorted "no signal" message drifting across the screen as if through an obscuring tide.

The sun went down. The sky turned indigo and then dark. On the western horizon, where the Chronolith had been, brushfires burned brightly.

I turned and walked the other way.

Twenty-seven

Lately I have visited two significant places: the Wyoming Crater and the Shipworks at Boca Raton. One a lake polluted with memory, the other a gateway to a greater sea.

And I thought—

But no, I'll get to that.

Ashlee had been released from the hospital by the time I made it back to Minneapolis.

I had been in the hospital myself, or at least a little overnight emergency-care clinic in Pine Ridge. Three days wandering with a head injury in the Wyoming backlands had left me sunburned, hungry, and too weak to climb stairs at any speed. My left arm was in a sling.

Ashlee was less fortunate.

She had warned me, of course, but I

wasn't prepared for what I found when I let myself into the apartment and she called my name from the bedroom.

The hurt to her body—the burns, the contusions—were invisible under the snowy white linen of the bed. But I winced at the sight of her face.

I won't catalog the damage. I reminded myself that it would heal, that the blood pooled in these bruises would fade away, that the broken skin would mend around the sutures and that one day soon she would be able to open her eyes all the way.

She looked at me through purple slits. "That bad?" she said.

Some of her teeth were missing.

"Ashlee," I said, "I'm so sorry."

She kissed me, wounded as she was, and I held her gently, despite my damaged arm.

She began to apologize in return. She had been worried that I wouldn't forgive her for having finally broken and told Adam Mills where to find me. God knows I wanted to apologize for having left her to this.

But I put my finger, delicately, delicately, against her swollen lips. Why dignify the horror with recrimination? We had survived. We were together. That was enough.

What I had not known—what I learned after I finally contacted Ashlee—was that Morris Torrance hadn't abandoned his post outside the apartment.

Adam Mills had identified Morris as a guard and had taken his men into the building through a rear entrance to avoid alerting him. Morris called Ash shortly before Adam arrived, placing her in the apartment, and he had seen no suspicious activity since then. He logged off after midnight and drove back to the Marriott for a few hours of sleep. He wore a tag alert in case Ashlee needed him in the interim. He received no such alarm. In the morning he called Ash again but couldn't get past her screen routine. He promptly drove to the apartment, not long after Kaitlin had arrived there, and unsuccessfully attempted another call. Deeply concerned now, Morris buzzed Ashlee from the lobby.

She answered the buzzer belatedly and her voice was slurred. Morris told Ashlee he was from a package delivery service and he needed her to sign his slate.

Ash, who must have recognized his voice, told him she couldn't come to the door right now and asked whether it would be all right if he came back another time.

He told her could come back but that the package was labeled "perishable."

Didn't matter, Ashlee said.

Morris then stepped out of camera range, phoned the local police and reported an assault in progress, and let himself into the lobby with the key I had given him. He identified himself (incorrectly and illegally) as a federal agent to the superintendent of the building and obtained a master key to the apartment.

He knew how long it might take for a police response and he elected not to wait. He rode the elevator to our floor, placed another call to the apartment so that the ringing of the phone would mask the sound of the key in the lock, and entered the apartment with his gun drawn. He was, as he had so often told me, a retired agent without field experience. But he had been trained and he had not forgotten his training.

Kaitlin, at this point, was locked in a bedroom closet and Ashlee was sprawled on the sofa where she had been left after a beating.

Without hesitation Morris shot the man who was standing over Ash, then turned his gun on the second Kuinist who had just stepped out of the kitchen.

The second man dropped a bottle of beer at the sound of the shot and drew his own gun. He took Morris off his feet with one shot but Morris was able to return fire after he had fallen. The dining-room table gave him a little cover. He placed two bullets in the assailant's head and neck.

Wounded in the leg—the bullet had carved a divot in his thigh, just like the bullet Sue Chopra took in Jerusalem—Morris was nevertheless able to comfort Ashlee and to release Kaitlin from the locked closet before he fainted.

Kait—who was mobile but had been beaten and raped—put a pressure bandage on the wound before the police arrived. Ashlee rose from the sofa and loped to the bathroom.

She soaked a cloth in water and daubed the blood from Morris's face, and then Kaitlin's, and then her own.

"It was foolhardy," Morris said when I went to the hospital to thank him.

"It was the right thing to do."

He shrugged. "Well, yeah, I think so too." He was in a wheelchair, his damaged leg suspended in front of him, swathed in regenerative gels and wrapped in a cast. "They ought to hang a red flag on this," he said.

"I owe you more than I can ever repay."

"Don't get sentimental, Scotty." But he seemed a little teary himself. "Ashlee's all right?"

"Improving," I said.

"Kaitlin?"

"It's hard to say. They're bringing David home from Little Rock."

He nodded. We sat silently for a time.

Then he said, "I saw it on the news. The Wyoming stone coming down. Took a while, but Sue got what she wanted, right?"

"She got what she wanted."

"Shame about Hitch and Ray."

I agreed.

"And Sue." He gave me a meaningful look. "Hard to believe she's really gone."

"Believe it," I said.

Because a secret isn't a secret if you share it.

"You know I'm an old-fashioned Christian, Scotty. I'm not sure exactly what Sue believed in, unless it was that Hindu Shiva bullshit. But she was a good person, wasn't she?"

"The best."

"Right. Well. I couldn't figure out why she asked me to stay here and took you to Wyoming with her. No offense, but that really bothered me. But I guess I served a purpose here."

"That you did, my friend."

"You think she had that in mind all along? I mean, she did have a thing for the future."

"I think she knew us both pretty well."

She took me, I thought, because Morris wouldn't have served in my place. He would never have let her walk into the jaws of the wolf. He would certainly not have killed Hitch Paley.

Morris was a good man.

Twenty-eight

Lately I have visited two significant places.

Traveling isn't easy for me these days. Medication keeps my various geriatric complaints under control—I'm healthier at seventy than my father was at fifty—but age breeds its own weariness. We are buckets of grief, I think, and eventually we fill to brimming.

I went alone to Wyoming.

The Wyoming Crater today is a minor, if unique, war memorial. For most Americans Wyoming was only the beginning of the twenty-year War of the Chronoliths. For that generation, Kait and David's generation, the memorable battles were the Persian Gulf, Canberra, First Beijing, Canton Province. After all . . . no one much died at Wyoming.

No one much.

The crater is fenced and managed as a national monument now. Tourists can climb to a platform at the summit of the bluff and gaze down on the ruins from a distance. But I wanted to get closer than that. I felt entitled.

The Parks Service guard at the main entrance told me that would be impossible, until I explained that I'd been here in 2039 and showed him the scar that runs up from my left ear to my receding hairline. The guard was a veteran—armored cav, Canton, the bloody winter of 2050. He told me to stick around until the visitors' center closed at five; then he'd see what he could do.

What he did was allow me to ride with him on the evening security inspection. We took a golf-cart-sized vehicle down a steep path and parked at the rim of the crater. The guard scrolled a newspaper and pretended not to keep an eye on me while I wandered a few minutes in the long shadows.

There had been almost an inch of rain this May. The shallow crater cupped a tiny brown pond at the bottom of it, and sagebrush bloomed along the rilled, eroded walls.

Some few fragments of the Kuin stone remained intact.

These had also eroded. Tau instability, the unraveling of complex Calabi-Yau knots, had rendered the final substance of the Chronolith as a simple fused silicate: gritty blue glass, nearly as fragile as sandstone.

There had been airstrikes here during the Western Secession, when American Kuinists had controlled these parts. The militias had claimed the state during the darkest hours of the War, had presumably (though there were no surviving witnesses) attempted to revise history by rebuilding and rebroadcasting the enormous Kuin of Wyoming. But they had been ill-advised. By someone. Someone who had convinced them to push the stability envelope past its limit.

History does not record the name of this benefactor.

A secret is a secret.

But, as Sue was also fond of saying, there is no such thing as a coincidence.

I stood for a time by a fragment of the Kuin's head, a weathered piece of his brow and one intact eye. The pupil of the eye was a concave depression as wide as a truck tire. Dust and rain had accumulated in the bowl of it and a wild thistle had sprouted there.

The Chronoliths have proven as impervious to history as they are to logic. The act of creating such a device is so fraught with tau turbulence and outright paradox—cause and effect so tightly entangled—that no single narrative has emerged. The past (Ray's "Minkowski ice," I suppose) is immutable but its structure has been finely fractured, layers compressed and upturned, in places rendered chaotic and uninterpretable.

The stone was cold to the touch.

I cannot truthfully say that I prayed. I don't know how to pray. But I pronounced a few names in the privacy of my mind, words addressed to the tau turbulence, if anything remains of it. Sue's name, among others. I thanked her.

Then I begged the dead to forgive me.

The park guard eventually grew impatient. He escorted me back to the cart as the sun touched the horizon. "Guess you have some stories to tell," he said.

A few. And a few I haven't told. Until now.

Was there ever a single, substantial Kuin—a human Kuin, I mean?

If so, he remains an elusive figure, overshadowed by the armies who fought in his name and invented his ideology. There surely must have been an original Kuin, but I suspect he was overthrown by any number of successors. Perhaps, as Sue had speculated, each Chronolith required its own Kuin. "Kuin" became little more than a name for the vacuum at the heart of the whirlwind. The king is unborn; long live the king.

After Ashlee's death late last year I was obliged to sort through her belongings. Deep in a box of ancient papers (expired ration coupons, tax forms, yellowed past-due notices from utility companies) I found Adam Mills' birth certificate. The only striking thing about this was that Adam's middle name happened to be Quinn, and that Ashlee had never mentioned it to me.

But this is, I think, at last, a genuine coincidence. At least, that's what I prefer to believe. I'm old enough now to believe what I choose. To believe what I can bear to believe.

Kait left David at home and joined me at Boca Raton that summer, an unplanned vacation. We hadn't seen each other since Ashlee's funeral in December. I had come to Boca Raton on a whim: I wanted to see the Shipworks while I was still able to travel.

Nowadays everyone talks about the postwar recovery. We're like terminal patients granted a miracle cure. Sunshine seems sunnier, the world (such as it is) is our oyster, and the future is infinitely bright. Inevitably, we will all be disappointed. But not, I hope, too badly.

And there are some things of which we are quite reasonably proud—the National Shipworks, for instance.

I remember, around the time of the Portillo arrival, Sue Chopra insisting that the technology of Calabi-Yau manipulation would yield a host of more enduring wonders than the Chronoliths. ("I mean, star travel, Scotty: that's a real possibility!") And Sue, as usual, had been right. She had an acute sense of the future.

Kait and I walked slowly up a long promenade to the observation level overlooking the launching bays, a vast half-moon-shaped structure walled with reinforced glass.

Kait took my arm—I need a little help on long walks. We talked some, but not about the large issues of our lives. This was a vacation.

So many things had changed. Foremost, of course, I had lost Ashlee. Ash had died of an unsuspected aneurysm late last year, and I was a widower now. But we had enjoyed many good years together despite the wartime privation and the financial crises. I miss her constantly, but I did not discuss this with Kaitlin. Nor did we discuss Kait's mother, retired and living relatively comfortably in Washington State; or Whit Delahunt, who was spending his declining years in a federal project outside St. Paul, serving a twenty-year home incarceration and community service sentence for sedition. All this was past.

Today we believed in the possibility of a future.

The observation deck was crowded with children, a school field trip come to witness the latest unmanned launch. The probe stood in its launch cradle a half mile away like a blue jewel, a sculpted glacier. "Time *is* space," the tour guide was saying. "If we can control one, we can control the other."

Sue might have quibbled with the word "control." But the kids didn't care about that. They had come for a spectacle, not a lecture. They talked and shifted restlessly from foot to foot; they pressed their hands (and some their noses) against the glass.

"They're not afraid," Kaitlin marveled.

Nor were they startled—at least not much—when the Tau Ceti probe rose as if by slow magic from its bay and glided noiselessly upward. They were impressed, I think, to see so massive an object lofted like a balloon into the cloudless Florida sky. A perceptive few might have been awed. But no, they were not afraid.

They know so little of the past.

I want them not to forget. Which is, I suppose, what all aged veterans want. But they'll forget. Of course they will. And their children will know less of us than they do, and their children's children will find us barely imaginable.

Which is as it should be. You can't stop time. Sue taught me that (and Ashlee, in her own way). You can give yourself to time. Or be taken by it.

It's not as hard a truth as it sounds—not on a clean bright day like this.

"Are you all right?" Kaitlin asked.

"I'm fine," I said. "Just a little breathless." We had walked a long way, and the day was warm.